LIPSTICK LOVERS

LIPSTICK LOVERS

A collection of twenty lesbian erotic stories

Edited by Elizabeth Coldwell

Published by Xcite Books Ltd – 2012
ISBN 9781908086686

Copyright © Xcite Books Ltd 2012

The stories contained within this book are works of fiction. Names and characters are the product of the authors' imaginations and any resemblance to actual persons, living or dead, is entirely coincidental

All rights reserved. No part of this book may be reproduced, stored in a retrieval system, or transmitted in any form or by any means, electronic, electrostatic, magnetic tape, mechanical, photocopying, recording or otherwise, without the written permission of the publishers: Xcite Books, Suite 11769, 2nd Floor, 145-157 St John Street, London EC1V 4PY

The stories contained within this book are works of fiction. Names and characters are the product of the authors' imaginations and any resemblance to actual persons, living or dead, is entirely coincidental

Printed and bound in the UK

Cover design by
Madamadari

Contents

A Woman's Touch	Kathleen Tudor	1
The Lock-in	Alice Candy	8
Overtime	Harper Bliss	17
Lam-dancing	Lynn Lake	27
Cherry Red	Jayne Wheatley	35
Anita and Angie Get Wet	Alex Jordaine	43
Lucky Charm	Kate Dominic	50
Fine Print	Emma Lydia Bates	60
A Change of Heart	Lucy Felthouse	70
Back to Square One	Angel Propps	82
Corsetry for Beginners	Medea Mor	95
Alison	Shea Lancaster	107
Feast	Rachel Charman	116
The Gift	Encarnita Round	127
The New Curiosity Shop	Jean-Philippe Aubourg	138
In Pearls	Giselle Renarde	149
The Wedding Singer	Anna Sansom	161
The Senator's Daughter	Valerie Alexander	170
Sealed	Elise Hepner	180
Rehearsing With Katarina	Elizabeth Coldwell	189

A Woman's Touch
by Kathleen Tudor

I twisted my wedding set around and around my finger, the diamond of my engagement ring scratching against my other fingers. The ring was not new. For over a decade I had worn it on my finger, and it bore the scratches and battle scars to prove it. It was a good ring, and it was a good marriage that it represented, at least in most ways. My husband was kind, patient, and dependable. Our relationship, even after all of these years, was warm. Comfortable.

I was preparing to throw it away.

Somehow the light of the bar looked smoky, even in smoke-free California. The sparkle off my rings was dull at best, and I sighed, slipped them off my finger, and carefully zipped them into an inner pocket in my purse. I had arrived here early to give myself time to back out. I was meeting Sam for the first time in ten minutes. I'd been there half an hour, and I was no closer to the door.

The next ten minutes passed like some sort of endurance competition. I sat on my hands. Put them in my lap. Picked at my cuticles. Sat on them again. Fifteen minutes. My stomach turned, and panic rose. *What am I doing here?*

Seventeen minutes. The door opened, and a goddess walked in. She was just a little taller than my five foot eight, curvy and sexy with short, spiked hair that – based on her smooth skin – could only have gotten that bright silver colour from a bottle. She saw me and her face lit up brighter than I would have imagined possible in the dim room.

'Cassie?' she asked me.

'Hello, Sam.' I nearly choked. She smiled and touched my arm gently, understanding.

'Would you like a beer?'

I nodded and sat back in my seat to practise breathing before she returned. I had just started getting the hang of it again when she walked up with two tall glasses in her hand. I took mine and downed two huge gulps without tasting a drop. I hadn't meant to do that.

'Are you having second thoughts?' She asked it with compassion, no clear sound of regret in her voice. I knew that all I had to say was I had changed my mind, and she would get up and leave, disappearing from my life for ever.

'And third, and fourth,' I answered. 'But I'm still here.' I smiled, feeling a little dizzy from the beer. I hadn't eaten.

'We don't have to do anything if you're not OK with it. We can just talk, right here, nice and safe.' She hadn't touched her beer. Since that first mad gulp, neither had I.

'I don't want to talk; I want you.' The blood all rushed out of my head, and then back up again, leaving me dizzy and blushing. I'd said it. She leant forward and touched my hand. This was the touch I was prepared to throw everything away for. A woman's touch. 'I'm ready.'

'Come on then,' she said, offering me her hand. I took it, marvelling at the softness as we abandoned our sweating beers on the small table.

'Your hands seem so small,' I said.

Sam smiled at me as she held the bar door open. 'No smaller than yours.'

I looked down and studied our hands, woven together like the reeds of a basket, intricate and beautiful. 'I guess you're right. May I touch your hair?'

'Of course.' Sam stopped right there on the sidewalk and bent her head toward me. I reached up with my free hand, unwilling to relinquish her soft grip, and ran my fingers through her spikes.

'Funny,' I said, 'they don't feel spiky.'

Sam laughed. 'I use mousse instead of gel.'

'I like it.' Stirring her hair had brushed the scent of it toward me, and I inhaled deeply. It was the scent of a woman, and tonight she would be my woman. It was the most intoxicating thing I had ever known.

This time I was the one pulling her along toward her car. She opened the passenger door for me with a chivalry that was softened by her knowing wink, and smiled at me as she pushed it shut. I closed my eyes in the sweet solitude of her car and breathed her in. The car smelled like her hair, and like lavender.

She got in a couple of seconds later, and I felt surrounded by her as we drove to her apartment. 'It's still not too late to change your mind. I can drive you home.'

'I want to go home with you,' I said firmly, and for the first time tonight I was completely, absolutely sure. 'I've been with my husband for 12 years, and I could never stand to have sex with him. I did my wifely duty, but now I need to know. I need to know what I've been robbing myself of for all this time.'

'I know,' she said, and her voice held all the same sadness and pain I knew was in mine. 'I won't ask again.'

'You were the same way, weren't you?' It was hardly a question. Her knuckles were tight on the steering wheel.

Sam sighed. 'I was married a decade. No kids, thank goodness. One day I got drunk in a bar and kissed a woman, and it was – magic. I never really knew what true arousal felt like before that.'

'I'm sorry.'

'Life has gotten better since then. Let me show you what it can be like,' Sam said. She parked the car in front of an unassuming little house, and I got out without waiting on her. I took her arm, though, and she led me up the walk like a princess. The house was decorated in a completely feminine and beautiful style. The furniture was simple and elegant, the colours somehow managed to be bold without being obtrusive, and tiny details – like a crystal vase full of colourful glass beads on a table – tied everything together.

'This is probably the most beautiful house I've ever been in,' I said. It looked gorgeous and lived in at the same time, and I envied the freedom to create a home like this even as I admired it.

'I'd offer you the grand tour, but I think we'd both rather just skip to the bedroom,' she joked, and I smiled nervously in agreement as I let her lead me down the hall and into a sumptuous bedroom.

'You knit,' I said, feeling silly as my mind picked out the basket of yarn in her bedroom and fixated on it.

'Crochet. I can show you later, if you want.'

I nodded mutely, staring at the basket rather than facing what was before me. It was my choice, but I was afraid. What if this couldn't break through my "frigidity" either? 'Sure,' I said. I felt lost.

Sam turned and stood directly in front of me, then reached for my chin and lifted my eyes until I had to look at her. 'You're safe,' she said. She leant forward and kissed my eyes shut, one hand on either side of my face grounding me to the moment. 'Trust me.'

I did.

Sam's hands lifted from my face, but her attention remained, and she petted and stroked, starting at my temples and tracing every contour of my face until I was so relaxed that I felt like I would melt into the carpet. Soon that relaxation turned into something else, and the touch of her hands left a wake of tingles across my face as her fingertips brushed lightly across my forehead, my cheeks, my nose, my lips. I sighed, swaying toward her.

I sailed away on a sea of pure tactile delight, discovering each touch like it was the first I had ever felt. I'd thought I'd known what arousal felt like – I'd been turned on over the years by books or movies or my own imagination – but that was a candle to the sun compared to what Sam was doing to me now, slowly stoking the fires of my body until I felt like my entire body was on fire. This was no warm tingle in my panties, but a flood of heat and desire and need that drove me to whimper her name.

I left my eyes closed as she slowly began to slip items of clothing off me, giving me time to protest – to change my mind – but my mind and heart were fixed on nothing but her, now. The way she touched me sent goosebumps up and down my arms and a chill up the back of my spine, and I was quivering from anticipation as she slowly undressed me.

'You're beautiful,' Sam whispered in my ear. 'Would you like to see?' I nodded, and she took me by the hand and led me to a full-length mirror in one corner. 'Look,' she whispered. She stood behind me, still brushing her fingers through my hair and across my exposed back as she watched me look at myself.

I had never seen myself this way. The woman in the mirror was a stranger, sexy and flushed and trembling from head to toe with a wild arousal. She was powerful, sexual, desirable. She was a stranger, and at the same time she was the truest version of myself that I had ever seen. She was my inner wild woman, finally allowed out to play. I breathed a sigh, and Sam smiled over my shoulder in the mirror.

'Exactly,' she said. She stepped back and I turned to face her as she peeled away her clothing, piece by piece. She was putting on a show for me, teasing and tempting as she exposed more and more of her beautiful skin.

At first I didn't know what to do with myself but, as she moved through her sensual striptease, my hands started to rise. I caressed my body in a way I had always avoided before, not sure where self-pleasure would lead and afraid to find out. My fingertips ran over my belly and up to cup my breasts, and Sam watched with satisfaction and desire and approval in her eyes.

When she was naked, Sam held out her arms for me. I came toward her, slow and shy, and she folded me in her arms, pressing our bodies together. I felt the way our breasts were crushed against one another, soft and warm. I felt our bellies press together before curving apart, and even our thighs met in an embrace that was as much comfort as it was sensuality and desire. Then she cupped my cheek with one hand, and she kissed me.

Our first kiss left me no room to doubt that I was not a frigid wife – just a mismatched one. Her lips were soft and gentle, and instead of being repelled, I couldn't help but let my tongue sweep out to taste her. The familiar taste of lipstick was followed quickly by a sweetness that left me craving more, deepening the kiss as if I could take in more of her essence though the actions of lip and tongue.

When she let out a soft sound of approval and pleasure, I thought my heart would burst. I pressed even more tightly up against her and abandoned myself to her whim as she took control of the kiss. We passed that gift back and forth for minutes, each taking a turn at dominating the embrace and submitting sweetly to the other, a subtle play of sensuality I had never experienced before and knew I would likely never experience with a man, no matter how many I kissed.

Sam surprised me when her hand drifted up from where it had rested on my waist, cupping my breast and kneading gently, smoothing her hand over my flesh, lifting it, and caressing gently. When her touch moved to my nipple it was neither too soft nor too rough, giving just enough pressure to turn my spine to jelly as I quivered obediently under her hand.

My nerves were gone, burned up in a storm of arousal as she drove me to heights I had never before dreamt could exist. When she stepped back – leading me subtly toward the bed – resisting was not even in my mind. She led me there step by slow step, her other hand on my breast, now. I shivered with pleasure as she teased and played, and finally she turned and urged me down onto the bed, parting from me at last.

I lay there exposed for her, and my breath was fast and hard as I waited for whatever came next. She smiled at me and ran her hand down my body once before she moved herself over me, tangling her legs with mine as she resumed our kiss. Then she pulled back, moving off the one side, her legs still wrapped up with mine.

'Do you want to touch me?' she asked.

'Yes.' I moved my hands up, suddenly shy, and cupped one of her breasts, feeling the weight and the curve and the softness of it. It was at once just like my own body and yet completely foreign, and I closed my eyes and breathed in her scent as I gently rolled her nipples between my fingers and massaged in the way I might have liked to do for myself.

She moaned as I touched her, and her pleasure made me bold. I moved one hand lower and found that pool of arousal between her legs, moving awkwardly because of the unfamiliar angle but growing bolder by the second as I found her clit and made her gasp and rock against my hand.

I found a rhythm, teasing and rubbing at her clit until she was moaning in a regular rhythm and thrusting into my hand, encouraging me as I touched her in exactly the ways I had always wished my husband knew how to touch me. Within minutes she added a whimpering cry to each exhale, and I found myself holding my breath as I watched her face, waiting for that transformation.

When she came it was like seeing the face of the divine.

I stopped moving, frozen in awe, and she laughed when she stopped moaning and opened her eyes to see my expression. 'Come here,' she said, opening her arms to me. I moved atop her and she showed me with gestures and a few words how to position myself so that I could move against her, my clit riding against her thigh. I felt her slickness against my hip and realised that she was reaching for her peak again too. The thought alone seemed to force me to a higher level of arousal, and I moaned as I felt my orgasm draw closer.

Being able to come with my husband was rare and I hadn't had high expectations for tonight, but as our bodies moved against one another and our breath merged in pants and sighs of pleasure, I knew that I was only seconds from that pinnacle of pleasure.

I held off for as long as I could, and was finally rewarded when Sam's eyes started to roll back and she began to shake like a leaf beneath me. I let myself go, then, feeling the pleasure roll over me and crash down, drowning me in powerful waves of ecstasy until I was nearly in tears from the intensity of it.

I did cry, when it was over, and Sam held me patiently, whispering soothing things to me. 'I'm going to have to leave him, aren't I?' Sam didn't say anything. She didn't have to. 'Will you help me?'

'Of course,' she whispered, and when she kissed me it brought back the memory of that life-changing wave of pleasure and a promise of all of the pleasure that awaited me in her arms.

The Lock-in
by Alice Candy

'The Highlands?' I'd almost choked on my goat's cheese salad when JJ suggested it.

'You'll love it, Roxy. I promise.'

'Ah, you know I'm a city girl. I'm allergic to the countryside. I'll get vertigo up there in Scotland.'

'I want to show you more of where I'm from. You'll get to know me better.'

'I'm not ready for the meeting the parents bit.'

'Neither am I. I'm not sure what my parents would make of you anyway. I'm not thinking of anywhere near my parents' place. This weekend is going to be purely about chilling out.'

I stretched lazily in the passenger seat of the hire car, feeling the cool early September breeze whip through my hair. Under the cover of my sunglasses I stole the chance to admire JJ, who was taking her turn in the driving seat beside me. She was lightly tanned in a black sleeveless vest and skinny jeans. Her arms were slim and taut. I loved her bright blue eyes and the short blonde bob that curled just above her chin. I still marvelled at my luck in finding her. I especially loved the contrast when I looked at photos of us together. The two of us laughing our way through the summer. Her delicate features nuzzled up to me with my dark skin, brown eyes, and black hair courtesy of my Greek mother. It had been quite a summer. We met just as spring was bursting in May and the long summer nights that followed had provided a perfect opportunity to explore each other. How we had explored, I smiled to myself. It was the hottest relationship I had had in a long time. JJ at 25 was 12 years younger than me. She was into experimenting and I was happy to rediscover my own enthusiasm for sexy adventures. This weekend had been very different, though, and I was delighted that away from the scene in London we seemed to be getting on better than ever.

'Yes, I have to admit I am enjoying myself. You were right, darling,' I said, dangling my arm out of the window to feel the cool air rush past on an evening milder than I ever expected in early September in Scotland. We were driving through a forest near Aviemore. It was lush and green, quite majestic in its beauty. It felt like a million miles from my usual North London stomping ground and I was loving every moment. We'd both needed this, at the end of a long summer in London of partying too much, working too hard, and indulging in extra partners a little too often. Things had got a little frenetic, and before one or both of us ended up needing a stint in rehab we decided we needed to chill.

So my sexy Scots girlfriend and I had flown into Inverness Airport in bright sunshine and hired a car for the drive to the cottage we'd rented for a long weekend. We had spent the weekend in bed having lazy couples' sex, leaving only to eat in little country pubs or walk alongside beautiful calm lochs. By the Sunday, our last full day, we were feeling totally and utterly relaxed.

'This summer has been pretty wild. Even by my standards,' I admitted.

'Great, though.'

'I feel like I've corrupted you, wee Scottish lassie.'

JJ bristled slightly. I'd started to notice it annoyed her a little when I teased her. 'You think I'm naïve,' she had told me once in a drink-fuelled argument, and accused me of being narrow-minded. I'd never been called that in my life. I'm just loud and opinionated. I thought she was pretty streetwise, really, and I was amazed at her appetite for trying all sorts of sex. She had only lived in London a year and was really just beginning to find her feet there.

We had partied practically since we met, my job as manager of a lesbian bar meaning we could get to know each other's friends. Sometimes a little too well. We had decided to have an open relationship at the start, both cool with each other exploring with other people, sometimes exploring someone else together. It had been an amazing time, but both of us agreed that we had come to the end of the summer feeling burnt out and keen to quieten things down just a little. I had begun to hanker for something more committed too. After a lot of red wine and feeling romantic this weekend, I had suggested being more exclusive with one another.

'I must be getting old. But I'm starting to feel I just want to be with you in bed. All these extra bodies are wearing me out, darling.'

'Hmm, I don't know.' She had mumbled a bit, and changed the subject. I'd tried my best to hide my disappointment that JJ had not felt the same way.

The weekend had been pretty much perfect. It was good to get away from all our friends just for a little while. We socialised in a group of party animals, and there was always something going on, plans being made. It made a change to be on our own and not have promised to be somewhere else.

'I'm switching off my phone. The reception's better than I thought it would be up here. I keep getting texts. "How's it going up there? Shagged any sheep yet? Are you the only lesbians in the village"?'

'I'm thirsty. Fancy stopping for a drink?' said JJ.

We passed a nondescript-looking place we didn't fancy on the road, so we consulted the guide book and headed for the nearest village, finding a little pub standing alone at the end of a street. Old sandstone, with flower beds to the front, it looked like a charming country pub, so JJ pulled over and parked up.

If the charming exterior had lured us in, the welcome when we entered the bar didn't match. A couple who looked in their 60s stood behind the bar, looking none too pleased to see us.

'We were closing early tonight.'

A couple of men sitting at the bar were finishing their pints and looking sheepish.

'A Coke and a gin and tonic, please,' I said cheerily. 'We drink fast.'

The barman, with barely disguised reluctance, sloshed some draught Coke into a glass and set it on the bar while the woman fixed a gin and tonic and eyed JJ and me suspiciously. We took our drinks and sat down at a table in the corner. The bar was cosy, if a little bit twee. It had tartan-covered stools and curtains, and a couple of Highland cow and sheep ornaments stood side by side on the shelf next to the optics in the bar. Apart from the frosty welcome, it was a nice little place for a pit stop.

'Things are looking up.' I grinned as an attractive young woman of about 20 walked into the bar. Her hair was white-blonde and short and she had a pretty, pixie-like face. She was slim but revealed an ample bosom when she took off her cardigan to reveal a tight, clinging T-shirt. JJ and I grinned at each other as we both sneaked a peek at her full, sexy breasts and clearly hard nipples poking through the fine cotton of her top. The girl caught sight of us admiring her and she smiled warmly at us.

'Hi.' She waved over. She walked behind the bar and tipped several bags of change into the till. Then she bounced off into the area behind the bar, which looked like the kitchen, and we got an unexpected treat when we saw her whip off her T-shirt and bound up a stairway topless, her breasts bouncing as she went.

'Hot,' said JJ.

'Smoking,' I agreed.

In seconds she had appeared back in the bar in a fresh T-shirt, but still braless, JJ and I were pleased to note.

'Want another?' she called over to us.

'We thought you were closing.'

The old couple were frowning by the bar.

'On you go up and watch the telly,' she told them. 'I'll finish off down here myself.'

I decided to order a whisky and JJ had another Coke.

The men at the bar had drained their pints and were making for the door. 'Night,' she called to them.

'Aye, night, Morag.'

She raised her eyebrows at us. 'I hate my name. My friends

call me Moo.'

The bar was now empty except for the three of us. Moo told us she worked in her parents' pub full time as bar manager.

'Doesn't it drive you mad, a young girl like you up here in the sticks?' I asked.

'I always find ways to make it fun.' Her eyes twinkled when she spoke and I couldn't help wondering what sort of fun she meant. 'Why don't you stay for a bit? We'll have a lock-in.'

She locked the pub door and bolted it. Moo brought a bottle of whisky and three fresh glasses with ice over to our table. She changed the bagpipe music to a Rihanna CD. Not a favourite of mine, but a welcome change anyway. JJ was sticking to her Coke, and we talked and drank and Moo and I got a little bit merry.

The mood was light and happy and then JJ suddenly blurted out, 'You have the most fantastic tits.'

Moo laughed. 'That's how I got the name Moo, because of my big udders.'

I cringed inwardly a little at that. The two of them were giggling, and with that, and Rihanna belting out *Only Girl in the World* in the background, I suddenly felt the age gap between JJ and me, something I hadn't thought about all weekend.

'Do you want to touch them?' I was surprised that Moo was directing her offer at me.

I looked at JJ. 'I can't resist.'

'I'm next.' JJ laughed.

She pulled up her top and we both took turns to fondle Moo's naked breasts. They were fantastic: bouncy and full. I sucked on her large, pink nipples, teasing and pulling them until they were erect. JJ pulled her own top off, and Moo turned round and started caressing her breasts.

Moo went off behind the bar and into the refrigerator and came back with a can of squirty cream. 'For the hot chocolate, normally,' she explained, and we all burst out laughing. She squirted the cream over her own breasts, and JJ and I took a breast each and licked it off.

We were getting louder and louder and JJ, the sober one, asked, 'Your parents. Won't they hear us?'

Moo seemed not to care.

'I don't think so. They're half deaf, I think, and they always have the telly up full volume.' By now the squirty cream was finished. There was a pause, then Moo stood up. 'Come with me.'

She pulled on her top and told us to follow her. She led us behind the bar and into the hallway, but headed for a door. She threw on a light which only dimly lit the way. She led us down a dingy stone stair into the cellar of the pub. We picked our way in the half-light through a maze of boxes and crates of bottles and barrels of beer. Moo picked up a torch from a shelf.

Moo was fumbling with a key at a door. An ordinary door that looked like it would be a storage cupboard. She turned the key in the lock and opened it.

'Welcome,' she said with amusement in her voice, 'to the dungeon.'

We could barely see a thing at first. Moo didn't bother to put on a light; instead, she used her torch and took a box of matches from a shelf. She then went round with her torch and lit masses of tea lights, and the secrets of the room were revealed. In the daylight and without the haze of drunkenness I suspected it would have looked murky and dingy, but in the glow of the tea lights and with a good whisky mist cast over it, it looked magical. A sofa lay in one corner, covered in a couple of velvet throws and various scatter cushions. But, most intriguing of all, was the contraption that lay in the corner opposite. It appeared to be an old dentist's chair. In the shadowy glow of the candlelight it had a sinister edge. Two large chains with a set of cuffs attached hung from its arms, tossed onto the seat of the chair. There were stirrups for the feet. I had seen stuff like this before, of course. At fetish clubs and even once in someone's basement in Shoreditch. Not what I expected, though, in the Highlands of Scotland. Maybe JJ was right. Maybe I was more narrow-minded than I thought.

'Look, darling. I can't speak for JJ, but this sort of thing ain't my scene,' I said.

JJ was cool and calm. 'I don't mind trying.'

Moo and JJ stood in front of the chair while they caressed

and kissed. Slowly they stripped each other until they both stood there completely naked, the kissing growing more intense as the excitement heightened. I sat on the sofa and, as I watched the two of them, I felt a short stab of jealousy. They looked beautiful together as their hands moved over each other's breasts and buttocks. But despite my feelings I felt hugely turned on too. I wanted JJ to have a good time and be who she is, even if that meant sharing her sometimes.

Moo sat herself in the seat and shackled herself in. She spread her legs wide apart and inserted her feet into the stirrups, exposing her pussy. JJ didn't need asking twice. She was over there and on her knees straight away. Her hands caressed Moo's thighs. Moo's naked body looked amazing with her legs spread wide. JJ was down on her knees, kissing her belly, her inner thighs. Teasing her before the main event. Then she moved slowly to her pussy and began kissing it and probing it with her tongue. I watched JJ's blonde head bob up and down; hearing the licking and smacking noises I grew so turned on I pulled down my jeans and knickers and began to touch myself.

The dungeon was full of the sound of female pleasure. Moo's moans grew louder and louder until, finally, she tensed against her shackles and cried out in one long sigh of bliss. Almost immediately after, I came too. I sat there, watching as JJ freed Moo from her restraints.

JJ was now sitting in the seat of the chair. Moo kissed her furiously. I moved toward the chair. Moo spread JJ's legs and put her feet into the cuffs and stirrups. I thought about taking a more active role, but Moo had other ideas. She was standing naked in front of JJ, fondling her breasts, squeezing them together, then letting them go. I realised I was a mere bystander as Moo made her way to the hot, sticky pussy of my girlfriend. I felt jealous, but I steeled myself and pushed it aside. I had to let this happen. I could see JJ was incredibly turned on. She was writing in her chains, gasping and crying out to Moo to make her come. Moo did, with incredible skill it seemed, for JJ came louder and harder than I had ever heard her. I felt an acidic sting of envy in the pit of my stomach.

Moo was looking at me now. The friendly demeanour had

evaporated a little, replaced with lustful desire. She was incredibly sexy. Moo went toward the unlocked cupboard and pulled something out I couldn't quite make out in the darkness. As she walked back into the glow of the candlelight it became clear.

'Ah, more my thing now.' I laughed, reaching out for the large brown leather dildo Moo held in her hands.

'Uh-uh. I'm wearing this, you're taking it.'

I couldn't help but laugh at the cheek of this foxy young thing. I was usually the one wearing the strap-on, but I am always prepared to take it when the occasion requires. I'm not naturally submissive, though, and I was starting to feel like an indulgent older woman who wanted to let the young ones have their fun.

Moo and I kissed and touched each other frantically. She almost tore my bra straps from my shoulders. Moo urged me toward the sofa. JJ came to the sofa and was stroking my face and hair and kissing me while Moo emerged from the shadows, the great strap-on lolling and slapping against her slim, white thighs.

Moo crouched over me on all fours, caressing me, her large, soft breasts falling softly against my own. In the muted light I was pleased to see our entangled bodies looked good together; Moo pale and soft against my dark, tanned, and still athletic body. Moo sucked on my nipples before making her way down my torso. She knelt up to separate my legs and then gently, softly, she started to kiss my pussy. Slowly flicking out her tongue and teasing me with small, light flicks of her tongue to her clitoris. I sighed loudly with pleasure. JJ was massaging my breasts and rubbing my nipples. Normally the more dominant one sexually, I lay there and let myself surrender to the moment. I realised I had forgotten how good it was to let someone else take charge.

Moo was kneeling up, holding the strap-on, and now that I was nice and juicy wet she was preparing to mount me. She pushed the dildo in slowly, gently at first, both of us enjoying the sensation of the huge leather appendage filling me. Moo started to rock her hips back and forth, clearly enjoying the sight of me gasping and writhing beneath her. Her gasps grew louder, more frantic, till she almost sounded like she was in pain, her face distorting. JJ was masturbating frantically and looked close to coming. With a few more mighty thrusts, we roared out our climax together.

As I lay sated on the sofa, JJ and Moo met each other's eyes and giggled.

'I could do with a drink. Got anything?' I asked with a wry smile.

Back in the bar, I remembered JJ was stone cold sober and she was wondering aloud when the parents would make an appearance. We had made a hell of a racket down there.

Moo fixed us both drinks, but it was clear she was ready now for us to leave. She was still friendly, but more efficient and functional. We drained our drinks, embraced each other, and said our goodbyes.

'Just one thing, if you don't mind me asking,' I said. 'That stuff down there is pretty – well, you know … Not what I ever expected to find in a remote country pub.'

Moo smiled. 'I think there's no better place.'

'Your parents –' JJ said, tentatively aware we might be overstepping the mark with our questions. 'How do you keep it hidden from them?'

Moo laughed heartily, unlocking the pub door for us and freeing the bolts.

'I don't. It's theirs. Luckily, they don't mind me borrowing it from time to time.'

Overtime
by Harper Bliss

Laura blinked twice. The letters in front of her started to swim. She'd been huddled over the document for hours, trying to find a loophole, a missed technicality, something that would give her an edge in tomorrow's meeting. An unusual office silence hummed around her, closing in. She guessed she was the only one left at this hour. Maybe her colleagues weren't so dead-set on pleasing Cathy, but it was all Laura lived for.

The triple beep of her office phone startled her. She checked the wall clock and wondered who would call her after 10 p.m.

'Burning the midnight oil?' The voice on the other end of the line was deep and throaty and, more than anything else, brimming with effortless authority.

'I'm struggling with the Wallace case.' Laura pinched her eyes shut in frustration. She could never keep her cool when Cathy called. Admitting to the boss, especially a boss like Cathy, who loathed weakness, that she was getting nowhere with a case was career suicide. 'But I'll get there.' She tried to correct herself.

'Maybe I can help?' Laura wondered what the slight, almost unnoticeable shift in Cathy's tone could mean. She couldn't be serious, though. It must be sarcasm.

'I'm sure you have better things to do, Miss Turner.' Another slip. Laura could hit herself for this one. She was supposed to address her boss as Cathy. Despite being a firm believer in scare tactics and strict hierarchy, Cathy insisted. She liked to play with people's minds like that. 'I mean Cathy,' she mumbled.

'My office in two minutes.' Cathy hung up with a dry click. Laura hated that sentence because, so far, it had always meant she was in trouble. She started mentally preparing for the tongue-lashing she was about to receive. If only she had left the office earlier. Her overtime hadn't produced anything useful and now she had Cathy to deal with as well.

She secured some stray strands of hair behind her ear and straightened the collar of her blouse in the reflection of her computer screen. A deep breath and Laura was on her feet. It was still a private audience with Cathy, she told herself. A late-night rendezvous. The psychological encouragement failed, and by the time Laura knocked on Cathy's door she was a nervous wreck, palms sweating and knees trembling. She was a grown woman, for God's sake. Graduated at the top of her class. Recruited by Cathy herself.

'Come.' Cathy's voice was always stern, but one-word commands made her sound like a vicious army lieutenant with too much power.

Laura opened the door and took a timid step inside. For a woman of her stature, Cathy had ridiculously bad posture. She hunched over her desk, her shoulders drawn up and her neck curved in an unnatural position. With icy-blue eyes she peered at Laura over dark-rimmed glasses that had slipped to the tip of her nose.

'I'm sorry, huh, Cathy.' It didn't feel right to address a superior like that, especially one as formidable as Cathy. 'I didn't mean to alarm you. I'm –'

'Shut the door.' Cathy put her pen down and leant back in her chair.

Her heart thumping in her throat, Laura turned around and gingerly closed the door. To her knowledge, they were the only ones left in the office, so shutting the door could only mean one thing. It was time for one of Cathy's infamous sugar-coated, smooth-voiced scoldings that worked best behind closed doors. Cathy Turner wasn't one to yell. She didn't need to raise her voice to get things done.

Laura shuffled toward one of the visitor chairs and pulled it back.

'I didn't say sit.' Cathy's eyes scanned Laura's face, her long lips drawn into her trademark sphinx-like smirk.

Laura withdrew her hand from the chair and didn't know what to do with it. What would appear least weak? Crossing her arms over her chest or clasping her hands together in a lady-like fashion in front of her belly?

'Do you have a girlfriend?'

Laura certainly wasn't expecting that question.

'What?' she stammered as her cheeks flamed pink.

'A boyfriend, maybe?' Cathy didn't show any emotion on her face. She asked it as if she were enquiring about the weather forecast, as if the answer didn't really matter.

'No. I'm single.' Laura had to force herself not to add a reverent "ma'am" at the end of her statement.

'I thought as much.' Cathy pushed her chair back. The scraping of its wheels over the floor made Laura jump.

Laura had steeled herself for a chastising speech and these personal questions were throwing her off guard. No doubt it was Cathy's plan to break down her defences completely before she went in for the kill. Nothing was ever straightforward with her, and if she couldn't make a game out of it, it wasn't worth investing any time in. At least Laura knew that much.

With a swift movement, Cathy pushed herself out of her chair. She briefly placed her hands on her desk, forcing the shoulder-pads of her navy pinstriped blazer to puff up. She reminded Laura of a lion about to pounce; the only thing missing was the audacious licking of lips.

'I see your ambition.'

Laura had a hard time keeping her eyes off Cathy's legs. Her boss strutted toward the front of the desk, toward her, and leant her behind against it. Cathy planted the palms of her hands on the table top and crossed her ankles. From day one, Laura had been enamoured with Cathy's glossy legs. Maybe because they stood in stark contrast to her overbearing, manipulative personality. Or maybe because, while always on display under Cathy's pencil skirts, they were so untouchable.

'It reminds me of me. When I was your age, I was always the last one to leave the office.' Cathy pushed a strand of perfectly coiffed blonde hair away from her forehead. 'I was single for a long time as well.'

Was this advice on romance? Laura's confusion grew.

'Of course, now I'm divorced.' At last, a sparse smile tugged at the corners of her mouth. Maybe she thought her divorce was funny – Laura believed Cathy didn't find anything funny. 'Don't make the same mistakes I did.' After removing her glasses, Cathy pinned her eyes back on Laura. 'In the end, it's not worth it.'

Laura couldn't believe she was in the middle of a heart-to-heart with the mighty Cathy Turner. Truth be told, it was more of a monologue, really, but still, Cathy was confiding in her. Clearly, she was suffering from some sort of melancholy that drove her to impart this nutshell of wisdom on Laura. Or maybe her divorce papers had just come through.

'I won't.' Laura felt it was a good time to speak, although she couldn't entirely relax. She never could around Cathy. Not just because she was her boss, but also because, even long after office hours, Laura had trouble getting her off her mind. 'It's just I'm still so young, and working here – '

'You don't have to explain.' Cathy pushed herself up from the desk and put her glasses, which she still held in one hand, behind her.

Laura was glad Cathy hadn't mentioned the Wallace case, but she had no idea what to do now Cathy marched toward her. Everything was quiet around them, the soft thuds of Cathy's heels on the wooden floor the only sound. Until Cathy was so close Laura could hear her breathe. Her own breathing was suffering, and she had to swallow hard. In a year of working for Cathy, they'd probably never stood this close together.

Instinctively, Laura took a step back. She didn't want to, and it wasn't a conscious decision, but she did. Perhaps her body thought it the logical next step in this late-night match of office Stratego, or whatever game they were playing.

'Lock the door.' Cathy's voice was low, a little menacing, and extremely sexy.

'What?'

'Turn the key to the right and lock the door.'

Laura stifled her natural reflexes to protest and did as Cathy ordered. When she spun around, her back against the door, Cathy stood mere inches away. Her eyes peered into Laura's as a small smile crept along her lips.

Before Laura had a chance to even consider what was happening, Cathy's hand was on her chest. Her fingers pressed against Laura's clavicle before finding their way down her blouse. Without warning or words, Cathy snuck her hand under Laura's bra and squeezed her nipple brutally between thumb and index finger.

Laura gasped for air. A sharp pain sped through her body as Cathy pinched harder.

Not allowing her eyes to leave Laura's, Cathy leant in a little closer.

'I'm only going to ask you once.' Cathy's lips found Laura's ear. 'Do you want me to fuck you?'

Laura nodded. Shaking her head was all she could muster. The power of speech seemed to have escaped her the moment Cathy's hand had landed on her skin. It was also hard to decline an offer like that when her boss' strong fingers were squashing her nipple. And besides, she wanted nothing more than to get fucked by Cathy Turner. The deemed impossible prospect of it had fed her fantasies for months.

'Good.' Cathy growled in her ear. She'd always had something animal-like about her, something feline. Sly as a cat. Reflexes honed to always come up with a sharp reply. Her eyes looked like they could burn through darkness. And then there was that cold, distant air, designed to keep people at bay and simultaneously lure them in, people like Laura at least.

Laura felt herself go damp between the legs as Cathy kissed her neck. She trailed a path of light pecks along her jaw until she reached Laura's trembling lips. The first thing Laura felt were teeth sinking into her bottom lip. Unsurprisingly, Cathy was not a gentle lover.

Laura responded greedily when Cathy slipped her tongue into her mouth. She latched on as if she'd never get an opportunity to taste it again. Pangs of lust shivered up her spine. Cathy roughly undid Laura's blouse, not caring about the delicacy of the fabric and the way the buttons were sewn into it. Laura was past wondering if she could ruffle her hands through Cathy's sculpted hair. It felt remarkably soft when she let it flow through her fingers, not at all like the hair-sprayed mass she had expected. Yet she was afraid to touch Cathy in any other place. Frightened to go near her breasts and explore their shape. Way too daunted to even think about opening a button of her starched blouse. It was clear who was in charge, who was always in charge.

Cathy yanked down the cups of Laura's bra, exposing one battered and one perky nipple to the air-conditioned office air. Electricity coursed through Laura's body. It wasn't so much Cathy's touches, which were sparse and rough at best – not that she minded – but the fact that she stood cornered against Cathy's locked office door, her boss all over her. Like most things that went on in this office, it was more a mind game than anything else. Maybe Cathy thought she had the winning hand again, but at least Laura knew that, for her, a massive orgasm was on its way. She felt it in the shortness of her breath, the goosebumps on her skin, and the heat between her legs.

Cathy's hand travelled down, to the button of her trousers. This pantsuit had cost a fortune but Laura didn't care if Cathy ripped it to shreds, as long as her fingers arrived where it mattered soon.

While amping up the pressure on Laura's tortured nipple, Cathy lowered her zipper in a slow and controlled manner – as if there was any other way. As unusual as this situation was, it was still a classic Cathy moment. A demonstration of power from the boss and an extreme act of obedience by the employee. Laura wondered what Cathy would taste like, feel like under her tongue, at her mercy. Despite what was going on, and the possible opening it might bring forth, Laura knew it would never happen.

'You're all wet for me.' Cathy's mouth went back and forth between Laura's lips and ear, nibbling and kissing both. 'Good girl.'

Cathy's fingers rubbed the soaking wet seam of her panties, inches away from Laura's throbbing clit. At last she released

Laura's nipple and used both her hands to tug Laura's pants down, underwear included. The sudden rush of air blowing between her legs made Laura's skin break out in goosebumps. Her clit swelled in the breeze of the AC and she could feel juices leaking from her pussy, moistening her upper thighs. She was more than ready for Cathy to fuck her.

Shaking her shoes and pants off, Laura searched for Cathy's eyes. Their icy stare seemed laced with a tiny sparkle, a glimmer of what usually stayed hidden. Apart from a tousled hairdo and a few creases in her blazer, Cathy's demeanour appeared unaffected. In stark contrast to Laura's dishevelled state, with her blouse torn open, her pants crumpled on the floor, and the cups of her bra pushing her breasts up from underneath.

Cathy repositioned. She pinned her gaze on Laura, unblinking and unwavering, like in a deposition with a hostile witness. One hand shot straight to Laura's neck, its thumb tracing the line of her collarbone. Laura couldn't see Cathy's other hand, but she sure felt it. Its fingers skated along her moist pussy lips with overwhelming tenderness. Up and down they travelled, only inviting more wetness to ooze from between Laura's legs.

During dull moments in meetings, Laura had often inadvertently stared at Cathy's fingers and wondered what they would feel like pressed inside her. Her breath hitched in her throat as Cathy parted her lips and slipped a finger between her folds, not too deep, merely probing.

'I'll fuck you.' Cathy peered into her eyes, as if she wanted to stare her down. 'Just like you want me to.' Her voice sounded lower than Laura had ever heard it. And just like that, Cathy pushed two fingers inside.

Laura gasped, feeling her pussy clench around Cathy's knuckles. She let her head fall back against the door, pulling her eyes away from Cathy's triumphant grin, looking up. Cathy retreated slowly, letting her fingers hover at the rim of Laura's pussy for a split second before slamming them inside again.

'Look at me,' she commanded and, as if she had no other choice in the world, Laura lowered her gaze and met Cathy's eyes. They shone with shameless bravado, but Laura swore she could make out something else in them as well. Something she'd never seen in Cathy's glance before, something fragile and akin to desire. Or maybe she was too caught up in her own lust, in her own world of pleasure at the mercy of Cathy's fingers, to see things clearly.

Cathy kept thrusting her fingers inside, pulling out gently and going in with hard determination. Each stroke delivered Laura to new heights. She focused on Cathy's eyes, let herself drown in the cold blue of them. Her pussy sucked Cathy's fingers in, accepting them eagerly, while her clit roared for attention. She wanted to touch herself. Her hands were idle anyway, hesitating between finding a grip on the door and tugging Cathy's clothes off. But she knew better than to take that kind of initiative.

A mild grimace took hold of Cathy's face every time she delved deeper inside Laura's pussy. Cathy's other hand dipped lower, to Laura's other breast, kneading it roughly before going to work on the nipple. The pinch of her fingers around Laura's nipple sent an electric jolt through her system, connecting with her pussy. Her blood seemed to sparkle, her entire body expanding and contracting around Cathy's fingers.

Just at the right time, just when Laura felt she couldn't take any more, Cathy flipped her thumb over Laura's engorged clit, setting off a round of fireworks in her brain. Fingers kept stroking her inside, touching her deep down, while the thumb of Cathy's hand expertly nudged her clit. Laura wanted to stay in this moment; the moment before all fuses blew, the moment before Cathy would retreat for ever.

As her climax approached, crashing into her from all angles, Laura had trouble looking into Cathy's eyes. Her eyelids fluttered, and in between the instances of darkness she noticed how Cathy's cheeks flushed. This crack in her boss' stoic air moved her more than anything. Laura let go and came all over Cathy's hands, no doubt staining the cuffs of her tailored blouse.

'God,' Laura murmured. When she opened her eyes, Cathy stared right back at her, a relaxed expression on her face.

Knowing this illicit office dalliance at least meant a little something to Cathy made it doubly satisfying for Laura. Carefully, Cathy let her fingers slip from Laura's pussy and lifted them between their faces. They glistened with juice and smelled of Laura's musky wetness.

'Open your mouth.' Cathy was back to giving orders again and Laura easily complied. She tasted herself on her lips as Cathy ran her fingers over them, before inserting them into her mouth. Laura licked and sucked, savouring the feeling of Cathy's fingers on her tongue. It was her turn to drill her eyes into Cathy's, who, try as she might, couldn't stop an almost inaudible gasp from escaping her.

With her fingers still in Laura's mouth, Cathy inched closer and pressed her lips against Laura's. Despite coming on her boss' fingers earlier, this was by far the most intimate moment they had shared. Laura felt her legs go weak again and this time she couldn't stop herself. Unhinged from her thoughts and inhibitions, her hands drifted to the waistband of Cathy's skirt. She'd barely touched Cathy and was consumed by the desire to do so, to give back. Cathy paid her, after all. Cathy stiffened at her touch and retracted her fingers as well as her lips.

'That's all right.' She placed her hands on top of Laura's. 'Unlike you, I can take care of myself.'

Just like that, Cathy slipped back into professional mode, as if this had been a business transaction, or a mere favour bestowed by a boss on a desperate employee. Laura knew fucking her had satisfied Cathy, though. Otherwise, she simply wouldn't have done it. With a last glimmer of goodwill, Cathy bent down and picked up Laura's pants.

'You'll need to get these dry-cleaned.'

Laura discarded her panties and slipped into her trousers, pulled up her bra cups, and quickly buttoned up her blouse. Cathy stood waiting at her desk, leaning against it like she had done before coming for her.

'Good night, Cathy.' Laura unlocked the door and cradled the handle in her hand.

'If you ever tell anyone about this, there will be consequences.' Cathy's voice had crept back into its most menacing register. 'Understood?'

Laura spun around and faced Cathy one last time. It seemed unreal – and certainly implausible – that she'd just given her such pleasure. The aura in the office had gone straight back to its usual frostiness, not leaving any room for sentiments.

'Of course.' She shot Cathy a smile she expected to be most unwelcome. 'Tomorrow I'll be working overtime again.' Laura licked her lips. 'I hope you approve.' With that, she turned the knob, and was out of the door.

Lam-dancing
by Lynn Lake

I smacked the clanging alarm clock off the nightstand and against the wall. It bounced, gave out one last shrill shriek, and then clattered to the floor. I stretched and yawned, wiggled my toes, rubbed my eyes, rolled over on the bed – and stared at the white empty space next to me.

Hot tears leapt into my swollen eyes, and my throat constricted with even more cotton.

Jenny was gone. And she wasn't coming back.

I rolled back over and up and slapped my bare feet down onto the floor, hung my head. She'd taken a powder on me and the whole sorry mess we'd called our life together – colleagues at the dime-a-dance dump, lovers in our lousy apartment.

I padded out of the bedroom and across to the bathroom, barely made it to the toilet in time.

Despite the cold shower, three cups of black coffee, and four French cigarettes, I was still as wobbly as an IWW member when I bumped into Mrs Stoyko on the second floor landing.

'You pay me my rent!' she demanded, dropping her slop bucket and sticking her hand out.

Mrs Stoyko was my slumlord, a short, stocky woman with hard blue eyes and even harder red features, her blonde hair bottled back from the old country. I silently cursed the Depression that had dropped me down into the dregs along with so many others, cursed Mrs Stoyko for having me in her clutches and never forgetting to squeeze. With Jenny gone, I was baffled as to how to make up her half of the 125 beans per month.

But then the fog lifted, and a dismal idea hit me, right where it hurts. It was slightly distasteful, somewhat immoral. Like bathtub gin.

I smiled sweet as muff pie and batted my eyelashes like I was warding off Cupid's arrows. Then I reached out and touched Mrs Stoyko's stolid shoulder, leant in and planted a soft kiss on her peasant lips.

She thawed like a Russian spring. The hardline dyke had been trying to make me and Jenny ever since we'd moved into her flophouse six months earlier.

'Well ... You come to my place tonight,' she allowed. 'We talk it over some more, no?'

'No,' I agreed, and disagreed, grinning and pinching one of her puffy cheeks.

Then I trotted off down the stairs, leaving her to figure out what I meant.

Leaving me a full work day to find a new dive to live.

'If it ain't Sleepin' Beauty,' Roscoe cracked, as soon as I shoved through the swinging doors of his dance joint.

I guess I did look kind of beat up after the bender I'd been on the night before. 'And if it ain't Prince Charmin',' I snapped right back. Jumping away when the lout tried to wrestle with me.

'Dime a dance, buster,' I taunted. 'Like all the other bozos not gettin' any.'

Roscoe wasn't a bad slob, as long as you knew how to talk back to him, and parry his pawing advances. He might own the shuffle emporium, but that didn't give him free access to my goodies. I strolled out of range of his leering eyes and mitts, making tracks across the gloomy dance floor and down the hallway in back.

'I-I was wondering when you were gonna show up, Sally,' Ruthie greeted me, as soon as I pushed into the dingy dressing room. She leapt off the chipped counter in front of the cracked mirror and stared at me with her big baby-blues.

The seven other girls lounging around laughed.

'Yeah, Ruthie's been pining away like a wooden nickel.' Earnestine made with the needle, taking a break from caking her homely face.

'Go climb your thumb,' I suggested.

'Oh my! What a mouth she has!' Earnestine feigned indignation, like the tramp had any dignity to start with. 'What a mouth has she – right, Ruthie?'

The girls cackled at that one too. Except Ruthie. She was still looking at me with her tongue hanging out.

She was 19, had a sexual appetite that just couldn't be satiated – for and by the same sex. She looked like a flapper from another, better era, tall and thin with bobbed black hair and long black lashes and smooth, pale skin.

She also had a connection in the bootlegging biz, and any girl who serviced her sex could get her fair share. I'd been making the oral transaction at both ends downright regular since Jenny had taken the air.

And that particular morning, I needed the hair of the dog something bad. Which meant the hair of Ruthie's pussy.

I gave her the nod and she squealed and ran after me out of the room. I met up with her legs in the tiny washroom at the end of the dank hallway. She hiked up the hem of her cocktail dress and jumped up onto the sink, just as my stockinged knees kissed the cracked floor tiles in front of her. I gripped her ivory thighs, swallowed hard, sunk my tongue into her dark-furred slit.

'Oh Sally!' Ruthie wailed, like my mouth and her mound hadn't been fornicatingly introduced ten times before.

I licked her pussy, stroking up and down through her downy fur and over her dewy pink flaps. She batted her high heels against the small of my back, grabbing onto my curls and rocking with delight. Two things you could say about Ruthie: she was always happy to see you, and she always delivered the goods.

Her perfumed, juicy pussy didn't make bad eating either, I had to admit. Especially for a girl operating on an empty stomach and love life. I dug my tongue deep into the task, spearing through Ruthie's petals and into her tunnel, then pumping back and forth in her honeypit with my hardened mouth-organ. She quivered and quavered, biting her lip and rolling her eyes, gushing all over my tongue work.

'Use your fingers, Sally! *And* your mouth!' she bleated, clawing my scalp and convulsing.

She was all ready to go off, shoot the works; but she wanted the knuckles-deep, sealed-button send-off.

I gave it to her, knowing she kept a quart in her purse. Eating was one thing, it kept you alive, but drinking kept you immune.

I lifted my head and traded in my tongue for two fingers, plunging three knuckles long into Ruthie's hot pussy. She shuddered, squealed. I dropped my head back closer and sucked up her swollen pink clit.

Ruthie gasped, shivered, as I pistoned her slit with my fingers, pulled on her clit with my lips. Her sexthusiasm was contagious, my face burning as red as the comrades in Coxey's Army, my own pussy tingling with a fervour I felt deep in the hole in my soul.

But Ruthie was ultimately all about Ruthie, the flapper frolic girl. She wasn't about to wait for me to build up my passion, or help me satisfy it. I tried to slow the thrust of my digits, ease the vacuum pressure of my mouth. But the dark-haired dyke was already too far gone. She screamed, stiffened, spasmed, squirted all around my fingers and against my chin.

So I let her have it hard and fast and sucksational again. She gave it back to me in convulsing hot waves.

And then she made with the real good stuff – 100 proof.

It was a busy day at the grope palace. The anxious guys and their clammy hands and clumsy feet were lined up two-deep along the near wall, dance tickets in hand and hard-ons ready to pop. I think there was an accounting convention in town or something.

Roscoe chewed his cigar and watched the dimes roll, dollar signs in his eyes, a thousand-watt grin on his 15-watt face. I kept going on a heady mixture of Long Island Lightning and fantasies of a rainbow just around the corner (like in the song).

'Let's dance, huh?'

'That's the ticket!' I yelped, half-crocked.

He was a little guy, with slick brown hair mostly hidden under a Homburg, a kind of delicate, pretty face half-hidden behind sunglasses. His black suit was cut baggy, and his spats hung sort of loose. He grabbed onto my waist and hand and I burped, 'All aboard!'

'Less mouth and more movement, huh, toots?' he grunted, his voice husky like he was working at being tough.

'You pays your dime, you gets your time! Oops!' I bopped my lips with my fingers, bulged my eyes Betty Boop-style. 'Sorry!'

'Some kind of lush, huh?'

'Some kind.'

He moved really well, whisking me around the dance floor, his form lithe and light-footed. But he shoved me back when I tried to shimmy closer, holding me off at arms' length.

Until two coppers suddenly barged in the front doors. Then the dapper little dancer pulled me tight, whirled the both of us away to a far corner of the dimly lit jive dive.

His body *was* lithe, slender and sinuous, almost curvy against me. And there was a pair of soft mounds pressing into my soft mounds from beneath that oversized suit jacket and white shirt of his.

'We're lookin' for a dame!' one of the cops roared at Roscoe, his bullhorn voice cutting through the muted music and sliding shoe leather.

'You come to the right place!' Roscoe cracked back.

The flatfoot gave him the frosty focus, his slab face congealing along angry lines.

'Just my dancers in here, officer!' Roscoe hastened to placate. 'And their dates.'

The other cop started muscling his way around the dance floor, giving the glare to all the coupled hoofers, me and my partner included. Before he moved on to check in the back.

'Any dames come in here in the last ten minutes!?'

Roscoe shook his jowls. 'Just gents, officer. I would've noticed any dames.' His grin was oiled.

The other lawman emerged from the back and shook his head, and the pair of coppers scanned the whole sleazy set-up one more time. I hugged my partner close. Those two soft mounds of "his" were sporting two hard points that butted up against my excited points quite pertly.

'You're a dame – a woman. Aren't you?' I breathed in her ear. 'The one they're after?'

No answer. Just quick, warm breaths bathing my neck from her hot face buried in my shoulder, breasts and nipples beating against my breasts and nipples.

'What'd you do? Tell me quick, or I squawk.'

A gasp. Her grip tightened on me, our heaving bodies moving as one. Then a hiss of hot air, 'I knocked over a bank 15 minutes ago. Changed into these clothes in an alley where I'd planted them. But the bulls are stopping everyone who looks suspicious, so I lammed into this hall to cool off.'

I held my tongue, holding the woman close, an idea brimming my noodle. 'Cut me in or I wail.'

She jerked her head off my shoulder and stared at me.

I opened my mouth, lifted my tongue.

She rasped, 'OK! You're in!'

The flatfoots finally shrugged and drifted.

We danced real close, my new pal and partner, our breasts bobbing together, nipples rubbing. I slid my hand onto the back of her slim neck and squeezed. She slid her hand onto my bum, and squeezed. We sealed our deal with a surreptitious kiss on the lips.

The music stopped, but we didn't. We waltzed right out the back door, when Roscoe had his back turned, and into the alley. I pushed her up against the worn brick and smacked a hard, wet one into her red lips. I had the advantage now like I'd never had it in my entire miserable lifetime before, and I was going to use it to get exactly what I wanted.

'What's your name?' I breathed, breaking the sticky liplock. I pulled away her sunglasses and brushed away her Homburg.

A pair of beautiful violet eyes looked into mine. She had thick, glossy, auburn hair for me to run my fingers through.

'Verona. Verona Massimillio.'

You couldn't make up a moniker like that. We were off to a good start.

'Sally Tompkins,' I replied throatily.

We kissed again, our mouths meeting, moving together by mutual consent. Her lips were soft and wet and supple. I dug my fingers into her lustrous hair, undulating my body against her body.

'I want you to suck my tits, eat my pussy!' I gasped, the air sucked out of me by our impassioned kiss.

The dame knew the score. She spun me around and pinned me up against the wall. She was strong, as well as agile. She pushed my dress off my shoulders and pulled it down, then my slip. My breasts spilled out into her hands.

I writhed against the wall, Verona squeezing my breasts with her hot hands, rolling my nipples with her slender fingers. I lit up like the city at night, my chest and body shimmering.

She dipped her head down and shot out her tongue, swirled the wet, pink appendage all around one of my stiffened nipples, the other one, adding to their aching joy and the aching want in my pussy. And when she sealed a throbbing tit-tip between her lips and sucked on it, I almost melted right into the wall.

She bobbed her head over and sucked on my other nipple, pushing my breasts and buds up in her clenching hands, so she could swallow and vacuum more of both. I could hardly take it, charged up already from the dirty dancing and my dripping session with Ruthie, the absence of my sex bunny Jenny; now electrified by Verona's tit fondling and sucking.

'Fuck me! Fuck me with your wet pussy!' I shrieked.

If she dressed like a man, she might as well fuck like one, bang me up against the alley wall. It was a naughty thought that occurred to me on the spurt of the moment.

Verona bought in, stripping away her jacket and tie and shirt, shoving down her pants. Revealing those soft, warm, pale, pink-tipped breasts that had first aroused my attention, a dark-furred pussy. I shimmied my dress and slip down to my ankles and clasped the near-nude 100 per cent woman to me. Our nipples kissed, bare breasts smooching, pussies touching and tickling and squishing.

She wrapped her arms around me and pumped her pussy against my pussy, our clits sparking. I dove my hands down her curved back and onto her humped, humping buttocks. I squeezed the taut, clutching cheeks, washing my tits against hers, thrusting my mound out to meet her thrusting mound, the pair of us grinding together. Happy days were here again!

'Fuck me, Verona! Fuck me!'

'Yes, Sally! Yes!'

She thumped against me, my nails embedded in her butt cheeks spurring her on. We kissed, frenched, our tongues leaping out and entwining in a slippery mass of pink budded passion. We humped harder and faster, pounding together. Until our tribbing clits triggered pure ecstasy.

Hot, wet waves of utter bliss rolled through our wildly shaking bodies, welling up from our scrunched, steaming cunts and melding us molten as one.

It was the most fun a girl could have on two feet. I'd found my perfect dance partner.

Verona wasn't sure what her next move should be.

I was sure, though. I'd hooked onto a honey with a load of sweet moolah and I wasn't about to let go.

'There's a marathon dance about to start down at the Hippodrome,' I told her. 'Let's enter as man and woman.' I winked at the naked lovely lying next to me. 'Those things can drag on for months. We can hide out there and have all kinds of fun two-stepping until the heat dies down.'

Verona grinned and nodded, then rolled over on top of me for another torrid horizontal tango; the pair of us in heat for the duration, my dance card now full.

Cherry Red
by Jayne Wheatley

I first caught her eye as she boarded the 6 a.m. Heathrow to JFK, the shift I always had hated. My colleague took her pass, and pointed to a triple seat toward the back of the double-decker plane. As she passed by me and I said my hello to her companions, my stomach flipped over. The dress she wore was cherry red and hung off her smooth curves. Her eyes sparkled as they passed over me, and she smiled. I felt a little winded as I chatted to the rest of the passengers. None of them seemed to notice her; she simply sat down, belted up, and shut her eyes. I was well accustomed to the tiredness now, but after we shut the plane doors and starting our prepping for take-off I too let my eyes drift shut as I leant against the wall. In reality, of course, I wasn't tired at all; my stomach had a little group of butterflies dancing in it. I hardly knew how I would talk to her normally; casually offer her drinks without sounding too obvious. Somewhere deep between my legs, a buzzing heat was forming.

'What's up Anna? Bored of the red-eye?' Danny, my best friend in the sky, asked as I caught my breath. I put on my best professional grin and turned back to him as I straightened my obligatory bow tie.

'Nah, course not,' I assured him, my normal South London accent slipping out in place of the usual clear-cut diction I possessed for work. Danny narrowed his eyes.

'Hmm, don't believe you. You're freaking out …'

As he tried to probe me further, the captain announced for us to be seated for take-off. I breathed a sigh of relief as I strapped in and watched the passengers settle in for the runway. I couldn't quite see her from my angle, so I focused on tapping the acupressure points in my wrists that stopped the nausea of a backwards take-off. Though it was raining hard, the take-off was gentle, and soon we'd climbed high enough for myself and the other cabin crew to prepare breakfast.

'OK, so it's not the take-offs, or early flights, what is it? Morning sickness? Oh my God, please tell me it is!' Danny squealed, flapping a little as we poured tea and coffee. I grabbed his arms.

'No! God, I've been single a year!'

He shrugged, pulling a diva pose.

'Oh come on, missy ...'

'Seriously, I'm fine,' I protested, taking a deep breath. His eyes gestured to the meal I was now preparing – it wasn't right.

'And a fruit salad goes on top of bacon, does it? Gimme that, and tell me about it.'

His hazel eyes darted out from behind the sleek fringe to watch my own face in anticipation of a reaction.

I pulled the silvery curtain back to reveal the whole of the ground floor of the plane

'OK, see the girl in, what, 38J?' I asked and he peeped out.

'Red dress, fidgety?'

I looked closer; she was moving around in her seat a lot. I wondered what was wrong.

'Yeah, she makes me feel strange.' I sighed.

Danny gasped. 'Like, scary strange?'

'No,' I replied, a little coldly at his constant hidden fear. 'She's so ... hot.'

He pulled the curtain back over my face and I shook my head. My heart was hammering, and the pulsing came back. I was hardly innocent and had been in intense relationships with both men and women, but I'd barely spoken to this girl and I was already feeling a little slick in my regulation underwear. I steeled myself and decided to check on the passengers in our section. I smiled politely as I made small talk with them, apologising for the little bumpy patches of turbulence we'd gone through so far. It was a bit unsettled, but I'd seen a lot worse. Everyone seemed happy enough, and I fetched glasses of water and orange juice in turn. As I approached the lovely woman in the red dress my breath caught in my chest, but I kept it together and gripped the seat headrest as I reached her row.

'How is everything?' I stopped myself from looking directly at her, but I could still see her hands tight on the chair arms. The older woman beside her, possibly a relation, leant in to me.

'Could you get her a wine or something? She's a bit terrified,' she whispered, and I nodded as I looked. The woman was shaking like a leaf in her seat, one hand holding her hair tightly while trying to compose herself. I gave her a smile and her dark eyes shone back, tears obviously desperate to break free as she looked almost past me.

'Please don't worry, this is very normal. I'll bring you a little wine in a moment,' I told her with my most soothing voice. As I walked away, I very nearly lost my footing as the plane banked. I had to pull myself together as I was experienced cabin crew. I turned back and she'd shut her eyes again, and seemed to be breathing heavily. I quickly poured her a white wine as Danny popped up behind me and made me jump.

'So, what's she like? Looks like she'd be a bit prissy.'

'Yeah, maybe, but she's petrified,' I replied as the captain switched on the seatbelt light. As this didn't apply to us yet, I carried on and took the wine out to her.

'Really, is this normal?' she muttered as I passed her the drink. I nodded, about to promise it, but then the captain sent a Tannoy asking all cabin crew to be seated too. As I took my seat next to Danny and belted up, he sighed loudly.

'Oh my God, we've still got five hours left on this one.'

'And yet you happily sat through *Les Mis*?' I giggled, and he elbowed me.

'That's something good to watch!'

'Pfft, well, I think we got a show here.'

'You're still watching her? Damn, girl, she'll be scared of you next!'

I shrugged, adjusting my seatbelt and admiring my Pandora bracelet, a Christmas present to myself, for the hundredth time.

As I tried to settle and rest my feet, turbulence began to make the plane shudder once more. The captain had just sent out a reassurance message, but I could see her panicking, and soon she would worry others.

As I unclipped my seat belt, cautious of the plane's movements, Danny nudged me again.

'Look,' he said under his breath. The woman was already up and moving down the aisle. Without hesitation, I moved toward her disappearing frame and caught up with her just as she entered the toilet. The lock read "engaged".

'Excuse me. You shouldn't be out of your seat until the captain has switched off the seatbelt light … Miss?' I tried my best to sound authoritative, but I was worried for her. She didn't answer as I continued to knock the door,

'Look, I promise it will be all right. Could you open the door, please?'

The lock light switched to "vacant" and the door swung open, but she didn't emerge. I peeped in and saw huge tears streaming down her face as she sat on the lid of the toilet.

'OK, look, can I come in …?'

'Lottie,' she offered through a sob. I squeezed into the tiny space and let the door snap shut. Even while crying, she made me feel hot and I tried to slow my quickening breath.

'OK, Lottie, listen to me. Relax. I've been flying quite a while and I've seen it much worse than this, and every time, we've been OK.'

'Really, though, you're not that old –' she protested. I laughed lightly.

'No, well, I'm 25. I've been with this airline since 18, so that's a while. But you can't be my age?' I suggested, trying to bring her a smile. She shook her head.

'Nope, 23.'

I was about to tell her she looked very good no matter her age, but a sudden shaking made her gasp, and I gripped her hand.

'See, now *you're* scared!' she cried out, and sobbed into her free hand.

'I'm not, I want to make you better …,' I offered, not sure what else to say. As she looked up at me I leant over and pulled her into a hug, out of instinct to protect if nothing else. For a moment she sobbed on my shoulder, but as she stood up with me, and I held her tight, an electrical buzz passed between us. Her wet eyes were of the darkest amber, and she had tiredness etched on her face. With a shaky hand I reached up and wiped tears from her cheek, as I became aware of her arm around my waist. Both my stomach and clit ached, as I wanted to hold her, touch her soft hair, and run my lips over her skin. I should perhaps have slapped myself to stop these thoughts, but there was a hook tied deep in my chest that pulled me closer to her.

My face almost touched her own as she whispered, 'What *are* you afraid of then?'

I swallowed hard, a lump in my throat and desire burning my chest. I opened my mouth and failed to speak at first, then, as I caught my breath, I replied, 'I'm afraid of doing something I want.'

My voice was a breathy shudder, but for the first time I saw a small smile creep over her face. It shone out in our tiny space and her eyes twinkled a little. She leant in even closer, her lips grazing across my neck as she said into my ear, 'Don't be afraid.'

I let my lips touch hers and placed a hand on her hip. She made a soft sound into my mouth as I kissed her. She tasted sweet, like bubblegum, and it mixed with the salty tears that had been streaming. I raised my other hand to her face and held her. Her pink cheek was very warm against my fingers. I couldn't help but stroke her skin, which sent a shiver through my whole body at the same time as she shuddered. I let my tongue dip onto her lower lip and she moaned into my mouth before pulling away. She bit down on her lip as though tasting me, and her tears had stopped. I breathed heavily, knowing I was so turned on by the moment that my cotton pants were damp. I kissed her again, harder this time and with a new sense of urgent longing. She traced across my waistcoat and work shirt, her fingers circling the buttons in a way that undid them. I was shocked at her response, but didn't argue when she ran her nails over my lace bra. I felt my nipples harden, and gasped lightly through the kiss. She almost panted in lust when I laid my hand on her exposed, creamy thigh. It ached to be bitten, but I refrained, and instead wound my way up her leg until I found her heat. The silk panties were in fact a thong, and her dress slipped around my arm as I rubbed at the silk underneath. I felt her writhe against my hand, wanting more and more. I shuddered as a pulse consumed me, and I played with the seam of her underwear. I licked her lip and her tongue met mine, just as I slipped my hand a little further.

'Do you like this?' I teased, and her eyes drifted shut.

'Yeah, don't stop, keep going.'

I needed no further encouragement and let my fingers meet her soft, slick cunt. She cried out a little as I touched the sensitive button, and gripped me tight. I tested the fire-hot hole and felt her wetness run over my fingers. Instinctively I raised my hand to my mouth and tasted her – she was sweet and musky. I guided her to perch on the edge of the sink, and kissed her once more before eagerly dropping to my knees. She didn't stop or even think twice, only threw her long hair behind as she leant back. I pulled the scarlet dress up around her waist and drank in the image of her thighs and the dislodged pants revealing plump, secret lips. I used my tongue to draw a line up her right thigh, just to the crease where thigh meets waist, then moved over and down the left side to her knee. She shook and gasped above me, making me want to relieve the building pressure in my own clit. I blew hot breath onto the highest point of her thigh and she trembled more violently, seeming to hold all her muscles in ultimate longing. I took deft little licks over her pants, my tongue not quite meeting skin, and revelled in the almost begging yet quiet moans that escaped her. She held her breath. I hooked her panties between my fingers and pulled them right down to let her step out of them. She had a small V shape of curls that rested on her mound, which I ran my fingers over, followed by the tip of my nose. It was only when I took a deep, exploratory lick from her wet hole to her already throbbing clit that she let out her breath, and began to moan again. Not loud, but enough to hear, and I relished each noise as I began to lick and suck on her clit. She wriggled in response to it and wound a hand into my neatly tied hair, pulling me in closer. Sweetness engulfed my tongue, which made the ache in my jaw easy to ignore. As she ground her sex onto my face I matched her rhythm and stayed wholly connected, my lips around hers, my tongue dancing on the hub of her lust. Her legs had tensed once again, her whole body quivering and clenched, nearly begging me to release her, to drop her into the waves of orgasm. Though as she came close to it, I licked ever so slightly to the side, pushing her into a frenzy. She fought against me, aching. I scarcely breathed, but not in effort; watching her mew and whimper above me caused a deep tension in my own clit. It burned and throbbed while I continued to chew and suck on her. The sensation seemed to start in her toes and work up as she bucked against me, crying out as pulsing pleasure threatened to consume her whole body. I licked harder still as she came on my tongue, a high moan escaping her mouth and her legs clamped tight around me. I drank her juices thirstily. As I caught my breath and stood up, a huge smile spread across her face.

'Fuck, I feel better.' She gasped, holding her chest. Sweat drops rested on her reddened cheeks and I kissed her hard. Then, as I straightened my hair back into shape, her small hands pushed me against the wall of the cubicle.

'Don't you want some fun, huh?'

It wasn't so much a question as a statement, and she knew the answer. I trembled, feeling wetter than ever as she kissed me, her tongue gently opening my mouth to accommodate. Her hands lifted my shirt and stroked over my waist, undoing the zip of my black pencil skirt. I moaned in longing as her fingers slid down under the fabric of my skirt. I shut my eyes and exhaled shakily. She paused for a moment, savouring my own reaction of panting in lust before her silky fingers reached under my panties and found my lower lips. I was beyond aroused; her single touch set me ablaze in electric pleasure. I bit my lip to hide my moans, as she rubbed against my clit, incessant in her quest. Layer on layer of exquisite pleasure built up inside me, and I was so ready that within what felt like moments she had me poised on the edge of climax. She kept whispering encouragement into my ear and it drove me wild. Even holding back from the release didn't stop the ripples begin to wash over me, a tiny scream leaving my mouth as I fell from an invisible mountain and succumbed to the pleasure, standing there in the tiny bathroom with her.

A look of total satisfaction crossed her face as I opened my eyes. When she stepped aside I was faced with my reflection in the little mirror – my hair had come loose and my clothes were all jumbled. I hardly cared, except for having to go back out to my job.

'So, how are you feeling now?' I asked politely, my voice still shuddering as I buttoned my shirt up and adjusted my waistcoat. She laughed as she fiddled with her long hair.

'Yes, very good, thanks,' she replied, her composure now restored, then she looked right at me. 'Do you do this often?' she asked, a little sadness in her eyes. She seemed to think she was just being used.

'No, not at all,' I answered honestly. She looked almost like she disbelieved me. I couldn't think what could convince her, but I took a small pen and a notebook from an oversized pocket of my waistcoat. I scribbled on it, then folded it and handed it to her.

'What …?'

'It's my international phone number. If you want to call me and meet again, is all,' I offered, and the beautiful smile returned. She said no more, and slipped out of the bathroom. I had no idea if that was the last moment we would have together, but as I preened my appearance further, there was a knocking on the door.

'Hey, Anna, babe, you good?' Danny called softly. I unlocked the door, still fiddling with my hair. A huge grin was plastered on my face. 'Look at your cheeks, they're scarlet! Oh God, you didn't …!' He squealed, full of excitement, as we returned to our duties, my tale slowly beginning to unfold.

Anita and Angie Get Wet
by Alex Jordaine

The creamy stuccoed Georgian terraced house was in a residential street just north of High Street Kensington in central London. The property had been converted at some stage into three solid, high-ceilinged apartments, and Anita and her lover, a submissive blonde called Angie, occupied the one on the ground floor.

It was early evening and the two beautiful young women were in the living room. Anita sat in a black leather armchair and was as naked as Angie, who knelt at her feet. Angie, whose backside was rosy-red from the robust spanking Anita had recently given it, was gazing out of the full-length, net-curtained window at the dark, wet dusk outside.

'You'd never know it was the middle of summer,' Angie said, looking at a sky stacked with clouds like black mountains. Rain crackled in the street and cars edged by slowly, water spilling out from their tyres, their windscreen wipers swishing. 'I wish I didn't have to go out this evening in such filthy weather,' she continued, still looking out at the relentless, dreary rain. She turned her blue-eyed gaze away from the window and looked up at Anita. 'And I especially wish I didn't have to visit my stepmother, of all people. I never could see what my dear father – God rest his soul – ever saw in that bloody woman. She's awful, you know, Anita: a snob, a bore, a prude ...'

'I can well understand your reluctance to visit her,' Anita interrupted, running her fingers through her lustrous auburn hair. 'I'll bet you'd much rather be here having great sex with me.'

'That's for sure,' Angie replied, her clitoris twitching at the thought. 'But needs must, I guess.'

'If you say so.' Anita smirked. There was a wicked glint in her hazel-green eyes.

'I need to make my way over to her place soon,' Angie said resignedly, glancing again out of the rain-splattered window. 'So I'd better get dressed.'

'I hope you won't be wearing any underwear,' Anita cautioned.

'I never do, not since you told me to stop wearing it,' Angie said, feeling another twinge between her legs. 'I'm very obedient to you, aren't I?'

'You are indeed,' Anita agreed.

Angie, despite her resigned statement a few moments earlier, had made no move so far to get up from her knees, never mind put any clothes on. 'Hey,' she said. 'Just think how disapproving my puritanical stepmother would be if she knew you and I are lovers rather than innocent "flat-mates".' She made quotation marks in the air with her fingers.

'Not to mention how she'd feel if she knew about all the other things we get up to.' A suggestive smile curled the corners of Anita's lips. 'Think how shocked she'd be during your visit if she knew you had nothing on under your dress, your wet pussy completely shaved, and your backside still aglow from the spanking yours truly gave it earlier. The thought of that should make a potentially very tedious evening a bit more interesting for you, wouldn't you agree?'

'I would.' Angie felt a real ache between her legs now. 'I'll be on my best behaviour with her, as I always am. But I'm afraid she's going to find me very distracted as company this time, the state you've got me into.'

'I'm sure she will,' Anita said. And I haven't even gone beyond first base yet, my sweet, she thought mischievously; just you wait and see. 'Then of course there'll be all those trips to the bathroom you'll have to make when you'll be returning all flushed.'

'I will?'

'Oh yes. You'll be wanking yourself stupid every time you go there. You're a horny little slut, Angie, what are you?'

'A horny little slut,' Angie agreed cheerfully. 'And what are you going to be doing while I'm away?'

'I think I'll just take myself in hand.'

'Take yourself in hand?'

'Yes,' Anita replied, spreading her thighs and rubbing her pussy ostentatiously. 'Read my hips: take myself in hand.' She teased the folds of her sex wide open and ran her fingertips against the pink flesh, concentrating on the hooded pearl of pleasure.

'What, you'll be masturbating for the *whole* time I'm away?' Angie asked, the idea of it – and the sight of what Anita was now doing – exciting her even more. It made her own clitoris pulse more insistently and her pussy dampen further.

'That's right. I'm going to have a real wankathon,' Anita said, continuing to roll her fingers actively over the stiffness of her clit before dipping them right into her wet pussy, plunging them in and out rhythmically. Then she stopped herself. Not yet, not yet.

She took her hand from her sex and pushed it into Angie's mouth. Angie sucked at her lover's sticky fingers until Anita pulled them away and ran them languorously up over her own erect nipples.

'Your fingers were nice and wet when you put them in my mouth,' Angie said, still savouring the taste of her lover's juices. 'Will you allow yourself to squirt when you wank?'

Anita could do that sometimes, but the circumstances had to be just right. She could only ejaculate by her own hand – nobody else's – and she had to get the pressure on her G-spot *just so*.

'I might squirt, I might not,' Anita said with a shrug. 'That's for me to know.'

'I suppose, one way or another, I'll find you in a state of complete sexual exhaustion on my return,' Angie said.

'More than likely, yes.' Anita returned her fingers to her sex and began to pleasure herself again, rubbing gently. 'Basically I'm going to wank and wank and wank until I'm all wanked out.'

'Will you be watching lesbian porno movies while you're jilling yourself off time and time again like that?' Angie and Anita had between them acquired quite a collection of such films, some with a BDSM theme, some without; all of them hot and steamy.

'I'll only be watching the lesbian porno movies in my head,' Anita replied, still slowly masturbating.

'Meaning?'

'One word,' Anita said. 'Memories.'

'Memories?'

'Uh-huh.'

'What sort?'

'Amazingly erotic ones,' Anita gently worked her fingers over her sex. 'That's because I'll be concentrating on my "first times". The first female to make love to me, to give you just one example, was a lovely porcelain-skinned redhead at college. Claire, her name was.'

'So what about this Claire?' asked Angie. Her pussy felt very slippery now.

'She was a year older than me, drop-dead gorgeous, and I had a huge crush on her. I'd an even bigger crush on her once she'd gone down on me. That was an incredible experience, I can tell you.'

'I'll bet!' Angie exclaimed. What are you trying to *do* to me, Anita? she thought. God, she felt horny.

'But I've so many sexy first time memories,' Anita went on as she continued slowly masturbating. 'Finger-fucking you up against that dark wall about half an hour after we'd met at that oh-so-respectable party. Remember that, do you, by any chance?' She took her hand away from her sex again; didn't want to have an orgasm yet, wanted to stay in control.

'Need you ask?' Angie replied breathlessly. Anita was making her so sexually excited she was now soaked. She could feel trickles of wetness running down the inside of her legs. 'I mean, do you really need to ask whether I remember that particular experience? For me it was mind-blowing, life changing.'

'No,' Anita replied, her eyes gleaming, 'I guess I don't need to ask.'

'Here's another memory for you,' Angie said. 'What about the time in that smart Italian restaurant in Old Compton Street when you told me to go into the ladies', remove my underwear, bin it, and never wear any again?'

'That's a good one,' said Anita. 'OK, what about the first time I spanked that tight, round butt of yours? Remember that? I'm sure you do.'

'I'll say I do,' Angie replied with a faraway look. It had been the first time she'd realised that Anita, the woman with whom she was already head over heels in love, could also give her what she wanted sexually, what she craved. Angie's clit was positively buzzing now and her pussy was *so* wet.

'It all came to me in a flash, I recall,' Anita said. 'You'd come out with some comment or other I'd found particularly irritating – can't for the life of me even remember what it was now – and I decided right there and then to punish you for it.'

Angie picked up the story. 'I can remember like it was yesterday what you did to me.' Her blue eyes shone. 'All of a sudden you told me to bend over the kitchen table, flicked up my short skirt to reveal my bare bottom, and started to spank me. And you didn't hold back. I mean, you really thrashed the living daylights out of me.'

'And, boy, did it have an effect,' Anita said. 'It made you climax so violently I thought you were having a fit.'

'I thought I was as well,' Angie replied, her heart beating faster at the vivid memory of that first spanking she'd received from her lover. Her body let out a little shiver, she was so excited. And all the while her clit throb-throb-throbbed and her pussy got wetter still.

'Anything else you recall about the experience?'

'Only that I'd so much love juice running down my thighs you told me you thought I'd wet myself,' Angie replied. 'And, while we're on the subject, Anita, what sort of effect do you think you've been having on me now with all this juicy first time stuff? You've got me so wet and horny I'm going out of my mind. Do I *have* to go and visit my God-awful stepmother this evening?' She briefly glanced out of the window. The rain had decreased somewhat but was still falling steadily.

'You're the one who said you had to go and see her, not me,' Anita reminded her, bringing her fingers back to her pussy and starting to masturbate again.

'Yeah, I know. She's expecting me, so I guess I'd better go.'

'It's up to you.' Anita shrugged, continuing to stroke her wet sex.

'If only there was some way I could get out of the visit without lying to her. You know what a lousy liar I am. I'm absolutely hopeless at it, couldn't fool anyone. I wish there was some way I could stay here with you instead, so you could fuck me senseless with your strap-on dildo.'

'Always assuming that's what I feel like doing,' Anita said, a slight edge to her voice. But still she kept masturbating, her fingers moving in tight, slippery circles.

'Oh yes,' Angie assured her respectfully. 'Only if that's what you want too, of course. What I'm really trying to say is that you could do anything you wanted to me – put me into bondage, beat me again and even harder this time – *anything*.' Her blonde hair was damp against her neck and her breathing was ragged as she stared imploringly into her lover's gleaming eyes.

'Well.' Anita pursed her lips as if in deep thought. 'There *might* be a way.' She removed her fingers from the dripping wetness of her pussy.

'Just say the word,' Angie replied, her own juicy sex pulsing at the possibility.

'Stand up,' Anita said, as she also got to her feet.

'Now what?' Angie asked, her heart beating rapidly. She could feel a thrill running through her body like an electric current. 'I'll do anything you say.'

Anita's eyebrows lifted eloquently. 'Will you indeed?'

'Yes, oh yes.' Angie's breath was coming quicker, her pulse racing wildly in her breast, her clit pulsing wildly in her sex.

'OK, what I want you to do is pick up the phone and call your stepmother.' Anita brought the hand with which she'd been masturbating to Angie's crotch and started to push upwards into her pussy. She found that it was sopping wet – as she'd known very well it would be. 'You're to tell her something has come up. In fact, you're to tell her,' she continued, pushing her fingers in and out of her lover's wetness with ever more vigour, 'that what's come up is very urgent.' Her fingers were like ramming rods now, sliding furiously in and out of Angie's sodden vagina. Then she started to grind them hard against her stiff clit.

'I'll do that.' Angie gasped, her whole body shaking. She was *this* close to orgasm, but she mustn't let that happen, she simply mustn't. 'I'll ph-phone straight away.'

'Tell her you'll be tied up for the next few hours,' Anita added. 'You won't be lying about that either.'

Lucky Charm
by Kate Dominic

From my princess perspective, no sane woman would sit on a frozen lake for hours on end, wrapped head to toe in insulated gear, staring into a hole while she waited for an icy cold fish to bite.

Maribelle and her butch hard water buddies were crazy enough to do it, and my Maribelle was very good with lures. From shiny silver spinners to wriggling live fish, she knew how to reel in what she wanted, even in the middle of January on the thick, snow-covered ice of Lake Minnetonka. I loved watching her firm, athletic hips roll beneath her blue and black snowmobile suit as she strode over the ice roads on the lake. Even through all those layers of insulation, I could still envision the way she looked naked under her clothing, her heated muscles moving effortlessly over her ripped, stocky body. And when she held up a prize-sized fish for a picture, her short brown cap of curls framing her strong, wind-reddened face as she grinned into my camera, my pussy tingled and I fell in love all over again.

It was just so damn cold out on the lake! I was once again perched on my camp chair in our hot pink wooden shack, watching the love of my life ladle slush from her freshly augured hole in the thick, grey-white ice. My nose had finally quit running, but the space heater Maribelle had gotten me for Christmas hadn't warmed up the interior of the shack enough for me to so much as loosen my scarf.

Maribelle was all about outdoor sports. I was learning to like being outdoors with her. Last summer, our first together, I'd loved hanging out at the beach in my splashy floral bikini. But I was finding it hard to be trendy in the layers upon layers of clothes under my insulated jacket, heavy snow pants, and insulated mittens. Instead of the sexy new calfskin boots with the three-inch spiked heels Santa had brought me, I was wearing black pack boots with insulated liners over my thick wool hiking socks. Even though my thermals were silk and my sweater merino wool, the only things that really felt right were my bright yellow cashmere scarf and my designer sunglasses.

Don't get me wrong, it's not that I really mind cold all that much. I'm a Minnesota girl through and through. But there's a big difference between dashing from a warm car into an even warmer club or snuggling in front of a fireplace with the woman of my dreams – and sitting on a camp chair inside a tiny, battered wooden ice house.

Last summer, Maribelle had painted the shack pink for me, much to her disgust. Pink was way too girly for her, but she'd humoured me when I pouted. I'd tossed my hair and told her something out there on the ice needed to be girly. She'd grabbed me right there in the middle of her back yard and kissed me until my eyes crossed, then she'd pulled the front of my sundress open with her paint-covered finger, peeked down the front, and said she was damn sure there was going to be something girly in her ice house. All summer long, the back of my favourite dress had sported her handprint from where she'd smacked me as she went back to work.

It was two weeks after Christmas, and Maribelle and her buddies were doing a private, dry-run competition, honing their skills for the big Brainerd ice fishing contest with its $150,000 in prizes. Maribelle had her sights set on the four-wheel drive pick-up truck grand prize. Her battered blue Nissan was showing signs of wear and tear from all the back country running around we did, every damn month of the year. She was feeling inspired.

I was determined to be her lucky charm, just like the ones in slinky short dresses the gamblers in Vegas had hanging on their arms when they competed for big stakes. I was still getting the feel for how to set the stage in our ten foot by ten foot ice house. From what I'd seen of the other structures in the shanty town on the lake, most were populated with beer-swilling guys who kept to themselves and spent the day staring at fish-finding underwater cameras or TVs perched on upturned five-gallon buckets. Our little enclave at the end of the row was all women, but Lydia, Carol, and Nakisha stuck to the bare essentials too, and everybody on the lake smelled of fish.

Maribelle had told me I could bring whatever I wanted to the shack to entertain myself, so long as all my junk fit in the car and I was willing to schlep it back and forth by myself. And it couldn't be loud or bright enough to scare the fish. At first I'd been bored, bored, *bored*! It was too cold for my brand new ebook reader, and I couldn't text with my mittens on. The first couple days we'd come to the shack, I'd sulked so much Maribelle had paddled me when we got home.

As usual, that had led to screaming hot sex. But when she threatened to leave me home if I didn't settle down, I'd changed my approach and started fixing up the shack into my own private ice castle. I'd added a folding table with a lacy tablecloth, picnic dishes and a couple of pans, and a propane camp stove to cook the stupid little pan fish Maribelle caught. Today's provisions box included cloth napkins, zippered bags of spices and breading, real butter, canned peaches, a single shot bottle of rum, a bar of Godiva chocolate, and thermoses of hot soup, coffee for Maribelle, and cocoa with marshmallows for me. When I took off the lid to the box, Maribelle rolled her eyes, muttered something about "too femme for words!" and went back to checking her jig line. But when I handed her a mug of coffee, her grin warmed me in all the right places.

Still, it didn't take me long to set up my little nest. This time, I'd brought a real book. And since I have to pee all the time in the cold, especially when I'm drinking cocoa, I'd even bought a little chemical toilet – and I'd gotten silk thermal long johns with old-fashioned drop-flap backs for both of us. I'd checked the little weather radio Maribelle had set up on an overturned bucket, making sure no unexpected storms were moving in. None were. With my book in my hand, I settled in to watch Maribelle fish.

Her auger and jig pole rested along the wall beside her. Maribelle was sitting on another bucket, tying a shiny new silver lure onto a line. The lure was part of her plan to perfect a new bouncing technique to entice bigger pan fish to take her bait. My fashionista was wearing her snowmobile suit, black pack boots, and her hunter orange hat with the furry ear flaps. Her black insulated gloves and a tackle box were on the snow beside her as she tied a series of tiny knots in the line.

'Are your fingernail clippers handy?'

'Yes, ma'am.' I took off my mitten and dutifully handed her the dedicated pair I had tucked in my pocket. I kept my short pink nails perfectly manicured, but there was no way I was putting a fishing tool in my make-up bag!

Maribelle clipped the line and handed the clippers back without looking up. I wrinkled my nose and put them in my pocket. The hut was starting to warm up, so I took my other mitten off and set them on the bucket by the radio. Despite my ridiculous attire, I couldn't help thinking about sex. My bottom tingled pleasantly from last night's spanking, and, well, Maribelle was right there in front of me. Looking at her always turned me on. I poured myself more cocoa, making sure I got some marshmallows, and when Maribelle dropped the line in the water, I topped off her mug with more steaming hot coffee.

'Thanks,' she smiled. Oh wow – that smile! As always, it sparkled all the way to her eyes. Heated tingles rushed to my pussy and I felt my face heat. God, I loved her!

A moment later, the line jerked. Maribelle set her mug down fast, coffee sloshing onto the snow as she landed a small but legal pan fish onto the ice. The hook was caught hard in its mouth. The fish flopped wildly toward the hole as she tried to dislodge the hook.

'Ew!'

'Quit being such a baby. Where the hell are the needle-nose pliers?'

I'd used them to fix part of the table. I retrieved them and daintily held them out to her. She expertly removed the hook, and got up to set the now nearly motionless fish in a small bank of snow she built up by the door.

'God, you are such a wuss.' Her face was red from the still nippy air and her eyes glowed with pleasure. 'First catch,' she called out, loud enough for her buddies to hear. Muffled cries of "damn!" echoed from the other shacks.

'But I'm your wuss.' I smiled, running my finger seductively up the front of my parka.

She laughed and shook her head at me. 'Don't take my tools, baby, unless you put them back. I need them.'

'Yes, ma'am.' I kept my gaze on her crotch, where she'd more than once strapped on a much-appreciated tool. 'I'll take good care of your tools.'

She rolled her eyes and sat back down on her bucket. The shack was finally getting warm. She unzipped the top of her snowmobile suit and shrugged out of it, letting it rest around her hips. The thick, cableknit sweater clung to her small, firm breasts. I loved playing with Maribelle's breasts. Her nipples were so sensitive. When I rolled the pointy tips between her fingers, her pussy creamed until her juices ran down the side of my hand, especially when I nibbled the side of her neck.

None of those areas were accessible to me at the moment, though my fingers itched to touch them. I pouted into my mug, my bottom surprisingly tender as I fidgeted against the uncomfortably firm camp chair. Last night, Maribelle had turned me over her knee and smacked me with the hairbrush when I sassed her back once too often about what my attire was going to be on the lake this weekend. That was the first time she'd used the brush, and damn, it turned me on! The flames in my backside fanned the heat building in my pussy. I loved watching Maribelle's breasts move as she jiggled the pole, the way her arms flexed and her hips twisted on her bucket as she lifted another stupid fish from the hole and tossed it to the pile by the door.

'God, you're gorgeous!'

'And you're distracting me.' She laughed, calling out "Got another one" to a chorus of muffled curses.

Maribelle had told me to remove layers when I got hot. So even though it was definitely still cool inside the shack, I peeled off my parka and sweater, shivering as I tossed the sweater on the table and quickly pulled my parka back on. My nipples stood up stiff against the thermal shirt. Beneath it, I'd worn only a form-fitting silk camisole. I circled my palms over my nipples, trembling as they tightened to stiff, shadowed points.

'I'm getting really turned on. I bet I could strip down to my boots in here, and nobody would notice.'

'I'd notice,' she growled. 'And you'd freeze when I turned you over my knee and unbuttoned the back of those fancy silk drawers. Your pretty little bottom would heat right back up when I commenced to paddle it. But I don't want to scare the fish, and if I have to stop fishing to paddle you, you're going to squeal!'

I knew my Maribelle, and I wasn't the only one who got wet when we talked about spanking. Her snowmobile suit unzipped from neck to crotch, and it could be opened from either end. I checked the weather report. Nothing had changed: clear and sunny and, of course, cold.

I moved my chair in back of her and sat down, my thighs spread against her hips as I settled my head comfortably on her shoulder. I carefully rested my hand on her thigh, making sure I didn't bump her arms. They moved up and down as she jiggled the rod. So did her breasts. Her nipples were as stiff as mine. I pretended not to notice.

'I have hat hair.' I sighed.

Maribelle's snort vibrated against me. 'You have very pretty hat hair. It looks like a lovely, brown mouse nest.'

My shriek had her chuckling even harder. Footsteps crunched on the snow outside the shack.

'What the hell are you two doing in there?' It was Maribelle's friend, Lydia.

'Nothing!' I wailed.

Maribelle hooted, 'Fishing!'

Lydia's snapped "You're scaring the fish!" had my Maribelle quietly laughing like a loon, and I was pouting all over again, though I couldn't quite make myself move away from the firm, strong body in front of me. Maribelle's breasts were so warm against my hands, and God, my pussy was hot!

'It's important to have attractive hair.' I sniffed. Maribelle turned her head, smiling as she kissed me.

'You always have beautiful hair, baby. It's just a little messy from your hood.' She reached around and patted the side of my bottom, hard enough to get my attention, though I couldn't really feel it through my snow pants. 'Now shush. The underwater camera showed there are fish here. I need to work on my speed.'

She picked up the ladle and scooped ice out of the hole, then, with a plunk, dropped the line into the water again. The silvery shimmer of the lure disappeared into the water. She'd barely begun to jiggle the rod when the line tightened.

'Got another one!' she grinned, pulling up a middle-sized pan fish. 'Crappie for dinner!'

I wrinkled my nose, averting my eyes as she removed the hook. When she'd cleaned them, I'd cook them. But until they were fillets, they were all Maribelle's. Moments later, the line was back in the water. In the next ten minutes, my love had two more keeper-sized fish lined up on the snow.

Maribelle's face glowed with excitement and her neck was damp with sweat. She worked the line, alternately jiggling it and letting it rest in patterns that made no sense to me. I loved seeing that happy look on her face. I quietly let my hand slide over her thigh and into her crotch.

Maribelle turned and gave me a look that promised a very hot bottom later. I smiled innocently and looked studiously at the window. Pretty soon her attention was focused on her line again. As she played with her fishing rod, I carefully slid the bottom of the zipper up. I got it almost to her waist before she noticed.

'Somebody's itching for a spanking.'

She had that right. But Maribelle's pants were finally open. I stroked my fingers lightly over the waistband of her thermals, under the edge of her plain white cotton underpants.

'I'm going to turn you over my knee.' She was trying to sound gruff, but her voice had that husky sound it got when she was getting really turned on.

'You will,' I murmured, 'but not now. You're fishing.' I gave her my prettiest smile and slid my hand down inside her underpants. Her skin was warm against my fingers. 'I'm fishing too.'

I teased my fingers between her pussy lips. Her panties were damp, her slit hot and drenched. I slid my fingers up, and up. Just as I touched her clit, she jumped and her arms jerked.

'Dammit!' she panted, her arms straining as she pulled in another fish. 'Dammit, I'm fishing!'

'So – fish,' I purred. I kept my finger perfectly still as she fought with the fish flopping on the ice. Her thighs tightened around my hand, but she didn't try to push me away. 'Pretend we're in Vegas. I'm your lucky charm.'

'It's warm in Vegas,' she muttered, pulling the fish free and tossing it with the others.

A shadow moved outside the house. Lydia's voice called, 'You having any luck?'

'Oh yeah,' Maribelle froze against me. She looked from the window to her crotch and shot me a grin. When she spoke, her voice was cool. 'You?'

'I've got a couple. Caro and Nakisha have one each. Nothing much is biting. How about we give it 15 more minutes, then call it a day? I've got a hot date tonight.'

I circled my fingers, then slid them down and into her. Maribelle shuddered against me.

'Fifteen minutes ought to do it,' Maribelle choked out.

'Fifteen minutes is good,' I whispered, nuzzling her scarf aside so I could bite her neck. I stroked between her now drenched pussy lips, alternately nipping and sucking her neck. I slipped my other hand up under her arm, lifting her sweater and thermal, pulling down the front of her bra. Her nipple stiffened in the cold. I pinched, warming the straining tip with the friction of my fingers, tugging it out into the chilly winter air.

'I going to paddle you with the hairbrush,' she choked. 'I'm going to paddle until you yell!'

'Um-hmm.' I sucked the side of her neck hard. 'I bet you'll really heat my bottom.'

'Like it's been too close to the fire,' she panted, arching into my fingers. 'Oh baby, that feels so good!'

I slid three fingers deep inside her, rubbing my thumb

relentlessly over her clit. 'I love it when you spank me, especially when you paddle me with your grandma's antique maple hairbrush. It sets my pussy on fire.'

Maribelle thrust rhythmically against my hand, letting me fuck her with my fingers as I milked her nipple. She turned her head to me, plunging her tongue into my mouth. Her pussy juice was running down the side of my hand. I curled my fingers inside her, ruthlessly rubbing her clit as I pressed up hard. I caught her scream into my mouth as she shuddered against me.

Suddenly, her arms jerked hard. Her velvety warm pussy walls clamped down around my fingers. She swore and leant harder into me, ignoring the straining rod as she trembled and groaned.

'I am paddling your ass good for this!' she gasped. 'And you are so replacing my lure!'

The rod had stopped jerking, the line obviously snapped. Swearing, Maribelle pulled away and put the rod under her foot.

'Stand up and pull those fancy snow pants down to your ankles. Then unbutton your drawers and bend over!'

'Yes, ma'am!' I grinned. My fingers flew over the ridiculous amount of clothes I wore, then I was bending over in front of her, my boots planted wide, my hands on my knees, my thermals unbuttoned, and my pussy backed up even with my Maribelle's wicked, lashing tongue. She snapped my thong with one yank, then grabbed my hips and buried her face in my slit. She tongued me until I was ready to scream. Then she sucked my clit until I wailed my orgasm into the fist I had stuffed in my face.

I was trembling so hard I had to sit down. I had barely stepped away from her when Maribelle's "Dammit!" echoed through the shack. The rod had jerked out from under her foot, catching on the edge of the hole. She grabbed it up, her arms bulging as she fought the rod that was now bent so far over I was certain it was going to break. I jerked my pants up right over my unbuttoned thermals, staring in shock as Maribelle fought to bring in her fish.

'Is everybody all right in here?' The door flew open as

Lydia and Caro and Nakisha ran in. We all stared in shock as a huge, ugly walleye head broke through the icy film that had been forming over the hole.

As the three of them yelled encouragement, handing her gaffs and hooks and God knows what else, Maribelle dragged a 15-inch walleye through the hole. If anybody noticed the condition of my Maribelle's pants, they politely didn't mention it. They were all too busy hooting and hollering and taking pictures and wondering why the line hadn't snapped and expounding on theories about what kind of bait she'd used. The general consensus was that the original crappie she'd caught hadn't broken the line, it had just become bait for the walleye, though nobody but me could quite figure out why she'd left the crappie in the water for so long.

Maribelle still paddled my butt with the hairbrush when we got home. She got my bottom so hot and tingly and sore, and she made me come so hard I howled like a wolf crying to the winter moon. And afterwards, my Maribelle told me that I could be her lucky charm and come as often as I liked every time we went ice fishing in our hot pink ice house, though I'd have to keep my clothes on at the actual competitions, since those were held out in the open.

I couldn't wait to go shopping for my new ice fishing wardrobe. We had weeks more of hard ice. I was so going to make the most of it.

Fine Print
by Emma Lydia Bates

It was the clothes that made me so uncomfortable. The starchiness of the suit jacket, the pinching of the shoes, the tight bun I'd dragged my hair into; it all contributed to making me feel ill at ease. Normal office wear was jeans, a button-down shirt and brightly coloured accessories – though given that there were only ever three people in the office and I was the boss, the only reason I didn't show up in pyjamas was to set a good example.

The boss. That still didn't sound quite right to me. I was far too young to be anyone's boss.

And it felt like everyone I encountered professionally agreed.

'Hi,' I'd said to the receptionist when I entered the vast, intimidating lobby of the country's leading book distributors. 'I'm Lily Reeves, from Lark Poetry Press. I'm here for my 12 o'clock appointment.'

She'd looked me up and down with an expression that mingled disdain and disbelief, but the terrifying meeting had gone well, and I'd walked back across the lobby with something of a sashay in my step. Though that might only have been because the shoes were getting very painful by then.

Maybe it was the discomfort from the clothes, or maybe it was the growing sense of elation that I might actually have pulled this off, but when I went to do the last errand I had left, my head was in a muddle. In my mind, I was already taking the train and heading back to the safety of my own little office, covered in author photos and pictures of cats falling over.

I was confident enough that I had dropped off the envelope with our recent sales data onto the right desk, but it was an old Edwardian building, and the office they were in was right at the top, and by the time I was two flights of stairs down I knew I wasn't going the same way as I had done when I'd gone up.

I headed down another flight, and concluded that I was, in fact, entirely lost. And the corridors were both anonymous and empty. That at least meant I could take off my shoes for a little while. I realised by now I should be at ground level, but there was no sign of an exit door, only more corridors. So I started trying door handles, to see if there was anyone who could direct me out.

The first two were locked. When the third door opened in front of me, I was so surprised I almost fell through it.

It seemed that the doors there led through to the adjacent house. I had found myself in a large room, which was clearly in the middle of being decorated. It had once been grand and opulent, with its elaborately moulded ceiling and broad sash windows, but now there were holes in the plasterwork and the ceiling was stripped of paint. The red marble of the fireplace at one end was grey with dust.

It took me a moment to notice the woman painting the wall in the far corner, and when I did, I couldn't help but let out a small cry.

She turned round. She was shorter than me, with a stocky figure, and her hair was pulled back into a messy ponytail, with several wayward strands escaping. She was wearing loose-fitting dungarees, with nothing underneath, and with the breast pocket full of heavy brushes, they were gaping open to one side.

'Take a picture, love,' she said, 'it'll last longer.'

I was probably staring. There was a hint of dark areola peeking from behind those dungarees, and she was standing like she owed the world nothing, and holy fuck, she was hot.

I turned into a gibbering mess. 'Erm ... I'm sorry ... I was just, y'know, looking for the exit ... I got lost ... Really sorry, and, erm, sorry ...'

She grinned at me and walked over, looking me up and down. 'Why aren't you wearing any shoes?'

That at least I could answer coherently. 'They really hurt.'

'Why wear them, then?'

'I was at a business meeting.'

We shared a grimace. 'Nice pin,' she said.

I looked down at myself, and realised that the last time I'd been wearing this suit, it had been to an excessively formal dinner for LGBT company heads, when Lark Poetry Press had only just hired me. It was a small, discreet rainbow, and I found myself feeling a little proud that I'd ended up wearing it to my Big Scary Meeting today, even if it had been by accident.

'Thanks,' I said.

She grinned and walked back over to where she'd been painting.

'What are you doing here?' I asked, trying to make the conversation last.

She turned around. 'Come and see.'

So I walked over to her, feeling ridiculous in my smart suit with my bare feet, and she put her hand on my shoulder and said, 'Look.'

'At what?'

'At all of it. Think about how beautiful it could be.'

I was having difficulty with that. I could imagine soaring ceilings, ornate chandeliers, couples whirling and dancing together across the varnished floorboards, but most of my thoughts were taken up by the knowledge of how close she was standing behind me, how near her lips were to my skin.

'The day is gone, and all its sweets are gone,' I quoted, almost instinctively.

'That's lovely,' she said.

'It's Keats.'

'Are you a poet?'

'Some of the time. I publish poetry.'

She smiled, biting her lip, her gaze running over me. 'Spending your time trying to make the world a bit more beautiful?'

'Something like that. Is that what you do?'

She nodded. I shifted my stance a little, looked over her body, willed her to want me too because I would never be able to find the courage in myself to make the first move. And then she said, 'Want to make the world more beautiful together?'

I must have gasped a little smile almost unconsciously, because she leant toward me, and just tasted my lips with her own. 'Do you have anywhere to be?' she asked.

I shook my head. 'Nowhere,' I said, 'not until the last train home.'

'And I'm self-employed, so I get to do what I want, more or less. So … Shall I lock the door?'

I stopped her, trying to make my legs tremble less. 'I have one concern.'

'Go on?'

'I don't sleep with women – even incredibly sexy ones – unless I know their names. I'm Lily.'

Her laugh echoed in the empty room. 'I'm Kate. As in "kiss me, Kate".'

I found the confidence to kiss her. Properly, this time, I wrapped my arms around her neck and let her pull me in close, my hands on her warm, bare skin, traces of some berry-themed scent lingering on her hair, and her lips on mine, gloriously.

She pulled away from me and found a heavy, old-fashioned key in her pocket. 'Sure about this?'

And I mumbled something that approached a yes as she marched off to lock the door.

I put my bags down awkwardly on the floor, and stood there watching her as she went over to the door, the dungaree straps falling off her bare shoulders, revealing a tattoo of a panther stalking across her shoulder blade. It arched as she locked the door.

She took my head when she came back over to me. 'You know, sweetie – Lily – you don't need to be nervous. I've never slept with a woman I've only just met in a semi-derelict building either.'

I smiled and bit my lip. She angled in to kiss me again.

I remembered some conference or other that I once went to, in the weeks just after I came out to everyone – friends had known for years, family for months, but that was the point at which I started correcting colleagues when they asked me if I had a boyfriend, and putting up pictures of my girlfriend of the time on my desk. I'd drifted into a very worthy phase of trying to be the perfect lesbian, and I attended seminars and conferences and read everything that Emma Donoghue and Sarah Waters have ever written.

I didn't know what I misguidedly thought that would achieve; I merely thought it was something I was obliged to do, to go along with my newfound identity. I'd gone through a brief (very brief) Goth phase in school and had done much the same thing, avidly reading magazine articles about the history of the trend, and lecturing uninterested friends on exactly what the upside-down cross meant as a symbol. But at one conference, I remembered a very forthright speaker who was constantly on the verge of shouting, who told us all that we needed to have random, spontaneous, casual sex, that that was the key to – something. To equality, probably, but I can't remember the line of reasoning now, and I doubt it made much sense to me at the time.

Still, standing there, awkward in my formal suit, with a woman I didn't know called Kate kissing me furiously, I had the odd flash of a thought that I was doing something right, and not just because of how good Kate's lips felt pressed against mine.

We broke apart, and she began unbuttoning my suit jacket. I pulled my hair out of the bun, and ran my fingers through it. She looked on appreciatively.

I kissed her neck. The skin was soft and warm underneath my lips, and she trembled slightly. I tried a small nip with my teeth, and it felt like she was melting a little underneath me.

Nerves had always been a problem for me. I found it a little tricky to believe that someone really wanted me, really desired me. I could look in the mirror and describe myself with poetic terms – pale porcelain skin and a cloud of long, dark hair, with brown eyes like deep pools, and a lithe, slender body, with feminine curves clinging to a narrow frame, or some such nonsense – but it was always a little harder to make myself believe it, and inevitably that made me nervous. It made me drop cutlery on first dates with pretty girls, and it made me blush furiously in front of the more forceful ones. It made me struggle to believe that when they said they liked me, they meant it.

But in that moment, with Kate there, I was in no doubt. I was kissing her neck and I could feel the heat of her panting breaths on my shoulder, her holding me, pressing me against her, whispering, 'Go on.'

So I bent a little lower, kissed downwards from her neck, across her shoulder, and then along the smooth curve of her breast, slowly – we had time. I found the fullness of her dark nipple, stiffened into an aroused peak that I took into my mouth and teased with long, slow licks of my tongue and the occasional graze of my teeth to turn a sigh into a whimper.

'Ohhh ...,' I heard her say, and her fingers curled in my hair. I trembled at that touch, just a little.

She pulled me back up toward her; I was a little taller than her and she raised her face to kiss me. 'I'm going to have you now,' she said firmly. 'You're ... oh, you're great.'

I let her lead me over to the stack of newspapers she'd been putting down to protect the floor. She picked up a fresh one and laid it out over the floor. 'I don't want to make a mess of your suit,' she explained. 'Not that you'll be keeping it on for much longer.'

Something in her straightforward, assertive tone was so phenomenally sexy I may have let a small sigh escape me. I could already feel how wet I was getting, and feel the hungry need pulsing in my clitoris.

But I sensed she was going to take this slow.

She sat down on the newspaper and pulled me after her, then took my wrist, pushed me down and swung herself over me so she sat straddling me, her breasts hanging down over me, spilling over the thick denim fabric of her dungarees. She pulled me out of my suit jacket, flung it to one side, and began with nimble fingers to unbutton my shirt.

'So you've never done this before?' I asked, as her fingers skimmed the curve of my breasts, just over the top of my bra. I was glad I'd worn a pretty one today; it was deep green satin, with a lace trim, intended to give my confidence a bit of a boost.

'It depends what you mean by "this" –' she said, trailing her tongue down my stomach.

I gasped. 'Erm ... Sleeping with a girl you've never met before, at work?'

She grinned. 'Well, obviously I've slept with girls before. And I've slept with girls I'd only just met before. But never at work.' She nibbled my earlobe. 'That's a new one for me.'

'Me too.'

'Really? You seem too straitlaced to actually be straitlaced, if you see what I mean.' She giggled against my neck. 'You seem like someone who might have dark secrets.'

'Not that many,' I murmured.

'That means some,' she said. She unzipped my skirt and climbed off me as I struggled awkwardly out of it, then rolled my tights down my legs as well. She was still wearing her dungarees, but then, I wasn't sure if she had anything at all on underneath.

'Classy,' she commented, running a hand over the outside of my knickers. Followed by, 'Shaved? You definitely can't be that straitlaced then ... It was always too itchy for me, but it feels *nice*.'

I mumbled something about my ex-girlfriend liking it that way, but the thoughts went out of my mind when her head dipped, and she began to lick me through the fabric of my knickers. I writhed, and she pulled them down to carry on, running a hand gently over the exposed skin, and trailing her finger through the wetness between my bare labia. She lapped at my clitoris until I moaned, and then just grazed it with her teeth. I groaned aloud.

'Is that good?' she asked.

She carried on without waiting for an answer; my moans, and the way my fingers were running across the newsprint in frantic tension, must have been more than enough to give it away.

She was lavish and decadent with me, holding my hand while I twisted with pleasure, curling our fingers together, tasting me indulgently. The slower, then faster motions of her lips and teeth and tongue created a thrumming tension deep inside me that built gloriously, until I yelped and my back arched and my hand squeezed hers, and the orgasm washed over me, leaving me panting and shaking, and her tongue still making little teasing motions that were almost agonising over my clitoris.

She moved to hold me and stroked my hair as I gasped and shook in afterglow.

She reached inside my bra to cup my breast, and made a little sound of surprise when her fingertips touched metal. 'Seriously?' she said. 'You're full of surprises …'

I unhooked my bra for her, to reveal the small silver bars going through each of my nipples. She played with them with her fingertips for a moment, making me shiver and moan, then took each nipple with its delicate piercing into her mouth, sliding the bars back and forth with her tongue and tasting the contrast between smooth metal and soft skin.

She leant back and surveyed me. 'So explain,' she said, 'go on. How is you manage to look like a librarian and yet that's what you've got underneath your clothes?'

I laughed. 'My university's LGBT society went on holiday together to Brighton. We went to a tattoo and piercing place, and everyone got a souvenir.' I gestured to my breasts, and said, 'Those were mine.'

Her hands skimmed over my breasts again. 'That's really fucking hot.'

And then she rolled me back on to my back, and giggled furiously.

'What is it?'

'Look at yourself,' she said.

I inspected my shoulder. Where I'd been lying, pressed against the newsprint, some of it had transferred on to my shoulder, so that thin black lines of text snaked their way across my body, marking it with words.

'It's all over you,' she said, turning me over so she could look at my back. She put a hand between my shoulder blades to hold me still.

And then I felt something cold on my back, and the

sensation of a brush, and I realised she was painting me.

'What are you doing?' I asked.

'Just adding a bit. I can't resist the canvas. This one's washable, don't worry.'

I rolled over nonetheless, and unclipped her dungarees. 'I want to see you naked,' I told her, finding some confidence from somewhere. She wriggled out of the dungarees, and I was proven right; she wasn't wearing a thing underneath. She was all smooth, luxuriant curves, with dark areolas, and wide hips. I slid one finger between her creamy thighs and found how wet she was; I played with her clitoris, but she pushed my hand back so that I was reaching into her vagina.

'I want to write on you while you make me come,' she said. 'Do you think we can do that?'

So I curved my fingers against her G-spot and thrust inside her, eliciting a little yelp every time I hit the spot, while she dipped the brush into the pot again and drew swirling letters on me, drawing little hearts around my nipples. She kissed them once the paint was dry; writing "I fucked Kate (and she loved it)" across my stomach, and "kiss me here" on my crotch. She was still giving a little yelp every time my fingers touched her G-spot, so I upped the pace a little, and her hands shook as she painted "and here" on the inside of my thighs.

I could feel her legs beginning to tremble; she lay down half on top of me, some of the paint, still wet, transferring on to her skin. As she wrote "beautiful and interesting – a rare combination" across my hips, she moaned, then dropped the brush and grabbed my thigh, as I became more forceful and the orgasm overcame her. When it was done, she lay on top of me, kissing all the words she'd written, and finally kissing my mouth, with lips slightly stained with paint.

'One more thing,' she said softly. 'Roll over.'

I did, and I felt the paintbrush touch my back again, though much as I tried to work out what she was writing, I couldn't figure it out from the motions of the brush. 'You can look at that when you get home,' she said. While it was drying, she gave me a back massage, strong hands working muscles in my shoulders that, until then, I hadn't even realised were tense.

When she was done, she rolled me over again and inspected her handiwork; delicate handwritten letters spiralling over my skin, the brushstroke hearts around my pierced nipples, and the faded newsprint, a background to all of this. She drew a finger from my neck, down between my breasts and over my stomach, and along my shaved pussy, and sighed a little.

'You are beautiful,' she said.

Looking at myself, in the fading light of the semi-derelict room, a gorgeous woman pressed against me and her handiwork marked all over my skin, I was inclined to agree.

I kissed her furiously. 'You're the best thing I ever found getting lost.'

We held each other until the sun went down, and I realised that my train was in danger of leaving without me. I pulled clothes back on, feeling oddly uncomfortable at them covering up the painted wonder of my skin. We kissed fervently; she was still naked, her skin soft underneath my hands. I dragged myself unwillingly away.

I managed to find my way out of the building on unsteady legs, though it took an improbable number of corridors and staircases to reach a door that led outside, and then, with a sprint, I just made it on to my train. I noticed that my suit had some splatters of paint on it. Hopefully the dry-cleaners would be able to deal with that. If not, it would be a fun souvenir. I hugged myself, and felt the press of the nipple piercings through my bra. I hadn't regretted most of the souvenirs I'd picked up over the years.

When I got home, I resisted going into the shower until I'd inspected my illustrated self a little more thoroughly. I was glad I did. Reading back to front in the mirror, I found on my back a number, followed by "love, Kate" and "call me".

The paint washed off easily enough. I called her the next morning.

A Change of Heart
by Lucy Felthouse

Alexis had taken some serious persuading to go to the local aerobics class. Her friend, Kelly, had laid on the guilt trips and nagged her until, eventually, Alexis gave in. It wasn't that she didn't want to do any exercise – hell, she was desperate to lose a few pounds and tone up – it was just that she hated the idea of jumping around in a room full of skinny women in Lycra. Alexis wasn't comfortable in that kind of clothing due to her size, and she knew that if she turned up in tracksuit bottoms and a loose fitting T-shirt, she'd stand out like a sore thumb. However, Kelly had worn her down and so she went, and that was the outfit she wore.

Sure enough, she was the only woman there who wasn't wearing skin-tight clothing. Even Kelly – fucking traitor – had totally dressed for the occasion in a sporty crop top and tiny shorts. But then she had the figure for it. Alexis looked around, shaking her head. It was odd: every woman in the room had a body to die for and yet they were all attending an aerobics class. Alexis was the only person, in her opinion, who *needed* to be there and yet she felt as awkward as fuck. Still, she'd promised Kelly that she'd give it a try and so she'd stick it out. For the first session, at least. She doubted she'd want to return for another one.

When the instructor walked into the mirrored room, Alexis rolled her eyes. The woman was flawless. She had the prerequisite athletic figure, wore all the right clothes, and her bouncy countenance was topped off by an equally bouncy ponytail. She was enough to make the less-than-flawless Alexis feel sick. Or, at the very least, completely inadequate. Kelly nudged Alexis as she muttered to herself about "fucking princesses".

'Shut up,' said Kelly, 'she'll hear you.'

'Whatever. This better be good. If I don't look like her by the end of the session, I'm outta here.'

Kelly shook her head and turned attentively to the front of the room as the instructor began to speak. She'd obviously noticed there were some new people in the group so she introduced herself – her name was Zoe – and encouraged everyone to exercise at their own pace. That was as far as Alexis got before tuning her out. They were just going to be jumping around a bit and waving their arms and legs to music – how fucking hard could it be?

By the end of the session, Alexis was panting like a dog and sweating like – something incredibly sweaty. Annoyingly, Kelly looked relatively fresh, with just a healthy-looking glow and slightly heaving chest giving away her exercised state.

Glancing to the front of the room, Alexis saw Zoe chatting with a couple of women, congratulating them on their progress. Their voices carried easily across the rapidly emptying room. Alexis snorted rudely. Progress? How could they be making any progress? They obviously came every week without fail and repeated the same workouts. It was the only way to explain the fact that Alexis was an unattractive, sweaty mess slumped at the back of the room, and all these perfect women were ... Well, perfect. Zoe in particular looked as flawless as she had when she'd first entered the room. There was not a hair out of place and her smile when she turned it on Alexis was genuine and warm. Alexis felt a jolt in her stomach, and an altogether more pleasant feeling between her legs.

Fuck, thought Alexis, I can seriously *not* be crushing on the fucking aerobics instructor! She's gorgeous, yes, but there's no way she'd ever look at me. Why would she? For starters, she's not a lesbian. And if she were, why would a hot, athletic chick like her want a chubby dyke like me?

Alexis'ss internal monologue was cut off abruptly when Zoe appeared in front of her and Kelly. Still smiling, she held a hand out to Alexis, who surreptitiously wiped her clammy palm on her trousers before shaking it.

'Hi, girls,' trilled Zoe, now reaching to shake Kelly's hand. 'How are you feeling after your first session? It's so nice to have some new people with us.'

Alexis smiled tightly, still trying to get her breath back. Luckily, Kelly piped up with the required praise and bullshit for the session Zoe had obviously been fishing for, as well as introducing the pair of them properly.

She might not have been up to chit-chat, but there was nothing wrong with Alexis's eyes. Zoe was looking at Kelly as they talked, so Alexis took the opportunity to study her more closely. Perhaps leching over her would have been a more apt description, though. She drank in every detail of the perky aerobics instructor; from her touchably shiny brunette hair down to her appropriately shod feet. Naturally, she paid special attention to the parts in between, particularly her tight thighs in skin-hugging shorts and her pert breasts, which were encased in a kind of sports-bra-cum-vest thing. She looked forward to the moment Zoe walked away, so she could get a good look at her ass too.

Despite her earlier grumbling outburst, Alexis liked what she saw. She didn't usually go for skinny chicks, instead preferring a girl with something to hold on to, but something about Zoe's physique indicated underlying strength. And that definitely got Alexis's motor revving. Visions of being pinned down on an exercise mat by Zoe flitted through Alexis's mind, and a fresh burst of heat zipped to her groin, making her grin involuntarily.

Zoe chose that moment to turn back to Alexis and, seeing her grin, asked, 'Are you feeling better now, Alexis? You looked a little wiped out earlier.'

Understatement of the century, thought Alexis. 'Yes,' she replied brightly, desperately trying to erase the filthy images which were still invading her mind, 'my lungs and heart seem to have caught up now!' She laughed heartily, then waved a nonchalant hand. 'I'm sure it'll get easier in time.'

Her sudden sunny and positive demeanour solicited a

suspicious look from Kelly, who obviously wondered what had brought about the change of attitude.

'It sure will!' replied Zoe, beaming at them both. 'So, I'll see you next week, then?'

Voicing their assent, Alexis and Kelly grabbed their stuff and headed toward the changing rooms.

'What was all that about?' asked Kelly as soon as they were out of earshot of the instructor. 'I thought you hated this! I was expecting you to do a runner and never come back again.'

'Well, I've had a change of heart. I'm entitled to that, aren't I? And besides, I *do* want to lose weight. It won't happen just because I *think* about it, will it? No, I'll be here next week, no probs!'

Kelly gave her friend a narrow-eyed stare. 'I don't buy it. You're usually as stubborn as a mule. What changed your mind?'

Before Alexis had a chance to answer, Zoe breezed past them into the changing room and called over her shoulder, 'See you next week, girls!'

Alexis nodded, grinning widely as she checked out the departing Zoe's pert backside. Following her friend's gaze, Kelly suddenly got it.

'Oh my God!' she said. 'You fancy her, don't you?'

An enigmatic smile from Alexis was all the answer she needed.

'Fucking hell, Lex! Earlier on you were calling her a "fucking princess" and now you're lusting after her? What is with you?'

'I don't know,' Alexis said, honestly. 'We can't help who we're attracted to, can we? There's just something about her.'

'Christ, you're not gonna go all lovesick puppy on me, are you? I don't think I could stand it if you suddenly became the model student in the class because you fancy the teacher. We're not going to have to go at the front next week, are we?'

By now, they were grabbing their gear out of their lockers. But, rather than heading for the showers like everyone else, Alexis said, 'You know what, I'm gonna head home. I'll be there in five minutes and I can shower without queuing then.'

Kelly shrugged, grabbing her wash bag. 'More like you want to avoid having this conversation. Suit yourself. I'll talk to you later, yeah?'

'Yeah,' replied Alexis, already heading out of the door and toward the exit of the leisure centre. She made a swift dash to the car park, unlocked her car, threw her stuff into it, then hopped into the driver's side. Gunning it a little more than was necessary, she was home in record time. Heading inside, she locked the door behind her, dumped her stuff on the kitchen table and made her way to the bathroom.

Once there, she hit the button on the shower and stripped off as she waited for the water to reach the right temperature. Seconds later, she was beneath the spray, heaving a sigh of both contentment and relief. Alexis hadn't been trying to avoid the conversation with Kelly – hell, if Kelly wanted it to happen then it would happen, if it was the last thing she did – she'd genuinely wanted to avoid queuing. And showering in public. As if it wasn't bad enough being in front of all those slim chicks in her frumpy tracksuit bottoms and T-shirt, she didn't want to have to get naked in front of them too. She'd feel like a bloody elephant amongst a herd of antelope.

Besides, she thought, reaching for her shower gel and squirting a healthy dollop into her hand, I wouldn't be able to do this in the leisure centre. With that, she slicked the liquid over her breasts and torso, then let her hand continue its southward journey. Dipping her fingers between her pussy lips, Alexis was not at all surprised to find that she was wet. Spreading her labia with her first and third fingers, she pressed her middle finger firmly to her clit, and gasped at the waves of sensation that rippled through her body. She was obviously more turned on than she'd first thought.

Alexis moved her hand to scoop up some of the soap she'd left on her breasts, then promptly jammed it back between her thighs. Her now lubricated fingers slipped easily back into the position they'd just vacated, and she had to use her other hand to steady herself against the shower wall as her middle finger worried at her rapidly swelling clit.

Visions of Zoe invaded her brain once more. The image of

being pinned to an exercise mat by that slim yet strong body spurred Alexis on to stroke her clit more rapidly. The fantasy continued to play out in her head as her body climbed toward its climax.

Zoe was still straddling Alexis, her thighs firm and solid on either side of Alexis's ample ones. Her chocolate-coloured eyes were peering into Alexis's rabbit-caught-in-headlights blue ones, pinning her to the spot as effectively as her limbs were. Then she licked her lips and dipped her head down, capturing the other girl's mouth in a slow and sensual kiss ...

Alexis yelped as hot cream gushed from her pussy. Slicking it over the madly sensitised bundle of nerves at the apex of her vulva, she redoubled her efforts, rubbing her clit desperately in her quest for climax. She didn't have to wait long. Squeezing her eyes tightly closed, she threw her head back, heedless of the water thundering onto her head and face. Biting her lip, she revelled in the familiar sensation overtaking her body, the tension not unlike a tightly wound spring.

Then, as the kiss that had been playing out in her imagination went from slow and sensual to hungry and downright dirty, Alexis came. She howled her release, the hand she still had against the wall barely holding her steady as waves of pleasure crashed through her body. Her pussy spasmed wildly. Oh, how she wished that her cunt was clenching around Zoe's graceful fingers, her clit grinding against that perfect mouth. Oh – how she wished all kinds of things.

Slumping down to the shower floor, Alexis leant against the wall, the cool tiles a shocking contrast to her heated skin, yet one she welcomed. As her climax abated, Alexis's mind continued to race down the track it had been following, seemingly unable to deviate.

Scenario after scenario flitted through her head, each one filthier than the last. After one particularly arousing thought about using Zoe's shorts and top to render her unable to move while Alexis parted her no doubt delectable pussy lips and licked her into blissful oblivion, she began to seriously wonder if she was in with a chance. Thinking back to the smiles and the idle chit-chat, she was still none the wiser.

Well, she thought as her hand slipped between her legs for round two, I'll just have to keep going to aerobics class to find out, won't I? Oh yes. I'll show that fucking sexy princess a thing or two. Oh fucking yes.

The following week, Alexis was at the leisure centre in plenty of time for the aerobics class. She was ridiculously early, in fact, but the excitement and anticipation of seeing Zoe again had made it impossible to sit around the house any longer. She sat in the cafeteria, idly flicking through a trashy celebrity magazine she'd found on an abandoned table. It was hardly engaging literature, but it kept her brain mildly occupied as the minutes ticked by.

Alexis was almost at the back page of the crappy magazine when she saw, from the corner of her eye, a slim figure with brunette hair making its way into the building. Her head snapped up. Zoe. An uncontrollable grin twisted the corners of Alexis'ss mouth up, and her heart rate increased.

Zoe was just as gorgeous as she'd been the previous week – hotter, perhaps, as Alexis had spent a great deal of time over the last seven days imagining the aerobics instructor in varying states of undress and sexual activity. They'd been some damn good fantasies, and seeing the subject of them in the flesh again sent a delicious frisson of arousal to her groin. Her clit throbbed, and Alexis squeezed her thighs together, grateful that nobody could see what she was doing. The action only served to make her clit swell more rapidly. Alexis gulped. At this rate, she was going to have to sneak into the toilets and rub one off before the aerobics class. Wriggling uncomfortably in her seat, Alexis was just wondering where the nearest disabled toilet was when Zoe finished whatever she'd been doing at the reception desk and strode over to her.

'Hi,' Zoe said, smiling, 'you're back! I didn't scare you off, then?'

Zoe wore a sweatshirt, which covered her perky tits and toned stomach, but her long, luscious legs in those sinfully tight shorts were on display. Alexis purposely kept her eyes fixed on Zoe's face. She could perv later, when the other woman wasn't looking straight back at her, waiting for an answer to her question.

'Huh? Oh no, of course not! Wild horses couldn't keep me away.'

Zoe's grin widened, and she looked at her watch. 'Well, you must be keen, you're an hour early!'

There was no way Alexis was going to admit she'd been sitting in the cafeteria for half an hour already. Instead, she gave what she hoped looked like a nonchalant shrug, and said, 'Well, I was out and I had to go past this place to get home, so it seemed silly to go home to come back again.'

'Fair enough,' Zoe replied. 'Why waste petrol, huh? Especially at the prices they're charging now! You wanna come and help me set up?'

Casting her mind back to the previous week, Alexis had no idea what Zoe meant. When she and Kelly had walked into the mirrored room, they'd had to grab their own exercise mats from a pile and put them where they wanted them. The only other equipment was a small speaker dock which sat in the corner of the room, ready to accommodate the iPod of whoever was running a particular session. Zoe might be a petite chick, but Alexis was pretty sure she could manage to carry her own iPod. Unless …

'Sure,' she said, grabbing her backpack from the floor and standing up. 'I'd be happy to.'

Following Zoe down the corridor and through a door marked "Staff Only", Alexis couldn't help but wish that the other woman's sweatshirt was shorter – it was hiding her arse in that skin-tight Lycra. Alexis found herself wondering if Zoe wore underwear beneath her shorts. Surely not, she'd get VPL.

Seconds later, she got her chance to find out. Zoe indicated Alexis should follow her into a tiny office space; once the door was shut behind them, she flipped the lock and turned to her.

'OK, we don't have much time, so I'm going to be blunt. Am I right in thinking that you've got the hots for me? If not, please say and I'll unlock that door and we'll never speak of this again.'

Alexis was stunned. Was Zoe actually coming on to her?

Her, a flabby dyke with no sense of style? Granted, she'd made a little more effort with her outfit since last week, but she was still no Kylie Minogue.

'Umm … No. Er, I mean yes! Yes! I have the hots for you.'

Suddenly suspicious, Alexis spoke again. 'Why?'

She'd been tricked. She knew it. There was just no way –

'What do you mean, why? I want to know if you've got the hots for me so I know it's OK to do this.'

She stepped forward until the two of them were face to face, then pressed a chaste kiss to Alexis's lips.

'Well,' Zoe said softly, 'was that OK?'

Alexis's eyebrows almost shot into her hairline. 'OK? Are you kidding?'

'I was hoping you'd say that,' Zoe replied with a smile. 'So, can I do it again? But, y'know, for longer.'

Alexis nodded vehemently. 'Just answer one question for me. Why me?'

Zoe frowned. 'Why you what?'

'Why kiss me? When there's a whole class of slim, attractive women to choose from.'

Zoe laughed. 'Oh, Alexis, you are funny. You of all people should know just because I like women doesn't mean I like *all* women! You don't fancy every other woman in the class, do you?'

Feeling suitably chastened, she shook her head. 'No, only you. But I never thought in a million years that I'd have a shot with you!'

'Well, you have. So stop being so self-deprecating. Is it so hard to believe that I like you?'

Spluttering, Alexis replied, 'Um – have you *seen* you? And, well, look at me.'

'Alexis,' Zoe replied, taking the other woman's face in her hands and looking into her eyes, 'listen to me. I like you. OK? I just kissed you, and I'd like to do it again in a second. So you're a big girl. So what? I happen to like my chicks with curves in all the right places. So shut up and kiss me.'

Alexis closed her eyes and did as she was told.

This time, their kiss was far from chaste. They wrapped their arms around one another and quickly lost themselves to lust. Soon, Zoe's hands moved to Alexis's waist and pulled down her tracksuit bottoms, and her thong with it. Alexis promptly returned the favour – she'd been right; Zoe wasn't wearing anything underneath the skimpy shorts.

As if by some unspoken command, both girls slipped their right hands between the other's legs. Alexis gasped at the first touch of Zoe's fingers against her swollen pout.

'Oh fuck,' she said, pulling away from their heated kiss. 'You're making me so fucking hot, it won't take me long to come.'

'Just as well,' replied Zoe, who was equally breathless, 'as we don't have much time!'

With that comment, Alexis decided that she wouldn't be the first to come. Her princess-turned-lover would crack first, she was determined of it. Sliding two fingers up and down between Zoe's pussy lips, she got them nice and wet with her juices. Then she trapped Zoe's clit and teased it, alternately circling it, stroking it, and pulling it. Given that Zoe was doing similarly delicious and dirty things to her pussy, Alexis found it hard to concentrate, but by the way her lover was panting and moaning, she was definitely still hitting the spot.

They continued to stroke and finger-fuck each other for a few minutes, until Alexis felt Zoe's cunt clench around her digits. She was close. She redoubled her efforts, still determined to make her lover come first. With her other hand, she reached around and grabbed Zoe's ponytail, pulling her head back so she could pepper her throat with heated kisses.

'Oh –' Zoe moaned. 'I'm ... Any second now ... Ohhh!'

Alexis gasped as she felt the iron grip of Zoe's muscles around her fingers, and she watched in glee as the other woman came apart at her touch. Zoe's hand had slipped from between Alexis's legs, but it didn't matter. Not right then. She was content to watch as Zoe's facial expression contorted into one of utter bliss as she climaxed against her lover's hand.

'Whoa,' Zoe said, when she finally came to. 'That was – just incredible.'

'It sure was. I didn't think it was possible, but you're even hotter when you come.'

Zoe swatted playfully at Alexis's arm, then said, 'Your turn now.'

'Wha –' Her words were cut off when Zoe pushed her against the wall. Kneeling in front of her, she reached up to part Alexis's pussy lips with her thumbs, then her pink tongue delved between them and sought out her clit.

It was all too much for Alexis. She began to come immediately, gripping and twisting the bottom of her T-shirt in her ecstasy. Quite forgetting where she was, she let out a throaty moan as the waves of pleasure crashed relentlessly through her body, leaving her trembling and boneless. She managed to summon just enough energy to reach for Zoe's hand, pull her up and into her arms.

They hugged tightly, breathing heavily and murmuring the odd expletive until, eventually, they felt able to function normally again.

'Wow,' Alexis gasped as the two of them disentangled and began pulling their clothes back on, 'that was one hell of a workout!'

'Yeah, and you'd better pull yourself together because you have another one in about ten minutes!' Zoe grinned.

The two of them scrambled to get ready, and once they were both decent, Zoe unlocked the office door and peered out to make sure no one was around. She beckoned to Alexis, and they left the room. They were heading a different way through the leisure centre and Alexis had no idea where she was, so she merely followed in silence.

Soon, they were standing outside the aerobics studio. Looking through the glass door, Alexis could see that the group was already assembled and waiting for Zoe. She turned to her.

Smiling, Zoe said, 'After you.'

Just as Alexis opened the door and walked through, she felt Zoe's hand on her arse. With a quick squeeze that nobody else could see, Zoe skipped away from Alexis and toward the front of the class.

'Hi, everyone! Now that all the stragglers are here –' she gave Alexis a pointed look '– we can start. I'm all fired up today, guys, so be prepared for one hell of a workout!'

Retrieving an exercise mat and walking to where Kelly sat, Alexis groaned. This was going to be torture – of the most delicious kind.

Back to Square One
by Angel Propps

She was hunting me through the streets, waiting for me to fuck up and make myself vulnerable. I knew that, but I didn't turn around to try to spot her. I knew she was out there, stalking around some corner or melting into some doorway that would render her invisible She had the advantage, and there was not much I could do about it but try to elude her as long as possible.

I ducked my neck lower into the collar of the overcoat that I wore, not for any extra warmth but to simply smell the fabric. Icy needles of rain slashed across the top of my umbrella and the wind blew up my skirt, making me grit my teeth in agony. The weather was ugly, grey, and bleak, but the buildings were beautiful thanks to the miniature rainbows created by the electric billboards that ringed the perimeter of Times Square. A group of tourists stopped in front of me to admire a flashing advertisement they could have seen on the television set in their hotel room; skirting around them, I muttered a curse, knowing that they would chalk me up as just another rude New Yorker.

But it wasn't just the tourists who made me swear, it was the fact that they were celebrating the death of the real Times Square, my Times Square, and admiring the cleaned up, sanitised version of it, that boring and overly done section that felt nothing like the place it used to be.

Times Square wasn't always just a testament to the willingness of the public to swallow down whatever trend was handed to them. It wasn't always wholesome and suitable for mass public consumption. No, once upon a time it had been a place where anything could happen, and usually did. I had been fucked hard and rough in a tucked-in little corner of the Square, my face pressed into brick and my ass and cunt exposed to cold February air. As I walked past the spot where that fuck had taken place, I winced at the sight of a mannequin in the window of an upscale clothing store that had once been a sex shop. The mannequin wore a violently purple dress with a multi-coloured woven belt and an expression of glazed-over boredom. I couldn't blame the mannequin; the new version of the Square made me feel jaded and tired too.

That mannequin also made me sad, as did the amusement park air pervading everything. I missed the hookers, the glitter of needles in the gutter, the fear that was really just desire starting to boil up under my skin as I walked through the Square of back then.

I had come to the city as a fresh-faced girl from a small town in rural Alabama. I had a college scholarship in one hand and a battered duffel bag in the other because my family was too poor to buy me a suitcase, and even if they had I would not have had anything to fill it with. I got off the bus and found myself staring in shock at the hordes of people, and then I got carried out the front door by the tide of bodies.

The sidewalk felt warm under my sneakers and the sky was not the same long expanse of blue it was back home. I could just barely see it in patches between the buildings and I had the oddest sensation that I was trapped in the bottom of some concrete fishbowl, looking up, gasping for air.

I could hear the men I had been warned about starting their pitches; pimps looking for fresh blood, their voices at once persuasive and hard. I pulled my duffel tighter to my body and started walking. I had memorised the directions, but what the map had been unable to tell me was how crowded the streets would be, how the smell of so many people would batter at me. Nobody in my town had known about the sheer volume of sound in the city so nobody had warned me. Voices came from everywhere, car horns honked, and tyres squealed. It was such a contrast to the sleepy, sun-struck sidewalks of my home town that I had to fight the urge to put my hands over my ears and burst into tears. I might have done so anyway, except that I had my duffel with all my precious and few belongings to consider. I couldn't put it down and I couldn't lift it that high either, so I kept my ears uncovered and walked toward my destination.

I wandered into Times Square just as dusk was falling. Neon flared gaudy and bright. A woman whose thinness reminded me of a cinnamon stick twirled past me, her too-big fur coat fluttering and her high heels clattering. I turned to look at her, at the scarlet heels that made her teeter and the long, black hair that had smelled like something both oily and rich when it flapped across my cheek for a brief moment.

Laughter sprang from somewhere, and there was an indefinable odour; it reminded me of the smell in the boxer shorts I had to wash in my lousy job in a laundry back home. It made me shiver for no reason at all, that smell, and I felt fear and something else mingling in my belly.

I walked past the sex shops, the theatres where men stood outside yelling at passers-by to come on in and check it out, get their dreams made true. I watched a few men staggering into those places and wondered what kind of dreams they could be having, and what was behind those doors that could make them come true.

Cars stalled in traffic, men yelled out windows, and on the sidewalks women bumped their pelvises at them. Words flew from both sides. I thought I knew about sex. I had a scar above my right eye, compliments of my former best friend's pissed-off dad. He found me trying out some moves we had seen on a porn flick on his daughter's pussy and he nearly put my eye out. Until the moment I saw that interaction between tricks and girls out in the Square I thought of myself as experienced in sex, as adventurous and knowledgeable. Walking through those blocks made me understand that nothing could have been further from the truth. I was a babe in the asphalt woods.

The days flew past those first few months. Like all scholarship kids I was terrified of not making the grade so I put my head down and studied, studied, studied. The city was always right outside my windows, but I pulled the shades and kept working.

Until a day in February that I woke up with a feeling of restlessness nothing would cure. By five that afternoon I was pacing like a caged animal, my work scattered across the desk and floor, and my nerves all twisted into a knot.

I decided there was no cure for it; I needed to get out. And not just out but *out*. I needed to party, to get drunk or laid. All the shoved-down emotions and hormones were tired of being ignored, and so I went to my meagre closet and began looking for something to wear.

I had my prom gown, a long, strapless thing that was a faultless soft pink. I cut the hem off it with scissors and then put it on, admiring the jagged edges that the cutting left behind. I found the fishnet stockings I had bought on a whim at a little store back in Alabama. I had hidden them in the very bottom of my duffel so that nobody would accidentally find them, and had never worn them, I didn't know how. I had to struggle to put them on; the little garter belt that went around my waist confused me and it took long minutes to figure it all out. I stared down at myself, at the wide delta of my hips and the patch of hair that puffed up from between my thighs. I looked in my drawer at the pile of neat and plain white or pink panties that I usually wore, and back down at my crotch. I could not cover the splendid little strips of lace and elastic with those panties, I just couldn't. I took a deep breath and decided to simply go out without panties. I could feel my pussy, the weight and slipperiness of it, without even touching it.

I put on thick-soled rain boots, painted on a brilliant red mouth and eyes shaded by a shimmery gold shadow, added thick eyeliner and mascara, and gave myself a pout in the cloudy mirror while I fluffed my red-gold curls with my fingers. I didn't look like myself; I looked like the girls I saw in the hallways, the ones who liked weird punk rock bands and talked about feminist theory in intense tones that always made me feel like they knew my mom and dad had been married since before time even began.

I had an old coat that practically screamed Southern. It was too thin for the weather, short and a cheerful orange. I wadded it up and stuffed it under my bed, at a loss as to what I could wear to keep myself from freezing to death while trying to look good.

In the common room I found the answer in a carelessly left behind overcoat, long and black. I picked it up and sniffed it. It smelled of cologne, not perfume, and I wondered what I would do if some guy appeared and demanded his coat back. Fight him for it?

The dorms were silent around me. It was a Friday night and early; everyone was still out at class or off for dinner. The parties I never went to had yet to crank up and the coat was already on my back, so I decided if someone had really wanted it they never would have left it in the first place.

Buoyed up by that thought, I headed out into the bleak remains of the day. Raindrops falling on my red umbrella managed to lend rhythm to my feet, the taps of rain a type of drumming that I followed up the avenues toward Times Square.

Hookers shifted their hips and cars honked at them. The air felt electrified and filled with possibility. There was an excitement in my belly that made me literally bounce on the tips of my boots. A laugh burst out of my mouth as I jumped off the curb and splashed into a puddle. Nobody noticed, or if they did they didn't care, and that made me feel even wilder. I began to sing at the top of my lungs and dance madly, doing an ass-shaking shimmy across the street.

'How much for a half-n-half?' someone yelled from a car, and I gave them a finger before darting onto a safer spot on the sidewalk.

'You certainly are not minding your lessons, now are you?'

I spun around at the question and found myself staring into the amused eyes of one of my professors, and not just any professor either, but the scariest damn professor on the campus.

Louise Hall had a reputation for being a hard-ass for a reason. She demanded her students give her everything they had, and she knew when we didn't. I turned in a short story assignment one afternoon and Professor Hall lobbed it back at me, literally, and told me I had 20 minutes to write something that would save my ass from being ejected from her class. I wrote "fuck I'm fucked" over and over, and burst into tears when she picked it up and read it out loud.

'Nice save,' she had said, slamming the crisp white paper with its crawling lines of black ink back down in front of me. 'Never go for less than the truth.'

The wind boomed down from the rooftops and across the tops of my nearly bare tits, making me very aware of the fact that my nipples were frozen into stiffness. The cheap material made them ache where it rubbed against them, and I bit down on my lip to keep from whimpering in painful pleasure.

'I like your dress; it reminds me of the colour of nipples. Are your nipples that colour?'

One minute she was standing half a foot in front of me, the next she was up close and in my face. Her raincoat was a thin yellow slicker; one of the fasteners was loose and it slapped against my tit when she leant closer. I gasped and shivered involuntarily, which made her grin, and I knew that it was deliberate. Then she began backing me toward the wall of the building, forcing herself into my space, putting her leg almost between mine until I was hitching backwards in an instinctive reaction that was only half fear.

I had heard that she liked girls, but then again the rumours about Professor Hall were rampant. It seemed like half the girls in the dorms wanted to fuck her and the other half had. She was sexy in a powerful way; she had short hair and jeans that always seemed to draw my eyes to her crotch. I had heard she wore a cock under there, but in my limited experience I had no idea of how that could have even been possible.

I wanted to find out, though, that I did know. So when my back hit the freezing bricks I tried to think of something witty and sexy to say, but all I could come up with was a squeak.

'I think you need a spanking.'

I blinked at her, then leant forward, turning my mouth into a circle. I bent my head until it was in the vapour that had been her words, and I dragged my breath in, trying to inhale her breath.

'I'll take that as a yes.'

Her husky alto was right in my ear. I wriggled my ass closer to the bricks as hot, squirmy sensations shot down my spine and into my very tailbone. Her fingers stroked my erect nipples through the dress. I found myself arching my back, struggling to get closer to her hands. Louise's mouth came dangerously close to mine; a distant streetlight gave a gleam to her teeth, and I had time to think that they were very white and very square before they were on the front of my dress.

There was a long burring sound. I blinked up at the interior of my umbrella and wondered what the hell had just happened, then the raw wind hit my nipples and I screamed. That sound was abruptly cut off by her hand.

She grabbed my umbrella and yanked it away from me, tossing it into the wind in one long, fluid motion. The wind snatched it and I watched it roll merrily away down the deserted corridor to my right, wondering what the hell I was doing, and why.

The kiss made me forget all questions. Her mouth sealed mine shut, then probed every corner, every crease. I could not breathe and didn't want to. My lips stung and ached; they were being pulped by the sheer weight of that kiss, and when she finally let me up for air I almost fell down from simple oxygen deprivation.

She turned me around and her hands slid up my thighs, leaving little shivers behind.

'No panties.' A gloating satisfaction tinged her voice. 'How did I know you would not wear them?'

Beats me, I wanted to say. Hell, I didn't know. I never got the chance to say that, though, because she grabbed me by the hair, arching my neck backwards while her knee came up into the spot where my spine and the top of my ass met. She pressed down on that sensitive bundle of nerves and a hand stuffed itself into my open mouth.

'Peel my fucking glove off, and don't you dare fucking bite me.'

I took the glove gently in my teeth, feeling the thin texture of it and smelling vaguely familiar cologne as I tugged at it. I felt like a puppy and, oddly enough, I liked it, wanted it. I wanted to curl up at her feet and simply be obedient.

The glove was all the way off. Her long, delicate fingers seemed at odds with her cruelty. I wanted to turn around, to ask her what was going to happen next, but her other hand was still in my hair and her knee was still holding my hips hostage against the bricks.

She moved her knee just then. I had no time to turn around, however, because she yanked my ass up while she bent my head down. I stared at the patch of glistening sidewalk between my rain boots and wondered why someone would smoke half a cigarette then toss it out, but that thought flew out of my head as my skirt was tossed over my back and night air hit my pussy and ass.

I had not known how wet I was until then. The cold hit fluid and made an unbearable ache. I would have run if it had not been for the first slap of that glove across my sensitive pussy.

Incredibly thin leather met wet flesh and heat exploded inside me. I wanted to run but I found myself pushing my arms against the bricks and shoving my ass up higher, spreading my legs wider and wider with each smack.

'I suppose you will definitely learn a lesson tonight, won't you?'

An insistent finger tickled at my clit and I began to cry. Tears ran down my face and dripped off my chin as a ticklish, itchy feeling came and went again and again while she alternated spanking me with the glove and circling my clit with her fingers.

'I asked you a question.'

'I will learn my lesson,' I hiccupped out although I had no idea of just what the hell it was I supposed to be learning.

'You will never steal my coat again.'

I had stolen her coat? I began to giggle helplessly and she halted all movement. I was instantly bereft; the imprint of her hands was still on my skin, hanging there phantom-like, but her warmth and the friction had gone.

'What's funny?'

'I stole your coat,' I got out, then a spasm of laughter took me over.

'Did you like me touching you?'

The streetlight flickered at her words and I stared at it; my cheek felt abraded and sticky where it lay against the building. I could feel a thudding little pulse in my neck and its twin down there in my pussy.

'Yes,' I said. 'I liked it a lot. I want you to keep doing it.'

She didn't use the glove that time. Her hand cracked against my ass cheek and I moaned in misery as I lurched up and forward. I could feel the heat growing in my flesh, not just lust but actual heat. My nipples scraped the wall and my lips too as I shook my head back and forth, trying not to weep, not to scream, and waiting for her to put her fingers back on my clit and make it all feel good.

I floated; there was this long emptiness. My nerves and muscles began translating the pain into pleasure and I found myself moving backward, hanging my head down again in surrender because I wanted those slaps. I didn't know what had changed, but it no longer hurt, or it did but it felt good too.

'That's a good girl, give it to me.'

I could hear the funny, ugly sounds coming out of my mouth as her fingers slid into my pussy. She didn't go slowly or easy; she worked her hands against my skin like it was enemy territory she was determined to divide and conquer. She pinched and tugged at my clit; she thrust and slammed into me. I could feel my pussy widening and stretching around her fingers. I kept pumping my ass back at her. My palms scraped the walls but I didn't care; the sting was nothing compared to the feeling of her inside me. I cried out every time she withdrew and whimpered when those hard fingers came back inside, pounding at my walls and crumbling me into defencelessness.

'I bet you could be fisted.'

'Yes, you can fist me, you can do anything you want, dammit,' I panted out even though I had no idea what she meant by fisting.

If she had said she wanted to kill me I would have said go ahead at that moment. I was sopping wet; I could feel pussy juice dripping down the insides of my thighs. Rain sluiced down, washing me all over, beating down on my bared tits and face. Friction bloomed, and my pussy clenched down on her fingers; I could feel it tightening.

'If you want to come you had better ask for it.'

'Please can I come?' I howled.

She moved the collar of the coat away from my shoulder, then she bit into it. My pussy started to spasm, opening and closing like the pain she was causing in the skin she was so furiously biting. I came, weeping against her mouth, my back curling and uncurling, my ass bobbing up and down and the top of my head grinding into brick.

She backed away, and laughter poured out of her. I stumbled back, and her warmth was a welcome haven. Her hands went to the collar of the coat and she closed it softly, easily around me as I stared at the faces lining the window of the sex store that inhabited the window we had been fucking next to.

The people in there were talking, but I could not hear them. I could see the giant Os of their mouths and one man had his hand on his crotch; he rubbed at it even as I watched.

'Let's go,' Louise said through laughter as she hauled me back out into the sea of humanity. 'I demand anyone who lets me fuck them in a public place at least allow me to buy them a cup of coffee after.'

'I don't drink coffee.'

'I'll get you some cocoa, then.'

I glanced at her face as we walked, taking in the strong jaw and the full lips. Her black hair glittered with raindrops; they looked like diamonds, and I wanted to touch one just to see if it was as precious as it looked.

'You can have your coat back,' I said.

'I will take it when you are in a cab.'

In a window, I saw our reflections and I felt my heart lurch. She was so masculine, her walk was a swagger. I was frail and drowned looking, even though I was hardly a small girl. My plump curves were evened out under the flow of that coat, and my hair was a contrasting sheet of colour hanging down the back of it. We looked good together, and that scared me. I had heard enough about Professor Hall to know she did not have the patience to deal with schoolgirl crushes.

'Here's your coat.'

I thrust it at her and ran away, pelting through the rain and mist toward my dorm. She didn't yell at me to stop; I had not expected her to either.

I crossed the intersection, picking up my pace, and took a turn down an alley for no reason at all, then cut through a side street that would take me almost back to the place I had been three minutes before. The evasive manoeuvre would not fool her for long, but it would give me a few moments to collect my thoughts.

The light turned and interrupted my trip down Memory Lane. A couple speaking German scurried past me and I stood still for a moment, watching them go, wondering how love would work if two people lived with it every damn day of their lives.

I had gone to class the following Monday, dragging my aching and scarred bones into my seat. Louise had been as distant and demanding as ever. I had refused to meet her eyes, and when I turned in my paper I had tossed it at her desk carelessly before sauntering out. Instinct told me Louise was a hunter, and maybe I did not understand things the other girls who had been raised in the city did, things like fashion and accessories and what was hot in the theatres and what the trends were before they ever happened, but hunters, oh those I understood.

Being raised in a small town where the men and even the women talked about their kills and the thrill of the hunt, being in the woods at five in the morning armed with a gun, those things had taught me much about hunting. And hunters.

Louise had no patience with those girls who fell in love with her, who chased her down. She had hunted me down in order to get her coat back and that ambush sex had been an extension of that hunting of me; she had not planned it but she had certainly liked it. So had I. I wanted her to do it again, and so I ran like prey will run and she came to hunt.

Twenty-three years later, I walked the streets of the city, pacing out the private preserve she and I shared once a year. My life had taken me from the city years before, and so our traditional hunt was born. Every February we met up for lunch in one of the little out of the way places, talked about books and art and what was going on in our lives.

And every year I stole her coat. She always came for it, always followed me through the city as the day turned to night. One year it snowed like hell; we could barely see an inch in front of our faces and we both had near falls that day. That year we fucked on a lonely side street while wind blew across the snow-covered pile of trash she threw me over. For years, the sight of a corrugated metal trashcan lid could make me laugh hysterically.

I came to a dark little section of sidewalk and paused. The crowds were sparse even in the Square itself at that hour, because it was between dinner and the opening times of the theatres. The noise was considerably less on the side streets and I glanced around warily, wondering if Louise had somehow gotten ahead of me, but I was sure she had not and that the dark could disguise me for a few more minutes.

I began to walk toward the deep shadows, feeling confident in the decision to go that way, until she came out of the stairwell that is.

Her hands were still strong; she yanked me forward by the collar of the coat I wore. Her coat and her mouth ground down against mine. I gasped for air and tried to run, but she caught me, tangling her hands into my hair.

She tied me to the black iron that served as banister for the stairs by my hair, and I found myself being thankful I had not had it cut off like I had been thinking of doing.

'I think you might just be a lost cause, little girl. I doubt seriously if you are ever going to learn.'

I sobbed in frustration and lust as her nails raked along the bare skin of my legs. The cold had left them sensitive and slightly swollen; the contact of her nails on them was almost unbearable.

I could see the lights twinkling in Times Square, that new and dandified Times Square. I could see them shining up there as her fists punched at my back and the backs of my legs and ass. The concrete steps I huddled on is my Times Square; the tourists can have that one farther up. The dirty, seedy little spots where anything can and usually will happen will always be Times Square for me, and every single February I will go back to square one for sex and for the hunt but mostly, mostly for the one I love.

Corsetry for Beginners
by Medea Mor

Every now and then, you know it's going to be a good day before you've even set a foot out of bed. The day I met Maisie was one such day for me. I woke up in the morning to bright sunshine, feeling well rested and cheerful, and not even the memory of the night before, when I'd seen my ex, Jenna, with her new girlfriend, was enough to dispel the optimism that I felt in my bones, despite the fact it had been a distinctly awkward meeting.

I hummed a jaunty tune as I unlocked the door of my shop and walked to the back of the L-shaped space, where my cutting table stood waiting for me. This same table, I recalled, had once been the subject of a heated debate between myself and Jenna. According to her, I shouldn't have my workplace in my shop because it looked messy and unsophisticated, but I disagreed. It made no sense to me to do all my sewing at home when I could do it in my shop during the long hours between customers. I'd never got the impression that my clients objected to my having a sewing machine in my shop; if anything, they seemed to enjoy watching me go about my work. They tended to respond very favourably to my explanations on panels, boning, lining, and flossing.

I'd earmarked this particular day to work on two garments. First I was supposed to put the finishing touches to a black-and-yellow PVC underbust corset for a ridiculously fit domme who owned more of my pieces than anyone else in the world. Then I'd get started on a Tudor-style corset for an American Ren-Faire enthusiast who, judging from her measurements, was rather less fit than the domme.

I spent about half an hour edging the PVC corset. Then I sewed a label into it, in a place where I knew it wouldn't chafe. LAUREN PRESTON, it read in a large and ornate font. And underneath, in smaller letters, BESPOKE CORSETS.

I had just secured the label in place when the telephone rang and a woman with a West Indian accent asked if I could close my shop this afternoon for a private fitting for her client, who was an international celebrity. Suspecting a hoax, I answered that I never closed my shop during the day, but that the lady's client was welcome to swing by a little after closing time if that was convenient for her. 'Just make sure she's here by six,' I added. 'If she's not here by six, I'll close up shop and go home.'

'She'll be there,' answered the voice on the other side of the line. 'She looks forward to meeting you.'

After I rang off, I spent a few minutes wondering if anyone would show up after closing time, and if so, whether she'd be someone I'd recognise as a celebrity, or rather some footballer's wife whose only claim to fame was marrying a man more talented than herself. I also wondered, a little anxiously, if I'd be home in time to watch the season finale of *True Blood*, to which I'd been looking forward for weeks. Ultimately, though, work demanded my attention, and I forced myself to focus on the patterning of the Tudor corset, forgetting all about the celebrity who was supposed to come and see me.

The day was over before I realised it, and at 5.45 – 15 minutes after closing time – I heard a soft knock on the door. I looked up and saw a short, black woman with shoulder-length straightened hair, dressed in black trousers and clutching an expensive-looking handbag. A chauffeur-driven car was parked behind her. Clearly, this was the customer I'd been waiting for.

I rose, unlocked the front door, and stared into a dark-chocolate-coloured face with bright, almond-shaped eyes. It looked familiar, but I couldn't place its owner until she opened her mouth and said in a melodious Jamaican accent, 'Hello. I hope you didn't mind staying open a bit later for me.'

There was no mistaking that voice, nor the accent for that

matter. Nor was there any mistaking the nervous smile I'd seen in the handful of TV interviews she'd given following the release of her second album, *Say It Like You Mean It*. This was multi-BRIT-Award-winning songstress Maisie James. I hadn't recognised her with her hair down – she usually wore it pinned back in her public appearances – but she looked amazing. And I had no doubt that she had enough money to buy out my shop if she wanted, so I was keen to make a good impression.

'Not at all,' I replied, not sure whether to let on that I'd recognised her or not. 'What can I do for you?'

She frowned as if that was a silly question to ask. 'I'd like to buy some corsets.'

'What kind?' I countered. 'Overbust, underbust, waist cincher? Period, modern, fetish?'

She smiled, clearly understanding now that her request hadn't been as straightforward as she'd probably believed it to be. 'I don't know. Can you show me some examples of the various styles?'

'Of course,' I said, leading her to the back of the shop to show her some samples of my work. 'I guess the first question we need to answer is whether you intend to wear your corsets as underwear or outerwear.'

'Both,' she answered at once. This didn't make my work any easier, but it did make it more likely that I'd be selling her more than one item. I liked the sound of that. If I was going to miss the season finale of *True Blood*, I might as well emerge with a handsome profit.

'Well, then. The second question that needs answering is whether you intend to wear your corsets while singing.' I was proud of myself for that question, which struck me as the perfect way to let her know that I'd recognised her without getting awkward or gushy about it.

She smiled. She had a gorgeous smile, I noticed, a little shy but ever so attractive. With a start, I realised it was exactly the kind of smile that had once attracted me to Jenna.

'Does it make any difference?'

Oh dear, I thought. 'I'm afraid it does. A tightly laced full-length corset reduces lung capacity by about 30 per cent, which makes it a bad choice for singers. You'd probably faint halfway through a concert if you were to wear one on stage, especially if you haven't practised chest breathing before.' For all I knew, Maisie James might be a pro at chest breathing, but I figured it was only fair to warn her.

'Oh,' she said, the disappointment plain on her face. I guess she hadn't really realised what corsets do to a woman's lungs.

Thankfully, I had something else that would serve her purpose. 'You could of course wear a waist cincher on stage, a broad belt that narrows your waist but stops under your ribs. Many singers wear them, either under or over their costume. They're designed to improve your figure without constricting your chest. They're supposed to help you improve your chest breathing too.' I inwardly thanked Nora Wilkinson, a regular customer who sang in a church choir, for that useful piece of information.

'Could you show me some of those, please?' Her voice was warm and hopeful. It sent a thrill through me, something I'd never experienced with another customer. Suddenly, I didn't care so much about the possibility of missing *True Blood* any more. Who needed *True Blood* when they had Maisie James standing next to them, in need of help and advice?

I lowered my eyes to Maisie's waist, trying to estimate the measurements of her hips, waist, and ribs, a skill all tailors learn once they've been in the business for a few years. I was suddenly glad that Maisie had come to my shop. She was a beautiful woman, but not dressed to her best advantage. If she could reduce her waist by four inches, her full breasts and round bottom would be accentuated in the most gorgeous way. I resolved to help her get that waist reduction, to help her make the most of her figure and become the siren she was born to be.

I walked to the shelf where I kept the waist cinchers and picked a handful that might fit her. One by one, I helped her put them on over her tight red shirt. The first one was too tight, the second a little too loose at the bottom. The third, a black satin belt with a subtle printed pattern, fitted her like a glove. She smiled approvingly as she turned around in front of the mirror, her enthusiasm so genuine that I couldn't help being infected by it. I could suddenly see why she'd become such an overnight success, apart from the fact that she had an amazing voice. She had a star's charisma, the kind where you find yourself smiling whenever they smile.

'I'll take this,' she said in her melodious voice. 'Would you also happen to have one in burgundy?'

I shook my head. 'Not at the moment. But I can make one to measure for you, if you can find a fabric you like.' I gestured to the left wall of my shop, which was lined with rolls of satin, silk, and velvet.

'I'll pick a fabric later,' she said. 'Could you show me some of your full-length corsets too? The ones you recommend I do not wear on stage?'

I laughed. 'What do you need them for?' I knew it was none of my business, but I was curious nonetheless.

'The cover of my new album,' she answered promptly. 'Promotional photos for my website. Promotional photos for magazines. The usual.'

Oh wow, I thought. One of my corsets may be pictured on the cover of Maisie James' new album. Does it get any better than this?

I grabbed a dozen plunges that I felt did a good job of showing off the variety of styles I offered. Some were straight-top push-ups; others had plunging V-necks or sweetheart-shaped tops. Some had shoulder straps, others didn't. Some wouldn't have looked amiss on a Victorian lady, while others looked considerably more modern. Yet others were hardcore fetish.

Maisie went through all of them, laughing at some of the more outlandish models and nodding appreciatively at a few others. I saw her look longingly at a purple taffeta halter-neck corset.

'This would look amazing on you,' I said, holding it in front of her and establishing that, yes, this shade of purple did indeed look wonderful on her dark skin. 'I don't think this particular corset will fit you, unfortunately, but I can make you one just like it if you'd like.'

She smiled gratefully. 'Thank you, Lauren,' she said,

blushing. 'Your name *is* Lauren, right?'

I was surprised, both at the blush and at the fact that she knew my name. 'It is. But how did you know that?'

She blushed again, so furiously that her face seemed to turn as purple as the corset I'd just shown her. 'I read a feature on you in *Diva*.'

I couldn't help staring at her. The fact that she read a magazine for lesbian women seemed to prove something I'd suspected for a while, but had never seen officially confirmed: Maisie James was a lesbian. If she'd read my feature – a two-page spread in which I'd waxed lyrical about Burmese silk and piano music – she knew that I was a lesbian too. And judging from her blush, something about all that was either very embarrassing or very significant to her.

'So it was the *Diva* feature that brought you here?' I asked.

She nodded. 'I loved the pictures of your work. And also … I wanted to meet you.' She looked at me a fraction of a second too long, then dropped her eyes as if she was afraid to meet my eyes any longer. Even her neck was purple now.

My jaw dropped when I understood what she was telling me. I was flabbergasted, so much so that I was rendered speechless for a minute.

Sure, I'd had a few crushes on people I'd never met over the years. As a teenager, I'd had a violent crush on a Hollywood starlet, which had been my first indication that I might be gay. As a student, I'd fallen in love with several book characters, and had deplored the fact that I never seemed to meet women like them in real life. Last but not least, my last partner before Jenna had been a girl I'd met on line, a girl with whom I'd fallen in love before I'd ever seen her photo or heard her voice. But the thought that Maisie James – Maisie James! – had felt similarly attracted to *me* after reading a feature on me in a magazine was mind-boggling. Mind-boggling and, I had to admit, a little arousing.

'Were you thinking of buying any underbust corsets, as well?' I asked eventually, trying to sound as if nothing out of the ordinary had happened, as if she hadn't just made the most extraordinary confession. 'They're short corsets which stop under your breasts. They're a bit more comfortable than full-length corsets, and they're very good for corset training, for getting your body used to wearing corsets.' All of this was true, of course, but the main reason why I was suggesting she buy an underbust corset was because I had a sudden craving to see Maisie James' breasts popping out from one of my pieces. Something told me it would be a spectacular sight.

Maisie had raised her eyes by now, and was looking at me a little shyly, but not anxiously. She was still blushing, though, and I had a feeling she would be for a while.

'Show me.'

I showed her a range of underbust corsets. She quickly settled on two styles and colours she liked, and then I convinced her to try one on, a stylish ivory-coloured one that I hoped one day to sell to a red-haired bride. 'I know this isn't your colour, but it's the only one of the lot which may fit you off the rack,' I said. 'Go on, try it on, just to get an idea of what you're buying.'

She stepped into my tiny fitting room, where I mischievously told her to take off her trousers as well as her top and bra. There was no real need for her to take off her trousers (the corset stopped above her hips), but I wasn't going to rob myself of the opportunity to get a close-up view of her glorious bottom.

When she was nearly naked, I went into the cubicle and wrapped the corset around her chest. As I helped her close the front fastenings, I stole a look at her firm, round breasts. They looked amazing above the ivory brocade, although I had no doubt they'd look even better above a jewel-toned garment.

I positioned myself behind her and began tightening the laces at the top of the corset. Being considerably taller than Maisie, I could watch her face in the mirror over her shoulder as I increased the tension on her chest. She seemed a little embarrassed by the intimacy of the situation, but at the same time I got the impression that she was a little aroused. I saw her nipples perk up when I smiled at her in the mirror, two dark brown nubs protruding from her taut, warm skin.

I began to pull at the laces at the bottom. She moaned softly as the corset grew tighter around her, reining in her flesh, ribs and lungs. I noted with appreciation that her moans were as melodious as her singing voice. They sent a thrill to my pussy, which had grown decidedly moist at the sight of Maisie's round orbs jutting from the ivory brocade below.

'I can see what you mean about singing while wearing one of these,' she said a little breathlessly as I hooked my fingers under the top crosses for a second round of tightening. She smiled at me in the mirror. 'I can barely breathe.'

A devil of an idea popped into my head. 'Show me,' I suggested as I pulled at the bottom laces one last time, smiling back at Maisie's mirror image. 'Sing me a song.' The prospect of Maisie James giving me a private concert while wearing a corset that left her pert bosom free to heave majestically was enough to send a trickle of wetness down my thigh.

She looked hesitant for a moment but, after an encouraging smile in the mirror, she opened her mouth. I half expected her to launch into *Saying Your Name* or *When the Lights Go Out*, her two greatest hits. To my amazement, she began to sing *Moon River* instead, sounding much like a black Audrey Hepburn. Soft and tremulous though it was, her voice echoed off the walls of the small cubicle, sending a shiver through my clit.

However, it was her facial expression which really did it for me. I'd never been able to resist a shy woman, and Maisie's shyness and vulnerability were just exquisite at that moment. I wanted to touch her so badly that I had trouble focusing on the lacing.

When I'd finally tied off the laces in the middle of the corset and Maisie's final "Moon River ... and me" had died away, I could no longer contain myself. Snaking my arms around her waist, I cupped the breasts that had been staring at me in the mirror. I lifted and kneaded them, revelling in their firmness and smoothness, relishing the way her erect nipples grew even harder under my thumbs' caresses. I could feel my own nipples throb under my shirt, craving a gentle hand of their own.

I watched Maisie's face for signs of disapproval, signs that I'd misinterpreted her words and blushes and steely nipples. For a moment, I feared I was doing something intensely stupid, something which would jeopardise a substantial order and all the publicity that would come with having Maisie James wear a garment of mine on the cover of her new album. But I didn't see any disapproval on Maisie's face. Instead, I saw need – need and desire and something I could only interpret as intense arousal. Clearly, she wanted this as much as I did – needed it, even. So I stepped in front of her, pressed her against the wall of the cubicle and claimed her gorgeous nipples, taking possession of them as if they'd been mine all along. I rolled them between my thumbs and forefingers, now tenderly, now a bit harder, all the while revelling in the soft moans emanating from Maisie's throat, the shallow moans of a woman who was laced so tightly that she couldn't breathe properly.

When I'd had my fill of her breasts, I ran my hands down her sides, so beautifully encased in the ivory brocade. The corset was a little too wide for her at the top, but fitted snugly around the waist. I estimated it took a full four inches from her waist. She looked stunning, even if the colouring of the garment was a little off.

The scent of arousal was thick in the air as I trailed my right hand downwards over her stomach until it reached her knickers, which were as damp as I suspected my own were. I wasn't sure whether the scent was hers or mine, but it didn't matter. I was caressing the first pussy I'd felt in months, and it so happened to belong to the über-lovely Maisie James, who was wet and wild for me and literally shaking with need against the wall. It was all I needed to know, all I needed to go on.

I cupped Maisie's pussy and, encouraged by her low moans, began massaging her clit with my thumb. I could feel it clearly through the fabric, a hard little nub at the top of her puffy lips. It pulsed as I pressed my thumb to it and traced minute circles around it, proving that she was every bit as aroused as I was.

I shot a brief look at Maisie, asking her with my eyebrows whether to proceed. She gave a curt nod which I interpreted as a sign to go ahead, so I pushed her knickers aside and smiled with approval when her bald pussy came into view. She'd clearly been waxed very recently. Goosebumps erupted on the skin of my neck as I felt how smooth she was, and how soft.

I spread her pussy lips and traced the velvety insides with my fingertips. Then, my head spinning with desire, I let my fingers glide over her sopping entrance. Maisie moaned at the contact, a desperate, guttural groan that set my pussy on fire.

Ignoring my own need for relief, I spread some of the wetness from Maisie's cunt to her clit. Then I teased a finger into her, quickly followed by another one. I could feel the walls of her tight pussy clenching around my digits as I pistoned them in and out of her, all the while massaging her hard clit with the heel of my hand.

Soon Maisie's moaning grew to a fever pitch. I vaguely wondered how a laced-up woman could produce so much noise, but loved the sound of her losing her inhibition. Since I didn't think she'd be able to come while standing up, I looked out of the cubicle, searching for a more comfortable place to continue my exploration of Maisie's body. To my regret, my sewing table, which doubled as my counter, was out. It was full of sewing equipment, rolls of fabric, and the dozen or so corsets I'd previously shown Maisie, and vacating its surface would undoubtedly take so much time that it would ruin the moment. Luckily, I had a comfy chair just outside the fitting room, where the partners of my clients generally waited while I laced the women up. I now led Maisie to this chair.

'Sit,' I told her, before giving her a gentle push. She gasped as her bottom hit the seat. I knelt in front of her, in between her muscular thighs, then gripped her hips and pulled her forward until her bottom met the edge of the seat. This probably wasn't the most comfortable position for her – the tightness of the corset meant she could neither arch nor bend her back – but she didn't protest. She just looked at me from under her long lashes as she draped her legs over my shoulders, a tiny smile playing across her lips. It was all the encouragement I needed.

I shoved my fingers into her again, searching and prodding. Then I bent forward and, without stopping the motion of my fingers inside her, ran my tongue over the flesh of her thighs, slowly and sensually. Her smell flooded my nostrils, making my mouth water for her taste.

I stole a look at Maisie's face before I dived in. With her eyes nearly closed and her lips slightly parted, her exposed breasts literally heaving with her shallow breaths, she was the most intoxicating sight I'd ever seen. I wanted to kiss her, own her, make her mine.

She tensed delightfully as I began to lap at her clit. I kept at it, stroking her with my tongue until her hips were grinding into my face and her hands were on my head, urging me on. I could feel her toes dig into my back, responding to the pressure of my tongue and fingers. It was the most erotic thing I'd ever felt.

Ignoring my own arousal, which was hungry for a release, I focused my attention on Maisie. I swiped long strokes over her clit with my tongue, concentrating on the spot that seemed to get the loudest response. At the same time, I curled my fingers toward me as I sawed them into her, trying to find her G-spot. Soon she began to wail, so loudly that I feared she might be heard outside. For a brief moment, I wondered if I'd locked the door behind her when I'd let her in. An unwelcome image of Maisie's driver storming into my shop at the sound of his mistress' cries flashed through my mind, but I didn't allow it to distract me from my purpose. I continued shoving my fingers into Maisie until I felt her thigh muscles twitch and heard her piercing cry of release. Her pussy tightened around my fingers as she came, and I could feel her juices trickle onto my hand as if to reward me for my hard work.

I gave her a moment to catch her breath before I withdrew my hand from her throbbing pussy. 'See? Good things happen to women who wear corsets,' I said jokingly. I carefully wiped my hand on my trousers, then began to undo the front fastenings of the ivory corset. I could hear Maisie's breathing become less ragged as the amount of air she could inhale into her lungs increased.

'Thank you,' she murmured when I took the corset off her. 'I needed that.'

I could tell from her face that she meant the orgasm rather than her increased lung capacity, so I nodded sympathetically and said, 'Must get lonely sometimes, being a star.'

She gave me an impenetrable look. 'You have no idea.'

The rest of Maisie's visit to my shop was a bit of a blur, partly because it was short and partly because I was so suffused with unsatisfied lust that I had a hard time concentrating on anything but the memory of her pussy contracting around my fingers. I know I took her measurements for the work I was about to do for her. I also know I laid out several rolls of fabric for her while she got dressed again, mostly jewel-coloured silks that I thought would look great on her dark skin, and that she picked her colours very quickly. And, last but not least, I know that I agreed to make three fancy overbust corsets for her, as well as a basic underbust corset and two waist cinchers, and that she seemed to be very disappointed when I told her how long it would take me to finish them. However, my abiding memory of that day is the way she smiled at me when I said she was welcome to come in earlier for a fitting. If I had any misgivings about what I'd just done to her, they dissolved when I saw that smile, which had lost all trace of shyness and had grown into pure delight.

As we exchanged phone numbers and promised to call each other soon, I came to the conclusion that it had been a very good day indeed. True, I did miss *True Blood* that night, but when I eventually got round to watching the episode, I did so with Maisie sitting next to me, looking resplendent in a red underbust corset I'd made for her. And what followed was even better than *True Blood*, but I'll leave that to your imagination.

Alison
by Shea Lancaster

The first pint is always the best. You know that feeling, when the barmaid puts the glass to the nozzle and the pump seems to take for ever. Yes, it may take 119 seconds to pour the perfect pint, but there's no need for her to be so methodical in her work when I have had such a horrendous day at mine. But, finally, the swirling black elixir floats over the counter and into my hand, as I sink into creamy happiness the way a nomad sinks into an oasis.

'Why can't you drink lager like most people?' my friend, Kate, complains, embarrassed by my "butch-looking" Guinness.

'Because it makes me burp,' I answer her frankly. She rolls her eyes at my uncouth demeanour and straightens her skirt for the thousandth time.

'Do I look OK?'

'You look beautiful.'

'You didn't even look at me!' Kate's bottom lip is quivering and she looks like she'll start bawling any minute. I fix her with a more thorough stare and make a point of looking her up and down.

'You really do look fine,' I insist. 'But he already knows what you look like when you're at your worst, so why make all the effort?'

'Because it's a *date*.' Kate's level of calmness has dipped drastically, and I fear that she is at breaking point. I decide not to test her any more and instead ask her about her plans for the evening. She tells me about Mike's need to avoid anyone he works with. Kate says it's "some stupid rule about staff and patient boundaries". I try so hard not to raise an eyebrow at this point. The Left Eyebrow of Withering Contempt has troubled many people and rocked many friendships. Although, in my defence, on such a subject as Kate's hot new man I feel I am allowed to be somewhat dubious. Mike is right to want to avoid people he works with. He met Kate as she was wheeled into the A and E department, screaming blue murder due to a horrendous kidney infection. It was while he was catheterising her that he remarked on her lovely long legs. Kate, as high as a kite on gas and air, promptly asked him for a date and he accepted and took her number, which she somehow managed to relay perfectly.

The eyebrow is not necessary, as Kate notices my scepticism.

'He was thoroughly professional the whole time.'

'Of course he was,' I reply dryly. 'Only he's touched your lady garden without having ever even kissed you.' Kate looks ready to kill me. I am saved by her sudden beaming smile directed over my shoulder, and I realise Mike is here. She stands up, gives him an awkward wave, and he comes over. The first thing I can't help but notice is how short he is, at least in comparison to Kate, who stands at five feet nine in just her stockinged feet. Tonight, she is wearing green patent shoes with six inches of heel slapped to them. Mike is about five feet four and obviously not in heels. It doesn't seem to faze either of them, however, and they can't keep their eyes off each other.

'You two lovebirds have a fabulous evening,' I say, shaking Mike's coolly perspiring palm and settling back into the comfortable leather chair with my pint. Kate barely says goodbye as she trots off her with her highly inappropriate nurse.

It's blissful to have this time to myself after the day of work I've had. Three restraints in one day will take their toll on anyone, but I am particularly sore after having been thrown across the bed by a highly paranoid patient. I thoroughly deserve this Guinness and am about to pull out my book when I look out of the window and notice how it's a really beautiful evening. I decide to go and sit in the beer garden. I sneak out my pint in its contraband glass by carefully placing it into the deep hip pocket of my uniform. If there's one thing I hate, it's watching my settled, unassuming pint unceremoniously dumped into a plastic beaker in order to go and sit outside. Now in my late 20s, I feel I have mastered the skill of holding on to a glass without breaking it. I walk out slowly, doing my best John Wayne impression, and sit at an empty bench.

The evening is quiet and still and the beer garden looks over a pretty canal with barges moored on its sides. The May sunshine is still going strong at six o'clock, and I pull out my book and begin to read. My drink begins to drain away all too quickly, and I muse over the chances of being able to sneak out another glass. As I sit debating with myself, a shadow falls over my book. I look up, squinting against the glare of the sun that surrounds a figure like a halo. The silhouette appears to be that of a woman with short blonde hair.

'You know you're not allowed out here with a glass, don't you?' A strong Northern Irish accent instructing me firmly is not something even I am careless enough to be flippant about. I decide feigning ignorance is going to be my best bet until her next comment takes me by surprise.

'How about I get you a plastic glass, with a fresh pint in it?'

'Eh?' My ignorant reply is mortifying, but this woman has floored me.

'There aren't many girls around who drink Guinness.'

'No – there aren't,' I concur, wondering if someone with a hidden camera is conducting research into the reactions of authoritative Irish women. Never one to refuse a free drink, however, when she repeats the offer I accept.

'Thank you. Is it on the house because of my blatant flouting of the establishment's rules?' The woman looks confused, then realisation dawns in her eyes.

'Oh, I don't work here,' she says. She notes my confusion and adds, 'I see a woman sitting alone with a pint of the black stuff and I feel compelled to support the cause.'

'Ha.' I am amazed at her forthrightness and her blatant flirting. What amazes me is that we're in a very straight bar in a very straight part of the city. I'm also a little perturbed at her apparent knowledge of my fondness for women without her even having said a word to me before now. Is it the drink I chose? The book I'm reading is innocuous enough. I'm wearing my nursing uniform, admittedly with comfortable, flat shoes, but I can't think of anything incriminating. I'm too bewildered to do anything but sit dumbly until the woman returns with two fresh pints, unfortunately in plastic glasses. She sets one of them down in front of me and stands in front of me hesitantly until I laugh.

'You're allowed to sit down, you know,' I offer. 'I don't bite people who buy me things.' She appears less challenging now; there is a hint of a blush on her cheeks, and a rather red neck. 'Fabulous opening gambit,' I add.

'Why, thank you,' she replies with enthusiasm. 'I've never even done that before, offer to buy a stranger a drink. I just saw you walk out with your pint in your pocket and I loved it. So I thought I'd take the plunge.'

'Ah, I failed in my discretion.' I shake my head in mock self-loathing. 'The thing is how did you know I'd say yes?'

'I didn't,' she admits. 'But I turn 30 in less than a week and I'm sick of waiting for life to come to me.'

'Good on you,' I say, genuinely in awe of her guts. 'I'm glad you came over. And not just for the drink,' I add. She nods, smiling. Nods some more, before looking around as though desperately searching for something to say. Damn it. She's cute.

'Introductions?' I offer. Her eyes light up and when her lips open in a wide smile I notice how stunning she is, and how straight her teeth are, with the added quirk of a twisted incisor. It gives her a cheeky look. She offers her hand.

'Alison.' It's a statement, and I welcome both it and her petite, soft hand in mine.

'Sarah. And thank you again for the beer.' Admittedly the plastic glass sullies the taste, but it's almost worth it, to be sat in the sunshine with her company.

We talk easily for well over an hour, and after a while I take stock of the scene playing out here. I've had a God-awful day at work, but sitting in front of me is the cutest woman I've seen in a long time, melting me a little bit more with every word she says. She has a sharp, sarcastic side that gives the Left Eyebrow of Withering Contempt a run for its money. She talks with a soft, Irish burr she says originates in Derry. I have tried to be nonchalant and cool, but she is making it harder for me. There's far too much I want to know about this woman than is appropriate for an hour-long acquaintance but, strangely, I feel she could ask me anything about myself and I'd tell her.

Suddenly, I realise I have not heard from Kate in a long while and make a mental note to text her next time I go to the loo to check everything is going well on her date. I realise that tonight is the closest I myself have been to a date in about six months. I swore off women for good at Christmas, after Lindsey cheated on me for the tenth and last time.

'Sarah?' Alison's voice snaps me back.

'Shit, I am so sorry,' I apologise. 'I've had the worst day, and then you are so lovely and you knock me for six by buying me a drink, and –'

'Sorry if I overstepped a line …' Alison looks genuinely crestfallen, and I feel terrible for having zoned out on her.

'No, really, you haven't.' I explain about the stress of the hospital, and the three restraints I battled my way through. She listens to everything I've said with genuine interest, the way she has for the past hour. I decide to take a leaf from her book and grab the bull by his proverbial gonads.

'I am in desperate need of a shower and am craving a pizza,' I announce. With only a slight hesitation I add, 'I can make it a large pizza if you'll forgive my ignorance just then and join me.'

'Where?' She looks shocked.

'My – flat.' I falter, feeling I may have been a little too forward. What I want to say to her is that this isn't a seedy, cheesy line I am feeding her to lure her back to my place. If anything, I just want to stay in her company. Her voice alone I could enjoy all evening. To say nothing of her mouth. I go red at the thought of feeling the twisted tooth bite my lip.

'OK …,' she says quietly.

'Look,' I say, looking her straight in the eyes. 'I don't do this every week or anything, invite people back to my flat. But I understand if you don't want to. I'll tell you exactly where I live, and you can ring a friend and tell them where you'll be. It's within walking distance from here.'

'It feels a wee bit strange,' Alison says and I nod. 'But I am having the best night I have had in ages,' she adds.

'Me too.' Admitting that to her is a huge relief. I was worried I would sound like a real idiot by telling her how I feel. We finish our drinks and stand up. Maybe it's a combination of the beer and the evening sun, or maybe it's simply that I cannot wait any longer, but I pull her toward me by her waist and she doesn't object when I lean in and kiss her.

I can tell she's taken by surprise, but she doesn't pull away. Instead, she slowly brings her arm around my neck and I feel her twisted incisor with my tongue. She smells divine and tastes even better. Her lips are soft and she kisses like nobody I have kissed before. Her mouth moves with a pulsating sensuality and I was right: feeling the twisted tooth graze me infuses me with an urgent sense of having to possess this woman and have her possess me.

I am aware of our surroundings as three labourers in dusty overalls and steel toe-capped boots start cheering appreciatively. Not wishing for one iota to be a fantasy for boys, I grasp Alison and we quickly exit the beer garden and head on to the main road. Alison's hand stays firmly in mine as I abandon the idea of a pizza and a stroll home by getting into one of two black cabs parked in the taxi rank. The driver sullenly swings the car around and heads to my flat, barely a mile down the road. He pulls up and I pay him and grab Alison's hand once more. I let us both into the main building and into the lift. We exit on the fifth floor, and I unlock my front door.

As we walk through the living area to the kitchen I consider what to do next. I tell Alison she should ring someone and let them know where she is. She sends a quick text as I rifle through my post; when she is finished, she puts her phone in her pocket and lifts her head to look straight at me.

'I feel I should offer you a drink …,' I begin, but my sentence is cut short as she walks the short distance between us, slides her arms around my neck, and pulls me in for an even more intense, delicious kiss. Thus begins a passionate devouring of one another, as her tongue swirls with mine, her hands on my face, my hands on her hips. My fingers snake around her back and dance on her spine until she pulls them from her and holds me by my wrists.

'Take me to your bedroom,' she instructs me in her commanding Irish accent. She makes me smile, and then asks me what is so funny.

'It's the Amanda Burton-esque way in which you tell me what to do.' I laugh. 'You know that bit in *Silent Witness*, when she says –'

'Don't touch that body!' she finishes for me. Her mock serious face cracks me up, and breaks into its own grin. And I have to kiss her again, as I mutter in between kisses that she has to turn around, follow the corridor, and make a left into the bedroom. She pulls me behind her, as though this is her house, and I am her guest, enticed into her lair. When we enter the bedroom she pushes me against the wall and kisses my neck softly, the action in itself a complete juxtaposition, yet intensely erotic. I can hear her breathing quickly as her lips wander up and down my neck, and I conclude she is both nervous and excited; the idea that she is turned on sends a chill through my body. I lift my hands to her hips once more but she pushes them away softly, exploring my mouth again with her tongue. We kiss and kiss; by now she lets me touch her and I steer us both to the bed, never once relenting on the kisses. I lie down and she straddles me, bringing her head lower to meet mine. Feeling her thighs wrapped around my waist is intensely powerful and makes me begin to move my hips up to meet her crotch. She moves with me, as though we are inside each other already, and she moans softly in time to the thrusts. She shifts to the left and lets one of her legs drop between mine, rubbing herself on my thigh as we frottage together, still kissing. My ache for her is becoming unbearable and I cry out in frustration. She smiles, and I plead with her with my eyes, silently begging her to relieve me from this rising craving.

'I'm going to fuck you,' she whispers in my ear, tickling me with her voice and making me groan even more. Her breath is hot and she tastes of alcohol, a flavour that always drives me wild.

'Please,' I croak. 'Please just have me.' I don't recognise what I'm saying. This isn't me. I do not get women buying me drinks. I don't bring them back to mine and I certainly don't let them top me like this. I'm bewildered by the strange, unfamiliar feeling of wanting to be dominated. But this woman demands, in some way, that I pay attention, that I submit to her. And by God, I want to. I stop her for a second and push her away gently, making her pause in her movement. I make her watch me unbutton my shirt. She watches as my fingers play with the buttons, and doesn't make a move until each one is slowly undone and my top falls open. Alison lowers her head and licks the top of my breasts, above my bra. She is driving me crazy, and she knows it. I lift myself onto my elbows and decide to play her at her own game, pushing my chest forward and running my tongue along her top lip, touching her teeth and nibbling at her. She responds by running her hands over my shoulders and pushing away my open top, and I wriggle free of it. She notices the scars on my right arm and retracts a little.

'They're nearly ten years old,' I tell her.

'Did you do them yourself?' she asks quietly.

'Yeah, it's a long story.'

'It's fine,' she reassures me. 'It doesn't change my plans.'

'Your plans?'

'To completely and utterly own you, for one night.'

'Then for Christ's sake, please just do it!'

She obliges by taking my hands and moving them to her own shirt, and I slip the buttons through their holes and slide the top off her. Her bra is turquoise with sequins and I stroke her breasts through it, feeling her nipples harden and watching her close her eyes and suck in her breath. I take the opportunity to catch her unawares and, with my right hand, I quickly snap open her bra from behind. Her eyes flick open and her mouth opens in what looks like horror, but then she grins and shakes her head.

'I got caught off guard,' she says, grimly, and pins my arms back down. She begins an all-out devouring of my body, licking my neck, and my chest, and my stomach. She undoes my bra with one hand impressively, and begins to tug at the button of my trousers, deftly opening it. Without stopping, she yanks down my trousers and leaves me lying on the bed, naked but for my knickers. The satin material is dark in its wetness, and she notices this and exhales, closing her eyes in rapture. I'm nervous and yet hugely complimented that this woman is clearly excited to see how turned on I am. She presses two fingers to my damp pants, and I groan in surprised pleasure when she licks her fingertips delicately and savours their flavour. I shift my legs slightly wider, blatantly inviting her to fuck me. She grabs my thighs and dives into my crotch, licking me through my pants crazily. I feel her tongue press against my clit and I begin to see stars, crying out, then clamping my hand over my mouth so as to hide the noises from my neighbours. She tugs at my knickers and pulls them down, over my thighs, my knees, and then my ankles, before tossing them off the bed. I am completely naked and exposed but I do not care.

'I can see your wetness,' Alison whispers, her eyes fixing on mine.

'You've got me unbelievably turned on,' I gasp, beginning to move my hips in their rhythmic motion, enticing her tongue once more. She nibbles my thighs and moves toward my crotch once more; with the tiniest tip of her tongue she slowly licks me from the hole to my clit, scooping up my juices and letting them dribble down her tongue. I am blown away that someone so new to me would do something so intimate, but it feels as though she has been doing this to me for ever. She is past teasing me now, and gently takes her fingers and opens my lips, exposing my throbbing clit. She whispers something I cannot decipher and begins to lick me slowly, sending electrifying bolts of lightning from my toes to the tips of my hair. She licks me rhythmically and I grab her head and push myself against her, panting loudly, not caring who hears me now.

'Oh Jesus,' I moan, as she reaches her hands up my chest and pinches my nipples hard. She makes me curl toward her with my body, holding her head with both hands, my shoulders off the pillow, my feet raised in the air. I can feel myself getting wetter and wetter but she deals with it like a professional, lapping up whatever I give her, sucking on my clit, grazing her teeth over the tip. The feeling is incredible, and I am finding it hard to breathe; with every exhalation I am moaning louder and louder, but there is something missing, something extra I need. My brain searches for what it is, but Alison answers me telepathically by taking her fingers from my nipple and introducing them to my cunt. She needs no lube and slides in two fingers, claiming me without permission. The feeling of sheer relief is overwhelming as she leaves her fingers still for at least ten seconds, as if to emphasise her action. Then she begins to stroke me from the inside, and instead of licking my clit she bites my thighs. The pain only intensifies the pleasure; as she presses on my G-spot with her fingers I can feel the pressure rising. She has been fucking me for barely five minutes and already the pleasure is becoming too much and I feel I am going to lose it.

'Wait,' I say, panting. 'I'm going to come.'

'And what's wrong with that?' Alison asks, between pushing her fingers inside deeper and biting my thighs.

'It's happening quickly ...' I don't even know why I am concerned, but I am shocked that she has got me this close so soon. I start to pull away slightly and she grabs my thigh quickly, pinching my skin.

'Don't you dare move,' she growls. 'You're going to come right now. You're going to feel me fuck you to within an inch of your life, and don't you even dare to stop me.'

I cannot do anything but surrender as she begins her rhythmic stroking of me from the inside, alternating between sucking my clit and biting my thighs and stomach. Once more the swirling intensity is building. I start to picture myself standing naked on the top of a hill in a vast expanse, and before I know it I am thrust forward and am tearing down the hill at the speed of light, and stars are showering me all over, and I realise I am coming, pushing against her as she pushes against me, fucking me so hard I feel myself explode on her hand, soaking her as she moans, feeling me pulsate from inside my cunt, until I can't take any more and collapse back onto the bed, panting, desperately trying to get my breath and pushing her hand away as I can't possibly stand to feel her fingers tease me any more. She begins to withdraw her hand but I stop her, enjoying the feel of her filling me up without moving. She is no longer predatory, and instead gives me tiny kisses where she has marked me with her teeth, sighing into my crotch and closing her eyes. I watch her lie there, between my legs, as though she has done this to me a thousand times, and I tap her on the head and beckon her to come up and lie with me. She slowly removes her fingers from inside me; as she does so, she makes me squirm. She giggles and, finally, her hand is free, and she crawls up to my chest, where she lies on my breasts and throws an arm over me.

'Holy shit,' is all I can say. I am utterly exhausted and cannot for the life of me move. I want to kiss her, touch her, explore her body the way she has mine, but I have nothing left. Not one iota of energy. The physical exertion of my shift and the fucking of a lifetime have taken every shred of life from me. But as I lie there, my hand across Alison as her head is on my breast, I hear the faintest snoring and realise she is asleep. I stare in wonderment at the mysterious lover who, in less than an evening, has stormed into my life, my bed, and my body, flooring me and leaving me as helpless as a child.

'Thanks for the drink,' I whisper to her, as she stirs in dreamy unconsciousness.

Feast
by Rachel Charman

I leave the house, giving her an hour to get ready in my absence. I have planned everything down to the last detail and she has been left instructions. When I return at eight o'clock on the dot, I feel a tense ache in my belly as I unlock the front door and go in.

I am starving.

As I enter the house I am hit by the heat and the scent of the food I have prepared. Passing the mirror, I check my appearance scrupulously. I am dressed in my black tuxedo, freshly dry-cleaned today, and my crisp white dress shirt, open at the throat. My hair was cut yesterday and sits closely cropped and slicked with wax so not a strand falls out of place. Satisfied, I move on into the kitchen.

I know she is in the dining room, but I do not call out. I don't need to. I know she will be listening to my every move. I check once more that everything is ready. With a final deep breath, I step through into the dining room.

Inside, the room is almost exactly as I left it. It is lit with candles in my best silver candlesticks. The dark wood mantelpiece and dining chairs gleam with beeswax polish. The tablecloth is sparkling white and starched into perfect folds so that it falls just so over the edges of the table. She has, however, made two important changes.

First, she has as instructed taken the champagne from the fridge and placed it in a silver ice bucket at the foot of the table. Second, she is lying along the length of the table, naked and waiting.

I feel a rush of excitement as I step closer to the table. I've always loved the formal indulgence of fine dining. I love the rules dictating courses that uphold the procession of sensations: the stiff, fresh blast of the aperitif; the teasing lightness of the starter; the rich carnal pleasure of the main dish, and the creamy luxury of the dessert. To see her spread out naked on my perfect table is the realisation of a dream; my two great loves in one sumptuous sitting.

She looks so good, lying with her hands by her side, skin shimmering in the candlelight, that I want to savour it as long as I can. My eyes sweep over her glossy, red-painted mouth, and I can smell her perfume and soap. I refuse to allow myself to touch her for now. Instead, I step around the table to the drinks cabinet and take out the vermouth, the vodka, and the ice shaker. Using ice from the champagne bucket I shake together two martinis, pour them into the correct glasses (checking them thoroughly first for spots and smears), and drop two olives in each. I turn back to the table, tasting my drink as my eyes rove over her.

Dining isn't just an oral experience. It should tease every sense in turn until you are entirely sated. Excellent food and drink provide the two most obvious treats of taste and smell, but there are plenty more. Sound is essential; think of the satisfying crackle of roasted fat under the knife, or the musical fizz and tinkle of champagne into a flute. Touch is equally important; consider the feel of starched linen under your hands or the cool delicacy of fine glassware against your lips. Then there is sight. Is there anything more handsome than a sizzling fillet of beef, warm and pink on the inside and oozing delicious red blood? Well, in this case there is: her laid before me, her hair spread out like glossy black treacle across the white cloth, totally still but for her toes curling in anticipation.

The martini loosens my shoulders as I step to the table and place her drink beside her. I watch her breastbone rise and fall as she breathes in the hot air of the room. I have heated the house so that she will be kept hot, even naked as she is; I want to taste her sweat. A trickle of my own is already creeping down my spine. Her full mouth twitches a little at the corner and she licks her lips as I watch her. Other than that, she does not acknowledge me, keeping her eyes closed.

Smiling to myself, I trace one finger over her warm lips. She shudders a little and opens her lips slightly. I take the olive from her drink and balance it with infinite care on her open mouth. She does nothing without instruction.

'Taste,' I say, quietly but firmly. Her pointed tongue appears, tickling the base of the olive.

'All right, you can have it,' I say. With considerable skill, she opens her mouth and gracefully lowers the olive inside.

Next, I place my hand gently behind her head and lift it so that I can tilt a sip of her martini into her mouth. She drinks gratefully – her throat must be parched in the hot room – and I delight as the condensation from the glass drips onto her throat, making her shiver.

I am forced to leave her after we finish our drinks to fetch the first dish. This is the only problem with my plans this evening. The true dining experience includes the pleasure of sitting languorously in a chair while you are served by a discreet but responsive waiter. I had suggested bringing in a third party tonight for exactly that purpose, but she drew the line there.

In the kitchen, I take the shucked oysters from the fridge and arrange them on a tray of ice. Returning to the dining room, I place them on the table, take the bottle of champagne from the ice bucket and open it. I pour two glasses and feed her a sip. I take a slick cube from the bucket and gently press it to her neck. She gasps as I run it smoothly over her skin, across her fine collarbones and skirting the lower curve of her breast. I see her resist the urge to squirm as I run it over the sensitive skin of her belly, leaving a trail of goosebumps in its wake.

I take the first oyster, enjoying the rough rasp of its shell against my palm. She watches me now as I tip the oyster, salty liquor and all, into my mouth, opening my throat and swallowing it in one move. I feel a rush of the intense freshness of the sea and immediately reach for another. This time, when I tip the shell to my lips I swallow the oyster and hold the liquor in my mouth. I bend over her and kiss her. She lets out a soft sigh, and explores my lips with her tongue. I open my mouth a fraction and share the icy saline liquor. She drinks it with relish. I feed her two oysters, delighting in the smooth motions of her throat as she swallows, and lick the salty juice from her lips. I bring her a taste of champagne in my mouth, and as I pass the freezing fizz between our lips I run my hand, cold from the glass, over her smooth thighs. She moans quietly, showing me she is hungry, but not yet ravenous. I pull myself away from her mouth, knowing I could easily kiss her for hours and spoil her appetite, and go back to the kitchen.

I take from the oven the lamb saddle, which I have rolled in a mixture of rosemary, thyme, tarragon, and garlic, and roasted. I cut it into slices, then cut the slices into smaller, bite-sized pieces, basking in the fragrant steam that rises from the meat. I place it on a platter and trickle a light jus from a saucepan over it. Next I switch off the pan of asparagus that has been gently steaming during our oyster course, and arrange the springy green spears around the lamb. I return to the dining room.

As I step in I catch her trailing her fingers over her thighs and belly, and chuckle. She looks at me with a smirk as she touches herself; usually, I can't resist watching her. I place the platter on the table beside her and gently push her hands to her sides.

'Not yet,' I say firmly. She gives a little whine but smiles. She turns her head to one side and sees the platter.

'My favourite,' she breathes, fixing her eyes on mine. I nod, and gesture to the platter. She takes a spear of asparagus and lowers it, tip first, to her mouth. She devours it in small, neat bites as I sip my champagne, watching her sharp white teeth and indecent red mouth. I take a slice of the lamb and eat it. Flavour overwhelms my mouth and I want to congratulate myself. It is just how I wanted it: tender and delicate, the juice bursting over my tongue, the scent of the herbs filling my nose. I place my fingers, smeared with juices, over her mouth and she takes them in, sucking the taste away with delight. Her mouth is hot and wet, and for a moment my stomach clenches with desire. She tickles my fingertips with her tongue and closes her lips around my knuckles. I take her hand away and feed her a slice of the meat. She gives a groan as she chews.

'How is it that you make it taste like sex?' she asks. I laugh, my mouth full, and sit in the chair nearest to her waist. I pour more champagne and we eat the dish like this, me taking a bite for myself, then feeding her as she lies in front of me. With each slice of lamb I give her my fingers to taste, and each time she sucks for longer. Each time she lowers a morsel to her mouth herself I trace my fingers, sticky with jus, over her breasts and stomach.

When the dish is finished, she props herself up on her elbow to drink her champagne. As she takes a sip I begin to lick the red smears from her skin, starting at her navel. I taste the rich, herbal flavour of the sauce and underneath it the distinctly sweet taste of her. I feel the prickle of invisible hairs rising against my lips and tongue. I glance up at her as I tease and she is still, her glass raised but forgotten, her eyes closed, breathing deeper as I move to her breasts. I lick and kiss away every trace of jus and take her nipple tenderly in my mouth. It tastes of rose water, fresh and saccharine beneath my tongue. She pulls me up by the hair to her mouth and I hold her as we kiss each other's mouths, cheeks, and throats.

I run a hand from her shoulders to her thighs and brush my fingers over the soft hair where they meet. She holds me tighter and pushes her hips toward my hand, parting her legs almost as a plea. I trace one finger lightly over her cunt and the hot, wet feel makes my chest contract with excitement. When I take my hand away she moans and her eyes flicker with surprise. I am not ready to give in totally, and I know she can want me more yet. I settle back into my chair and reach into my jacket pocket for my pack of cigarettes.

I place one in my mouth and light it. An old-fashioned diner, I appreciate the pleasure of smoking between courses. The rush of intense, bitter smoke into my system makes me lightheaded. She is watching me in confusion.

'Oh, where are my manners?' I say innocently. I light another cigarette from the tip of mine and place it between her lips. She smiles, understanding, and takes a deep drag, pinching the cigarette delicately between her index and middle fingers.

As she exhales I take her free hand and draw it between her legs. She laughs and begins to caress herself, smoke curling from her mouth with each sigh and groan. With her legs splayed, her hand working slowly between them, her breasts rising and falling with each deep breath and the cigarette smouldering between her fingers, she looks debauched. I smoke my cigarette, stub it out, and pull off my jacket. My shirt is plastered with sweat at the small of my back and, as she begins to move her hips fractionally up and down, I can see drops of perspiration forming between her breasts, on her brow, and on the backs of her raised knees.

She finishes her cigarette and I take it from her to stub it out. She looks up at me with half-closed eyes and reaches for me with her free hand. She wants everything at once, but I know how to wait. I shake my head and take a seat at in the carver chair at the foot of the table. I beckon to her. She shuffles down toward me until she can rest her feet on the arms of my chair. I am half tempted to tuck a napkin into my collar, purely for tradition's sake. Instead, I bend my head and take her in my mouth.

Being the glutton that I am, I have always delighted in the feel of her cunt in my mouth. The ever-changing parade of flavours fascinates me. Sometimes it is the most succulent, tart, tempting fruit; others times it is a rude, scintillating, saline sea-creature begging to be coaxed out and devoured.

Now, in the height of her arousal, her taste is deep, rounded, and sweet, like cherry brandy. I roll my tongue around her slick clit and she cries out, lifting her hips to press harder against my mouth. I feel drunk on her as I watch the length of her undulate in time with my tongue. When I push my tongue lower and slide the tip inside her the taste changes again; saltier, with a moreish tang. She cries out again and grips at my hair as I ease my tongue in and out, a little further in each time. Just as we relax into a rhythm I slide my tongue out and up to her clit again. She jerks and gives out a little growl of frustration, and I smile into her. That was the growl I had been waiting for.

She sits up and shoves me back into my chair with her foot. In one movement, she springs off the table and into my lap on the chair. I think fleetingly of the dessert, abandoned in the freezer, but she kisses me hard, biting my lips hungrily. She is hot and damp against my clothes. I make to hold her but she grabs my hand and guides it to her cunt.

'Stop thinking about the semifreddo,' she breathes as I tease her clit. She pushes hard against my hand, but I refuse to come inside, laughing. She rolls her eyes.

'You and your fucking menu,' she says as she jumps from my lap and disappears from the room.

When she returns she is holding the semifreddo in a plastic cup, and a long-handled ice-cream spoon. I had frozen it in the cup so that I could squeeze it out onto a plate in a pleasing conical shape, but she has dispensed with the aesthetics. She is a much earthier diner than I.

She slips into my lap, her smile full of mischief. She dips the spoon into the creamy dessert and carves out a mouthful before holding it out to me. I make to take it in my mouth, and she darts the spoon away and eats it herself. She rolls her eyes back into her head and mimes ecstasy, mocking me. She gives me my own spoonful as she swallows.

'Good isn't it?' she says. I nod, mouth full. Before I can protest she has put the dessert down on the table and is tearing open my shirt and pulling it from my back, exposing my bare chest. She lavishes kisses and caresses over my breasts and throat, and the sudden rush of attention makes my head spin.

Reaching behind her, she retrieves the semifreddo but not the spoon. With her fingers she smears a glob across my mouth. The cold is almost painful on the raw nerves of my lips, but she kisses and laps it away with her hot tongue. When it is gone she dips her fingers into the pot again, and spreads the freezing mixture across my breasts.

The sudden chill makes me gasp and arch my back. My skin wants to get away from her freezing fingers but never wants her to stop either. When I am covered in it, she kisses me again, and says, 'Fuck me.'

Obediently, I push my fingers into her and she moans as we kiss again. Inside, I marvel at how she is soft and tight at the same time. As she twists around my hand, she lowers her head and licks the semifreddo from my skin. She laps hungrily at the creamy confection covering my breasts and throat, then kisses me, smearing it onto my mouth and spreading it from my chest to hers, before returning to my chest for more. The feel of her sucking hungrily at my breasts and groaning louder, the sounds she makes vibrating through me, is almost more than I can bear. As she grinds harder against my hand she sucks harder at my skin, and I delight in the bruises I can feel starting to form. She starts to nip at the softest flesh of my breasts; with each sharp little bite I gasp and squirm. I lean back in my chair and keep my hand still and firm so that she can devour me and fuck my hand as she pleases.

When she has eaten the semifreddo from my skin, she returns to my mouth and kisses hard, biting my lips and forcing her tongue deep into my mouth. She pulls back to look at me. She looks gloriously crazed. Her hair has curled in the heat and stands out in waves around her face. Her eyes are half-closed in rapture, and her cheeks and chin are smeared with the white, creamy dessert. She is panting hard.

'More,' she growls, and I twist my hand to slide my thumb inside her. I push in my hand up to the knuckles and she gives a yell, tightening the grip of her legs around my hips. She leans back against the table for balance as she lifts her dark hair from her shoulders and grinds her hips in my lap. I feast my eyes on her curved body. I reach out to press her breast and she covers my hand with her own, pushing harder. Her cries grow louder and higher in pitch. I use my hips to drive my hand harder into her, groaning with each thrust as we move faster.

I see a trickle of sweat drip from a strand of her hair to her chest. As it runs between her breasts I lunge for it, desperate to taste it and to feel her heart thudding against my cheek. As I press my lips to her skin she clutches my head and screams. Her hips and insides lock still and tight and I feel the hot flow of her come over my thighs. I cry out as well, loving the feel of her spilling over me. I hold still inside her for a long time as she twitches and gasps. Gradually, I feel her relax. She quivers as I twirl my fingers inside her, and slowly withdraw. She rests her head against my neck, relaxing her weight against me. I hold her close, smoothing her hair as she catches her breath.

When she is able, she leans back and smiles at me. I reach for a napkin to dab my mouth and forehead, and say, 'Coffee?'

The Gift
by Encarnita Round

'Happy birthday, Rose!' Rachel and Debbie proclaimed loudly. After two bottles of wine it was a wonder that they could sit upright, never mind remember that it was my birthday. They gave me a card, and inside I found a gold-trimmed, professionally printed voucher with dotted lines where my details had been handwritten. 'This entitles Rose Marie to the stress reliever package at 4.30 p.m. on her birthday. Come along to the Simply Beautiful Salon and let us ease your stresses away.'

It really was a nice gesture, and I thanked them, of course. They, of all people, knew how hectic my life had been, and this was a perfect treat; if only I had the time for it. Time was the one luxury I could not afford to spare, and although the appointment was only an hour away, that, in addition to the late lunch with wine, did not leave me much time to rearrange my schedule.

At that point I must have looked overly thoughtful, guilty even, and that gave me away. 'Don't even think about going back to that damned office of yours,' Debbie told me, wagging one heavily decorated false nail at my face. I was less than an inch away from having my eye poked out, so I was grateful that we'd stopped at just the two bottles of Viura. 'You will go,' she insisted, her tone emphatic and implacable.

'Yes,' Rachel chimed in. 'You need this, Rose, it'll do you good.'

'Oh yes,' Debbie added, and enthusiastically so. 'You'll be a changed woman afterwards.'

I couldn't help but note the knowing, secretive look that passed between them, nor could I miss the barely suppressed giggle. They shared something, something I didn't know about, and although we were all good friends for just a moment I felt like an outsider. It was a sobering thought, and that didn't do my disposition any good, especially when I was about to waste precious time being subjected to the blathering of some beautician with a brain the size of a peanut.

My life was already full of crises that varied in magnitude, and I really didn't have the time to spare on beautification or idle and pointless chitter-chatter. Unless the beautician had a cure for sleeping; then I would be more than ready to listen. But I didn't think that the secret to extending the working day was going to be found amongst the bottles of nail polish. It amused me to think that it could, even though it made me sound mean, which isn't like me, not really. In my defence, it has been a tough year, and I think my edges are just a little frayed. So, instead of being callous and unkind, I concentrated my thoughts on ways to get out of the appointment, all without upsetting anyone.

When we left the wine bar, Debbie and Rachel not only anticipated my refusal, they'd planned for it. The moment we were outside I found myself manhandled and thrown over Debbie's shoulder in a more than competent fireman's lift. 'Put me down!' I screeched. 'You'll break your legs in those heels!'

Rachel didn't help, but she carried the handbags and made sure that I didn't struggle too hard.

'I've not seen your arse from this angle,' I said, trying a different strategy, 'it's very nice.' Then I squeezed it.

Debbie didn't even slow down. 'I know,' she answered calmly, albeit a little breathily. 'You can feel it some more if it makes you feel better.'

She dumped me right outside the saloon. 'There you are, now inside you go.' My friends didn't wait around, bless them, they abandoned me as soon as I turned my back. Probably because they took one look at the receptionist and decided they needed to be elsewhere. I didn't blame them; I took one look at the receptionist and I wanted to be elsewhere with them. She was one of those "too-much" types: too much fake tan, too much make-up, too much peroxide, and way too much attitude. She chomped at her gum and looked disdainfully down her nose at everything, including me.

'Oh yeah,' she almost snorted, looking at the voucher and calling over her shoulder at the same time, 'One of *yours*, Nina.'

Having performed her duty, she gave me a brisk once-over, and then flounced off with not a word. I was left at reception feeling like a spare part with not a clue as to what was next. 'I'm going home now,' the dulcet tones of the receptionist announced from somewhere in the back of the building. 'You'll lock up.' Then she raced through the salon as though her life depended on it.

I heard a quiet "wait a minute". But the door slammed shut before another word could be said. It was not an auspicious start, and if I were the one paying the bill I think I would have followed the receptionist. I didn't, but only because I didn't want the girls to catch me escaping.

'Sorry to keep you waiting.' A new, softer voice interrupted my train of thought. 'Some things always take longer than expected.'

'That's OK,' I answered as a small and rather petite woman moved behind the reception desk. She had long, deep brown hair that was so dark and shiny it was almost black. Her eyes were just as dark; they burned intensely. She wore a simple cotton tunic that fitted her so well it looked tailored to her body. Starched white, the uniform contrasted with her olive colouring. She looked stunning. If truth be told, it was hard not to drool and say "Wow!" out loud. If I thought I was being discreet in my appraisal, I wasn't, because she noticed anyway, smiling so broadly that the whole salon brightened. She could smile at any time she wanted. What a great start.

'I hope you're here for the stress buster,' she started, and she spoke so quietly that I had to listen carefully to hear every word. I just nodded, because I was too busy listening to her voice to be able to speak. It had a soft, soothing quality that made you feel at ease; she could recite the telephone directory for all I cared and I would still listen. 'Then you must be Rose? Rose Marie?' I nodded like one of those Churchill dogs in the back of a car. 'And this is a gift.' I nodded some more. 'My name is Nina,' she said, 'let me show you to the changing room where you can get ready.'

'I have no idea what I'm here for,' I said quietly. It was not an easy admission to make. I hate it when I don't know what's happening; it's embarrassing, and I feel all out of sorts. I suppose it's a control thing.

'I'm sorry,' Nina apologised. 'It is supposed to be a surprise.' That made it all a little better. Actually, her smiling made me feel better, and if all it took to get her to smile was for me to look an idiot, then I would readily do that some more.

I stripped off in the changing room, and wrapped myself in the fluffy white towel provided. It was a large sheet, more than big enough to cover everything. Muted pan pipes played in the background, and although that's not my thing it was discreet enough that I could still listen to Nina moving about and humming as she worked. Obviously she liked her work, and that made me feel even more comfortable.

The treatment room was clean and contemporary, with white walls, black floor tiles, and bright red accessories to offer a contrast. In the centre of the room a big, black leather-look massage table had so many levers it would probably look perfect in an operating theatre. 'Get yourself settled on the table,' Nina directed, as she placed a new towel over the top of the leather. 'I need to lock up at the front so that we won't be disturbed.'

The table didn't appear particularly comfortable, so I was surprised when I lay down that it was so much better than I'd expected. The padded top was extra soft, and it kind of moulded itself to my shape. In fact, it was so comfortable that, as I stared at the ceiling, my eyes automatically began to close and I could have just gone to sleep right there and then. The two glasses of wine I'd had earlier probably had something to do with that.

'We'll start with a head massage,' Nina said in that soft and dreamy voice of hers. She ran her fingers through my hair, and – well, that was it, I was all hers. I am so very easy, it seems.

I'd not paid much attention to Nina's hands, but it was immediately apparent that she had strong, supple fingers. She pressed them firmly against my scalp, and massaged every inch with just the tips of her fingers. Occasionally she simply ran her hands through my hair to keep it out of the way, and that was wonderful in itself. She had this way of moving her fingers in small, delicate circles around my temples, and along the side of my face. It had been a while since anyone touched my face that way and it was bliss; exciting too.

When those firm and competent hands worked on the back of my neck I could have melted, and I admit that I wondered just how competent they could be in other places. Her fingertips were soft around my ears and the side of my neck, and that's when I grew hot enough to perspire. It was all so very intimate, and I had not expected Nina's hands to be so thorough, and demanding. Well, I am no innocent, of course, and I know exactly what a woman's hands are capable of doing. I just had not expected it here and now. Did Nina know what kind of effect she had on me? I hoped not, because that made the whole situation more illicit, and I enjoyed that feeling most of all.

'How's that feel?' Nina asked, so quietly that I thought she was whispering against my ear. I could almost feel her breath against the side of my face and it felt so good I didn't want to ruin it by opening my eyes.

'Wonderful,' I whispered. 'Perfect.'

No wonder the girls raved about this so much. I knew that when I saw them again I would rave about it too. I wouldn't go into too many details; for a start, I probably wouldn't mention that I thought Nina was incredibly sexy, and I definitely wouldn't mention that I was aroused almost from the start, but I would admit that I liked it. Half an hour of this and I would indeed be a new woman.

Nina laughed as she drew the tips of her fingers along my chin. Her nails, trimmed short, hardly touched the skin, but it was enough. 'Oh, this is just the start,' she promised, and she chuckled again, but it sounded throaty and decidedly dirty.

'You are so tense,' Nina observed. I'm sure she was

smirking, but it was hard to be sure with her soft voice set so low that it sent shivers along my spine. 'I think we should get you turned over and spend a little more time on your back. Is that OK for you?'

'Fine,' I said somewhat blandly, although the thought of Nina spending time on my back sounded delicious. Still, I didn't want to sound overly keen; that just made me seem a bit desperate. 'I am in your hands.'

There was no mistaking the tremor of excitement that wavered in my voice.

'Yes, you are,' she answered, and I did not know how to take that. 'Now, over you go,' she ordered.

When all you are wearing is a towel, it is amazingly difficult to turn over and be modest at the same time. The towel never does what you want, and always reveals far more than seems decent. You need two or three hands to grip the towel, two hands to turn over, and another hand to straighten things out. Unfortunately, I am no multi-armed Kali, but Nina helped and took care of the towel. She even folded it so that it formed a narrow band across the base of my spine and revealed nothing. I think. Even so, I have to admit that lying down naked, apart from a bit of fluffy material, left me feeling a little exposed and more than a little self-conscious. Nina seemed oblivious, but I supposed it was an everyday thing for her. I wondered just how many naked women she got to see on a daily basis, and how many of them came back begging for more.

The oils Nina rubbed into her hands filled the room with a spicy, almost musky aroma. It was a wonderfully evocative smell, and it made me think of hot places: of sand dunes and tents, of spice bazaars, sweaty naked bodies, and skin heated by a hot sun. I liked that imagery, but it did nothing to calm either my pulse or other parts of my body. Given the rate at which those other parts were starting to throb, dwelling on them was probably not a good idea.

Any discomfort or uncertainty that I might have felt vanished the moment she put her hands to my shoulders and her fingers began to work on the kinks in my muscles. She was a miracle worker, her hands like magic, and tensions that I didn't know I had vanished. Relaxed of mind and body, my thoughts wandered, but only so far as Nina's hands upon my back and all the places that she touched. It was relaxing, but oh so very exciting, and I burned and shivered all at the same time.

It all changed when I felt the tips of her fingers brushing along my sides. My mind came back to the here and now with a decided *thunk*. My eyes flew open and I am sure I forgot to take a breath for a moment. I can't even remember if I made a sound, but as her fingertips, oiled to glide, slid smoothly across the sides of my breasts I was incapable of thinking of anything beyond my breasts. How hard my nipples had become; how I could feel every fibre of the towel underneath me rubbing against sensitive skin, the material abrading my nipples until they felt raw.

She was slow now, her hands deliberate, and it felt as though every cell of my skin strained to meet her hand. I'd been trying to ignore what my body was saying, but it was so difficult when she was doing all the right things and in just the right way. I know it is inappropriate, but I couldn't help but wish that she had lingered along my sides for just a little bit longer. Better yet, I wished that she had been more direct, that she had filled her hands with my aching breasts and lavished upon them the level of attention she had elsewhere.

I scrunched my eyes tightly together, as though that would make it all go away, but inside the pressure continued to mount. The tingle between my legs had blossomed into something more insistent and, like my hardened nipples, my groin throbbed plainly and inescapably. Screwing my eyes closed didn't help at all, not with Nina so close, not now that I was aware of her whole body and not just her hands. My mind was filled with her, and my thoughts were lustily driven. I felt the heel of Nina's hands pushing into my back, and it seemed the only way to get to just that angle would be if she climbed upon the table with me.

I could almost feel her there, on the table, straddling my hips as she leant forward to use both hands. It felt so good that I wiggled my hips just so she was in the right position. I felt her lean back, sitting on the backs of my legs, and from the heat of her I knew she was as excited as I.

I could see her starched white uniform open, the studs popping with dull cracks as she pulled the material apart until she was completely revealed in all of her glory. Her tunic would slip off her shoulders and fall away, so that I could fully appreciate the naked woman beneath. So convincing was this thought that I could feel the cotton land on the backs of my legs and then slither to the floor. I liked this development even more, and I knew that between my legs the signs of my arousal would be glistening invitingly.

Now she had nothing on, she used her whole body to massage, and I definitely liked that. Her hands rested on the table just below my arms and I could feel her breasts pressing into my back. They were soft, but firmly uplifted, I decided as I fantasised, with puckered nipples to show she was enjoying herself. I don't know what happened to the towel, but it was not in the way as Nina slithered sinuously over the length of my back. I felt her breasts press into the backs of my thighs, over my buttocks, and slide across my skin to my shoulders. Her nipples racked over my skin, leaving tracks in the glistening oil. Then she pressed herself fully against my back, moulded herself to my shape; with her full weight upon me she pressed her groin firmly into my arse. I could tell from the way she ground into me that she was aroused; I could hear that hitch in her breathing, a little moan, a little whimper, and all for me.

I think she kissed the back of my neck then. I could already feel her breath upon my skin, her lips hot and moist, as she nipped the skin. She nuzzled the skin just right, just as perfectly as her hands, and I know that I moaned and whimpered, revealing my appreciation.

I was so consumed by this thought that reality and imagination blurred; I wanted so much more that I could feel myself pushing upward and arching back into her. I felt wetness oozing between my legs and I whimpered; it was definitely not a quiet one.

'Are you all right?' Nina asked, her husky voice breaking into my dream.

'Fine, yes,' I answered, but it was forced, because I could

not bring myself to face reality.

'Are you sure?' she asked.

'I was dreaming,' I answered, and that was enough.

'I hope it was a good one?'

'Oh yes, the best,' I answered, but I kept thinking, please God, don't let her ask me to turn over; if she does then one of us is in terrible trouble. At the very least I will beg her to stop what she's doing and just fuck me.

She stopped attending to my back then, and moved to my legs. It was not really where I wanted attention, but it was surely safer than anywhere else. I sighed, showing frustration and relief in equal measure, but I hoped that Nina did not misconstrue and think that I was not happy. She started with my ankles, a nice, innocent zone for those soothing and gentle fingers of hers. Even my racing heart began to beat just a little slower. She did not touch my feet, but she worked her way slowly upward. She used two hands on my left calf as she applied gentle pressure with her thumbs, working out the kinks and the tightness. She moved slowly to my knees, and she massaged them most efficiently and thoroughly. I felt my heart rate step up a notch again. Then the right leg; ankle, then calf, and at the knee she lavished a great deal of attention. I have never considered my knees to be sensitive, but with Nina they were, and I am sure that my legs parted a little bit further. Just so she had the space to work on my knees, you understand. Perhaps a little air would help other parts of my anatomy to cool off just a little.

She didn't stop, and I could hardly breathe as her fingers slid along the back of my thighs and almost under the towel. I was deafened by the thudding of my own heart, and I knew that my temperature was rising so fast I was surely turning red. I wanted her to stop, to do it some more, to go further, to stop. All of these things, Goddammit! Then warm hands started on the inside of my thigh and I know that I barely managed to suppress a moan. Please God, more, less, higher, lower, stop, don't stop. Nina moved lower, and I slumped against the table. Then the other leg. She seemed to reach higher; I swear I could feel her hands reach under the towel. Did I imagine her fingers extend just a little too far? Did those fingertips find evidence of the wetness waiting there?

Then she moved away and settled as far away from my groin as she could, working on my feet. She was particularly gentle, but firm. It was easy, settling, until she pressed in just the right spots I felt as though I'd been plugged into the mains. I was on fire and about ready to beg for more. That's when Nina stopped. She placed a cool hand at the base of my spine, but it felt as though she was much lower. I am positive that she stroked my arse, but then my judgement was a little skewed. 'Are you all right?' she asked quietly, and rather than answer, I concentrated on trying not to pant.

'That was not what I expected,' I admitted, when I was finally able to take a slow breath. It took every ounce of willpower I had to sit up and still keep a towel in the right place. My heart did not settle, and it took even more deep breaths before I could look up. Nina stared at me with those intense eyes of hers, her pupils so dilated that I could hardly tell where the iris ended and the pupil began.

'Are you all right?' she asked again and her voice sounded husky, her breath a little ragged. She did look decidedly dishevelled. She rested her hand on my knee and I stared at it as though I expected my skin to burst into flames. 'You look …' And she waved her one hand around as though that would put things into perspective. But she knew what effect she had, and I need say nothing.

'Do you always have this effect?' I asked.

'Do you?' she countered.

That confused me for just a moment, because I'd done nothing but maybe wiggle a bit.

'Rose –' she started, but I put a finger to her lips.

'I don't want this to stop,' I said, because I am a determined woman and I know what I want.

'No …' She sounded wistful even with just that one word. 'I have to be. To be professional.'

I stared at her hand on my knee. I understood. 'We should go for a drink, then. Do something social away from here.'

I knew, even without looking, that she was nodding her

agreement.

'You know you can't ever come here again.'

'I know,' I agreed sadly. 'I could never impinge on your professionalism.'

'Good.' She laughed loudly. 'Rose,' she said, pushing between my knees, 'I can't wait for later. Now you are no longer a client, I don't have to wait.' She positioned herself so her face was inches from mine. 'Let me give you a gift you'll never forget.'

The girls had been so sure that I'd be changed after a stress buster with Nina, but I wonder if they knew just how much. I wanted to ask her if she knew a way to get more hours out of the day, but her mouth was busy and I was no longer sure I could form a sentence. Nina knew a lot about the female form, and she was showing me everything she knew right now.

The New Curiosity Shop
by Jean-Philippe Aubourg

It was the watch that caught Maggie's attention.

She had always believed it was the small details which told you the most about a person. Not that you could describe this watch as small. It was a cuff watch, a thick brown leather strap much wider than the watch's classic face, probably meant for a man, making it look all the more incongruous on the girl's slim wrist.

She had seen the watch as the arm attached to the wrist was raised, the hand reaching for a high shelf, to place a scented candle alongside several others. Maggie's heart had skipped a beat when she saw the timepiece, and its strap. It so consumed her that it was several seconds before she looked at the girl.

She was slim, almost skinny, with long arms and legs. Her hair, brown and straight, was parted in the centre and plaited into pigtails which hung either side of a face somewhere between pretty and plain, long, with a slightly pointed nose. "Interesting" was the word which sprang to Maggie's mind. The girl wore flat sandals of brown leather, almost the same colour as her watch, faded blue jeans which fit snugly around a small bottom, and a blue T-shirt. Her right arm was curled around a box containing more candles, her left hand dipping into it every few seconds.

The woman became aware of Maggie's stare. She turned and smiled, sizing up a potential customer. Maggie squirmed, knowing she was being assessed in the same manner she that she had the shopkeeper, her appearance scanned and conclusions leapt to. She wondered if some of the thoughts she had been enjoying could be read on her face. It might save a lot of time and embarrassment.

A pair of hazel eyes took in her blonde hair, elfin short, her white short-sleeve blouse and black miniskirt, which left her legs bare to the top of her black cowboy boots. She brought her hands to her front, grasping the strap of her shoulder bag, her intention to display the adornments on her own wrists. On her left she wore her watch, also a man's model, a metallic silver Breitling. On her right was a leather cuff, a designer wristlet, also expensive, also thick, and secured with two silver buckles. As she gripped the strap of her bag she pulled back her shoulders, pushing out her large breasts.

'Anything particular you're after?' The shopkeeper's voice was soft, gentle, and friendly. Oh, I know exactly what I want, thought Maggie, but those were not the words which came out.

'Just browsing. You're new, aren't you?'

'Opened this month. I've been travelling, India and the Far East. I thought it was time I came home and used some of what I picked up to launch my own business.'

'Well, you've done a great job!' Maggie did what she felt was natural. She browsed. Moving about the shop, she picked up the occasional item: a bottle of essential oils; incense sticks; a statue of Ganesh. By the time she had worked her way back to the candles, the shopkeeper was behind the counter, checking off items on a clipboard.

By now Maggie had a plan, but it would take nerve. She took a deep breath and reached for a candle, then carried it to the counter.

The woman looked up as it was set down. 'Just that?'

'This time. I'll be back. You have such wonderful stock!'

The shopkeeper reached under the counter for a sheet of purple tissue paper, which she rolled around the candle. Maggie watched her hands at work, and suddenly made her move. 'This is wonderful too!' Her right hand had grabbed the shopkeeper's, her fingers on the leather of her watchstrap. It was smooth and supple, many years of loving wear behind it.

'Oh!' The woman was startled, but Maggie felt no move away, no attempt to escape. 'It's really old,' she said. 'I got it in a shop in London, one which specialises in second-hand watches. It's from the early 70s, I think.'

'Much older than this!' Maggie turned her wrist to show off the decorative cuff. The two bands of leather touched.

'Oh, but that's lovely too! I'm considering expanding into jewellery, and that's just the kind of thing I'd like to stock. Nothing too girly, even if it is a little …' The sentence was left hanging, as if she were waiting for Maggie to punctuate it.

'Butch?'

'Yes, butch! And maybe,' the woman went on, her voice dropping, even though they were alone, 'kinky. I'm Cindy, by the way.'

Maggie barely registered the name. Her heart had been sent pounding by the previous sentence.

'Kinky?' she repeated, before adding, 'Oh, I'm Maggie.' She had been keyed up to make the running, use her best seduction techniques; now she was off balance.

'Yes, kinky. There are so many more uses for a thick length of leather than just holding a watch around a wrist.' Maggie's face flushed as Cindy spoke, calmly and without embarrassment. 'Some people make assumptions when they see my watch,' she went on. 'Is that what you did?'

Maggie's voice cracked, her mouth suddenly dry. 'It was – more of a hope than an assumption.'

'Then it was either justified or correct.' Cindy smiled again, the broad grin of a potential lover, rather than a retailer making a sale. She took her hand away and Maggie enjoyed the feel of the leather sliding underneath her fingertips. 'You seem like you're going to be a good customer. I've got a few things in the stockroom I'd like to show you. Would you like to see them?' The last sentence was said slowly, each word emphasised, so there could be no misunderstanding.

'Yes! I'd love that!' Maggie loaded her own reply with the same meaning.

'I'm due a lunch break – let me shut the door.' Cindy came out from behind the counter, walked across the shop, turned the sign to "closed", and snapped the lock. She came back to a mesmerised Maggie, raising her left hand for Maggie to slip her right hand into. She was led past the counter and into the small room behind it.

There were boxes stacked against three of the walls, and more placed on shelves. The room smelt airless but it had been thoroughly cleaned before the stock was moved in. Most of the floor was clear and there was a tall, backless bar stool in one corner. For taking things down from shelves, Maggie assumed, although her over-excited mind was conjuring up all kinds of alternative uses. She placed her bag carefully on the floor and turned to face Cindy.

'So what did you want to ...?' Before she could finish, Cindy's hands had clasped her face and pulled it toward her. Their lips met, Cindy forcing her mouth onto Maggie's with an unexpected violence. But Maggie was no shrinking violet, and had no intention of being taken passively. Grabbing Cindy's shoulders, she squeezed them, and tried to pull her body as close as possible, returning the kiss with equal passion. In seconds, their lips had parted and their tongues were fencing.

They stood in a glorified cupboard, French kissing, revelling in the moment. It seemed neither wanted their first kiss to end, but eventually Cindy broke away. She leant back, Maggie's face still gripped firmly in her hands, before closing back in and placing her mouth right next to Maggie's left ear. Her voice was just audible. 'What are you? Sub, domme, or switch?'

Maggie was wrong-footed again by Cindy's directness. It took a few seconds before she could answer. 'Switch – yes, I'm a switch!'

'Excellent!' Cindy's voice was still so low it could barely be heard, even right in her ear. 'Do you want to give or take first?'

Maggie had only planned to ask the shopkeeper out for a drink, and had never imagined she would be asked this question so soon, but it was a question which had to have an answer. She thought, before placing her own mouth next to Cindy's ear. 'Take,' she whispered.

'Hmm. We are going to get on, with so much in common!' Suddenly Cindy's face was in hers again, the passionate kiss resumed. Then Maggie's head was pulled back and she found herself looking into eyes which brimmed with frightening excitement. 'So,' said a voice which brooked no argument, 'pull your skirt up, your knickers down, and get over that stool.'

Cindy took her hands away from Maggie's face, stepped back and waited, her fists resting on her hips, her feet planted apart. The loss of contact was almost as alarming as the harsh words, and the sudden sharpening of tone, but Maggie's head was now firmly in the scene, and she obeyed quickly.

Picking up the stool, she placed it carefully in the middle of the available space, then stood before it. Bending her knees, she took the hem of her skirt and wriggled her hips as she eased it over her plump bottom. She blushed as her knickers were revealed, thanking providence that today she had worn a good pair; high-cut, lilac, and decorated with white flowers. Cindy's face showed her approval, and at the moment her opinion was the only one which mattered. Her instructions, of course, had been "knickers down" – Maggie hooked her thumbs into the waistband and followed them to the letter.

Her stomach flipped as she exposed her bottom to her new lover. Once prone to self-criticism, Maggie had grown to love her curves as she accepted her sexuality, and took pleasure in the moment she revealed them to a woman for the first time.

She left her underwear around her thighs, hoping Cindy would find the line they drew against her pale skin appealing. She reached down and gripped the stool's crossbar, her eyes focused on her watch and wristlet, as her fists squeezed the wood. Her breathing was heavy and she trembled.

The sound of Cindy's feet on the floor, and the feel of her hands on her exposed bottom, only made that increase. She sucked in her breath as fingernails traced lines up and down her buttocks. The hands left her, and a second later Maggie's breath was knocked from her by a sharp slap to her left cheek. 'Ow!' she hissed. But her bottom wiggled, telling Cindy she wanted more.

The next spank was naturally on her right cheek, a stinging slap which rang around the confined space. Maggie felt her buttocks wobble and hoped Cindy was the kind of spanker who looked at an ample bottom and thought "more to spank"! It certainly seemed like it, when Cindy's left hand was placed was placed in the small of her back, as the shopkeeper steadied herself in the classic bottom-smacking position. Her palm went against Maggie's naked skin, slipping underneath her blouse.

Maggie's classic bottom-smacking began in earnest, Cindy's hand bouncing as if it were on a trampoline. It was fast but perfectly paced, and Maggie felt the sting and heat grow at exactly the correct rate. She continued to wriggle her hips and make appreciative noises. A spanker needs to know when they are getting it right.

It stopped at just the right time too, when the burning was still comfortable. Cindy's hand was taken from Maggie's back and Maggie heard her step around the stool. Lifting her head as far as she could, she was just about able to take in all of Cindy. She was blowing on her right palm, which must have been nearly as sore by now as Maggie's bottom.

Without speaking, Cindy lifted the hem of her T-shirt to show the waistband of her jeans. She wore a thick leather belt, brown, gnarled at the edges and so wide it was only just able to fit through the loops. It had a large silver buckle and its tail, which extended almost halfway round Cindy's waist, was curled and worn. The leather itself appeared shiny and smooth. Clearly, it was very old, very used, and very long. Cindy started to unbuckle it slowly, and Maggie licked her lips.

'I told you,' said Cindy, as the belt slithered through the loops, 'there are so many more uses for a nice, thick length of leather.' Her eyes smouldered as she doubled the belt and gripped the buckle and tail in her right fist. She held out her left palm and slapped the looped belt hard against her own skin, making Maggie jump as she lay waiting for it to be used on her.

Cindy stepped back behind her. Maggie lowered her head, pleased not to have to crane her neck any more, but knowing that very soon her bottom would be on fire. She braced the toes of her cowboy boots against the floorboards and held her breath.

There was a faint swish, and the belt cracked right across the centre of Maggie's cheeks. She howled as the pain sank in, reigniting the sting of the spanking while bringing an agony all of its own.

'Nothing like it, is there?' came the voice from above. 'The feel of real leather. It's what I get from my watchstrap all day, a bit of kink I can carry around with me in the real world. I know it's what you get from that wristlet too. But there's nothing like using it for what it's meant to be used for, and I don't mean holding up my jeans!' A second stroke landed on Maggie's bottom, almost dead on top of the first, making her howl. 'You're getting a dozen, by the way. Ten to go,' Cindy added, matter-of-factly.

All ten were given with strength and perfect timing, Cindy knowing how long to wait for the pain to dissipate, without waiting so long that the delicious anticipation was overdone. It was the mark of a true switch, Maggie knew; someone totally aware of the effect of the implement she wielded. Maggie groaned and howled her way through her sentence, feeling the cathartic release of asked-for-and-got corporal punishment, as Cindy laid the belt across different parts of her bottom, covering her whole behind by the time the 12th stroke had landed. Despite her enjoyment of the strapping, Maggie still breathed a sigh that it was over.

She stayed over the stool, waiting for instructions. She was sure she was not going to get any more punishment, but she would be submissive until Cindy told her she was not, and not a second earlier.

There were noises behind her. The thud of the belt buckle on the floor. The rustle of clothing. Her tummy flipped again and her breathing, almost back to normal, became heavy again. She prayed her guess was right.

'You can stand up now.'

Maggie eased herself off the stool, rubbing her bottom as she straightened. She turned to see that her prayer had been answered. Cindy was naked.

She was facing the wall, her thin arms raised, her fingers interlocked on top of her head. All she wore was her cuff watch, the overpowering piece of leather around her wrist even more obvious now she was nude. Maggie drank in the sight of the slender figure: a pair of long legs; a back which curved elegantly, and, at their meeting point, an apple-shaped bottom, prominent on her small body, despite its modest size.

Maggie took a step toward her, and realised her skirt was still around her waist and her knickers around her thighs. She thought about straightening them, then snapped open the catch, pulled down the zipper, and let the skirt drop to the floor, taking the underwear with it. She stepped out of both, naked from the waist down.

Now Cindy was within reach. She put out an arm and extended her index finger. She touched her spine, at the nape of her neck, and felt Cindy shiver. Applying only a tiny bit more pressure, Maggie traced the outline of Cindy's backbone, drawing a sigh. She stopped at the cleft of her bottom, sorely tempted to grope it, but deciding to deny herself that pleasure till the last possible moment.

Instead, she drew the finger back up, then let it travel across both Cindy's shoulders in turn, up and down her right arm, then her left, lingering at the wrist, touching the leather of the cuff watch again. Cindy turned her head and grinned.

'When I bought it,' she said, 'I took it home and put it on. After I stripped naked. Then I stood like this, for half an hour, fantasising I had someone like you doing this to me.'

Maggie smiled at the image of an excited Cindy, with no one to share her passion. 'No more frustration,' she told her. 'In your fantasy, what happened next?'

Cindy said nothing, but looked at the belt coiled on the floor.

'I see,' said Maggie. 'Although I'm sure there was some spanking first.'

Cindy grinned and nodded, her eyes going to the stool in an unspoken question. Maggie shook her head. 'Right where you are will do.' She cupped the beautiful bottom with her right palm. It was smooth and elastic, filling her hand gloriously. Now she knew for sure this woman could fulfil her.

Cindy faced forward again, throwing back her shoulders and shuffling her feet a little further apart. Her breasts became more prominent, although they were tiny, conical little mounds with pointy nipples, which were, of course, rock hard. Maggie cupped the left breast, her whole hand more than enough to cover it. Cindy closed her eyes and exhaled as her as her breast was squeezed, gently, but with enough menace to tell her that it was she who was now under control.

Maggie lifted her right hand to shoulder-height, then brought it down, hard and quick. Cindy gasped and Maggie felt her nipple push against her palm. A second spank, a little harder, tested Cindy's limits a tiny bit more.

Maggie smiled and spanked in earnest, safe in the knowledge that fate had found her another serious player, one who shared her view of the world. The tight little buttocks barely yielded to each slap. Her hand almost bounced off the small bottom. It felt delicious, and Maggie revelled in the way she and Cindy complimented one another.

Spanking Cindy was a pleasure, but Maggie knew a greater joy was to come, one which was hers whenever she wanted it. She teased herself a little, continuing to smack Cindy's bottom for a minute or two longer than she really ought, until the poor woman was gasping and fighting to keep herself in check. Only then did Maggie stop, although they both knew it was a pause before her mettle was tested properly.

Smoothing her palm over the hot mounds, Maggie leant in to whisper into Cindy's ear. 'Hands on knees, feet apart, bottom well out. You're also getting 12.' She stooped to pick up the belt and found Cindy had eagerly assumed the position in the centre of the room. Her pigtails dangled and her sex was visible, pouting between her slender thighs.

Maggie doubled the belt over and gripped the buckle and tail in her right hand. Cindy had handled it expertly. She carried it everywhere with her, around her waist; it could be assumed she got a lot of practice. By contrast this would be the first time Maggie had used a belt in this way. She focused on getting it right.

She lifted it level with her head, then let her right arm swing. The belt sailed in a wide arc and landed with a satisfying *crack*! Cindy squealed and rocked forward on her toes, then back on her heels, before coming to a stop.

Maggie looked at the rectangular mark she had left. It was a little high. She aimed her second stroke lower and, when Cindy had come to rest once more, was surprised to see it had landed much lower, a clear gap between the two broad lines. The third she aimed meticulously, and was delighted to see the evidence of its landing clearly between numbers one and two, joining them up.

She began to enjoy herself, putting a real belt against a willing bottom, and Cindy made a wonderful playmate, oohing and aahing in appreciation, adding the occasional "oh yes, harder!" and "hmmm, that's sooo good, thank you, miss".

All too soon, the full 12 had been delivered. Maggie touched the tortured bottom, now bright crimson and covered in lines and ridges, an exact match for hers. Cindy twitched and gave a little cry as her fingers made contact, but quickly shuffled her thighs further apart. 'Yes please!' she hissed 'Touch me!'

Her labia, which looked large as they peeked through her small bottom, seemed to be offering themselves without asking their owner. Maggie's finger walked over the glowing skin and touched the pouting folds, which were wet and hot, like Cindy's bottom.

Maggie slid two fingers inside and heard a groan. The bending woman wobbled, so she moved closer, slipping her left arm underneath Cindy's waist, gripping her right hip. She was as light as a feather, and many future over-the-knee spankings flashed before her eyes.

She quickly found Cindy's clitoris. There was a gasp, then a long moan, as Maggie started to rub. The woman was excited beyond belief, and Maggie knew exactly what she was doing. This would not take long.

Maggie felt the skinny body tense and stretch within her encircling arm as a guttural groan dragged itself from Cindy's throat. The vagina around Maggie's finger pulsed and tightened, pumping for several seconds until it came to a stop, Cindy's body sagging as her almighty orgasm flooded her body.

Maggie allowed Cindy to slip to her knees, then forward onto her hands. Cindy rested for some time on all fours, then raised her head, a filthy grin stretching from ear to ear. 'Fantastic!' she said huskily. 'Magic fingers, and a proper strapping. My guardian angel must have sent you to my shop.'

'And it's still your lunch break,' said Maggie, looking down at the naked woman, crouched at her feet like a faithful dog. Cindy looked puzzled. 'I mean,' Maggie explained, 'that you haven't eaten yet. I think you should eat something.' She unbuttoned her blouse and slipped it off, tossing it onto the floor and to hell with the dirt. She parted her thighs and smoothed her hands over her neatly trimmed mound, its curly hairs the same light shade as those on her head.

Cindy got her meaning. Pushing herself onto her knees, she rested her hands on Maggie's thighs, opened her mouth, poked out her tongue, and angled her head, aiming it at the waiting sex. Maggie shivered as Cindy made contact, her fingers tangling in the light brown hair …

That was three months ago. This morning Maggie is still in the shop. She stands exactly where Cindy did when Maggie first saw her. Her left arm holds the box of scented candles, her right rhythmically taking each one out and setting it on the shelf.

Gone are her office clothes. They went with the tedious job, in exchange for a good redundancy, which she used to buy into the business, a business she now runs with her girlfriend. Now she can wear what she likes. Today it's a T-shirt and jeans, which are held up by the thick leather belt. They take turns to wear it, and this week she is dominant.

Her girlfriend is in the stockroom, checking a delivery. She is wearing a kaftan, brought back from India, and underneath it, nothing. That was Maggie's idea, and besides, knickers would only chafe against the sore red bottom she is certain to have for the next couple of days, at least, after last night.

Something else Cindy will not be wearing this week is her cuff watch, the butch, kinky timepiece which first attracted Maggie. As she reaches for the last candle, Maggie checks to see if it's lunchtime yet.

Curled around her left wrist, the cuff watch tells her that it is.

In Pearls
by Giselle Renarde

The day Davina moved in with me, I carried her across the threshold and brought her all the way to the couch. Kneeling before her, I said, 'This is *our* home now, yours and mine.'

'That's fine,' she said with a flick of the wrist. 'But I don't do windows.'

It turned out that she didn't do dishes either, or carpets or floors, or laundry. She didn't make beds, she didn't make dinners. She didn't scrub tubs or plant flowers or dust bookshelves. Household chores were not her style.

And my Davina had style, that was for damn sure. She was a fame-hungry femme if ever there was one. She wanted a taste of celebrity, and though she probably knew in her heart of hearts she'd never reach that particular pinnacle, she didn't mind acting as if. That's not to say she didn't have her own successes. Davina was much loved at the talent agency where she worked as receptionist, but she was obviously waiting for the break that would never come.

My girl was a butterfly beauty: stunning, but fragile.

So I laughed along when she went on her little "imaginings" about us as the next lesbian power couple. She'd joke about unleashing a sex tape (at least, I hope that was a joke) or she'd host a house tour for make-believe talk show cameras.

'You never know where the paparazzi's going to find you,' she'd say as she pulled me into the shower. Her perfect, perky breasts would bounce as she rustled her hair beneath the spray. 'That's why I need to look my best at all times.'

'You always look incredible,' I'd tell her, cupping her

mound and squeezing. 'All the time.'

I'd kiss her under the stream of shower water, and she'd pull away, laughing. 'You really think so?'

'God, yes.' I'd crush her fine form to my hefty body, kissing her until the wetness between her pussy lips let me glide right in. Her body devoured me finger by finger.

I've probably made my girl out to sound like a total nutbar, but everybody has a fantasy life, right? Davina just daydreams out loud. If you knew her as deeply as I do, you'd understand that the flashy colours and designer flair are all a mask. Davina lived through horrors she wouldn't want mentioned here, and if she needs to paint the world a little brighter to make it through the day, all power to her.

That said, every relationship reaches its points of frustration, and ours is no exception. I love Davina, but love and everyday practicalities don't always go hand in hand. When one partner doesn't contribute to the household, when she racks up credit card debt buying clothes but refuses to help with the rent, when she's never washed a dish in her whole damn life, the other partner's bound to get a little testy.

One day, it came to a head.

'Just pick up after yourself for once! You're not a poodle, princess.'

'But I *am* a princess,' she shot back, hands on hips. 'You're supposed to take care of me, Greer. I'm yours, to have and to hold!'

'You are not *mine*, Davina.' How could I make her understand? 'You're not just a trophy that sits on my shelf. You're a person in your own right, and this is a partnership, not ownership. This is *our* house that *we* need to maintain.'

She perched precariously at the edge of the couch. When her lip started quivering, that did me in. I was a sucker for Davina's tears, crocodile or otherwise. She brought out the hero in me, the nurturing rescuer of damsels in distress.

Still, I had a point to make. I got on my knees and softened my tone to ask, 'Do you really want me to see you as just another finicky houseplant? You're so much more, honey.'

Gazing down at me, she batted her glistening lashes and

dabbed at the corners of her eyes. She was so precious, so beautiful, so delicate.

'I'm sorry,' Davina said. Her voice cracked, and that's how I knew the tears were real. 'You're right. I haven't been much of a partner. No excuses this time.'

The pity I felt for her made me want to clean the whole damn castle for my queen, but I wouldn't let our weaknesses win. 'You might enjoy a taste of domesticity if you gave it a try.'

She laughed, scrunching up her nose. '*Like* is a strong word.'

Something about the straightness of her spine gave me a brilliant idea, and I ran up the stairs, shouting, 'Wait right there!' I riffled through her drawers, pulled things from the closet. When I'd laid out the absolute perfect homemaker outfit, I called Davina up to take a look.

She gasped, then giggled. 'Oh Greer! You naughty thing. You expect me to clean the house wearing this?'

I raised an eyebrow. 'I'll be waiting downstairs with the vacuum.'

Davina was still chuckling in the bedroom when I skidded down the stairs. I grabbed the vacuum from the broom closet and set myself down on the couch. As usual, she made me wait, but the waiting only got me so hot and wet and ready that the second I heard the click of her heels on the stairs I just about soaked my shorts.

'Fuck, woman.' I tried to whistle, but I'd never quite mastered that particular art form. Instead, I clapped my hands. 'You look like a million bucks.'

Most red-blooded dykes would probably have laid out a French maid's outfit for their sweetie, but not me. I wanted something altogether different, something to fulfil a fetish I never knew I had.

I wanted my woman to vacuum in pearls.

Not just pearls, mind. High heels too, and fine silk stockings with garters, an A-line skirt, a minty green sweater set. She was a ghost of the mid-century modern mom. I almost couldn't keep it in my pants when she grabbed hold of the vacuum like she knew just how to handle it.

'Nice day at the office, Greer?' Davina winked, as if to tell me she knew exactly what I wanted. 'Shall I fix you a drink, darling?'

'No, no. I'm happy just to watch my lady work.' I reached out to cup her ass, a perfect handful.

She giggled, smacking my hand away. 'Why, Greer, it's still daylight out! What if the neighbours see?'

'If we've got neighbours skulking in the bushes, a few dust bunnies are the least of our concerns.'

Davina gasped as I traced my fingers down her thigh, past the hem of her skirt, and across the sensual silk of her stockings. Her calf muscles were so taut in those heels that I just wanted to rub my throbbing pussy all down her legs. Waiting was the sweetest torture.

Stretching both arms across the back of the sofa, I spread my legs wide. My pussy was aching so badly I couldn't have kept my thighs shut if I tried. But I wasn't going to touch myself. I'd wait until she came to me, even if it took all night.

'Do you know how to start that thing?' I asked, nodding to the vacuum.

'Why, surely I do!' Davina said with a fluttering giggle. She looked the vacuum up and down, still chuckling with nerves, until she finally found the foot pedal. She pressed down with the toe of her designer shoe, but nothing happened.

'Problem?' I asked. My pussy was raging so hard I could have sworn I heard it through the silence.

'Well I …' She looked at me sheepishly. 'I'm afraid it must be broken.'

I pointed to the electrical cord wrapped around the side. 'Why don't you try plugging it in?'

'Oh.' Davina's face went instantly pink – a pleasant shade on her. 'Greer, darling, what would I do without you?'

'Live in a dirty house,' I teased.

As she leant forward to unwrap the length of cord, I watched the sweet sway of those gorgeous tits under too many layers of fabric.

'Hey, why don't you take that off?' I pointed to her top.

'Don't want to ruin your clothes if you work up a sweat.'

'Women don't sweat, we glow.' Davina shot me a sneaky sort of smile. 'But I'll do as you wish, darling.'

She undid her sweater slowly, pressing each mother of pearl button through its rightful hole, and then pausing to glance at me. I must have looked mesmerised, or lost in space, because she laughed every time. She did a sort of shimmy to shrug the sweater from her shoulders, and then she tossed it at my head.

'This too?' she asked, grabbing the hem of her green camisole.

I nodded slowly, deliberately. No sense rushing things.

'I'll have nothing on but my brassière.'

'Good.' I could feel my gaze darkening, intensifying.

With a shrug, she said, 'You're the boss,' and pulled the knit camisole over her head, tossing it into my lap.

The bra I'd picked out was dusty rose mesh, a vintage style with cone cups. It matched the high-waisted panties I'd laid out for her, and the more I thought about the ensemble, the more I had to see it.

'Take off the skirt too,' I said as she leant down to pick up the vacuum cord.

'Whatever you say.' She turned around, backing up until her perky ass was right there in front of me. 'Unzip me, will you?'

How could I say no? I unfastened the little clip at the top, then slid the zipper down until her skirt fell to a puddle on the floor. The sight of her nearly naked ass made me want to bend her over and lick her perfect little rosebud. I wanted to take her right then, but I restrained myself. I'd wait until after she'd vacuumed.

'Thank you,' she said, and stepped beyond the skirt's borders.

Her ass cheeks writhed inside her see-through panties as she walked away from me. When she bent at the hips, her beige garters spread around the sides of her ass, showcasing her squeezable cheeks. A groan burbled up in me, but I bit my tongue, watching in tortured silence as she plugged the vacuum into the wall socket. That border of flesh where her stocking gave way to skin was the most awe-inspiring image I could fathom.

'Are you ready?' she asked, taking hold of the vacuum. Her heel dug into the carpet, but her toe hovered over the pedal. 'Shall I start now?'

My throat felt like cotton. It took all I had to mumble, 'Uh-huh, yeah.'

She stepped down on the pedal, bringing the vacuum to life. Obviously she didn't realise what a monster it was, because its suction drew her forward and she struggled to overpower it. The behemoth was loud. I didn't try to speak over it, and neither did she. She just vacuumed and I just watched, lost in desire.

I didn't know where to look. Her calves were so muscular, but her ankles were strong too, and I loved the way they gave in to her feet, letting them showcase her high-heeled shoes. But then there were her breasts in that vivacious vintage lingerie, swinging and swaying each time Davina pushed the vacuum forward. Of course, if I let my gaze slide down her front, I could watch the eager contortions of her abdomen with every pull. There were those panties, gorgeous mesh overlaid by a classic garter belt, and then I was back down at her stockings.

More than anything, I loved the way her pearls hung stoically around her neck. When she bent forward, they swung away, and when she straightened up, they slapped against her chest. The string wasn't terribly long, but the pearls themselves were perfect, smooth spheres, white like innocence itself.

It wasn't long before the carpet was clean. When Davina turned off the machine and its engine whirled toward silence, mine was just getting revved up.

'Nice work,' I said.

She unplugged the vacuum and smiled. 'I think I'm getting the hang of this cleaning game.'

'You just need an audience.'

Her expression fell for a split second, then revived with a grin. '*Touché.*'

'You know what else you need?' I was so turned on I could barely breathe.

Davina took two steps forward and asked, 'What?'

Grabbing her wrist, I tugged her into my lap so her beautiful bum waved in the air. 'A spanking!'

'Oh Greer!' She propped her head up off the carpet to look at me tenderly. 'A hard one, please.'

'My pleasure.' I slapped her ass, feeling her flesh rebound inside the pink mesh of her panties. The garters looked good, but I felt like they were in the way, so I struggled with those finicky little latches until I could flip them up.

'Another one?' she pleaded, panting already.

'Anything for my girl.' I let my next spank fall against her ass, and she gasped. That was a good one. 'Even more?'

'Yes!' She answered without pause, so I smacked her hard; same cheek, same spot. I could feel her muscles tensing in anticipation now. She wanted it so bad I could feel her ache as strongly as my own. My breath came slow and hard as I traced my palm up her spine, all the way past her bra, until my fingers met the latch of her necklace. I don't know what inspired my nasty little move, but I took off her pearls and held them in front of her face.

'Suck on these,' I said. 'Get 'em good and wet, because they're going in your ass.'

She gasped, but slurped the string of pearls like spaghetti. I expected her to fight me, and when she didn't it was like dawn breaking through an open window. It was the start of a new day.

I spanked her again, and because she'd waited so patiently I didn't stop at just one. I punished her ass until my hand started to buzz, and then I took a break to glide my palm across the fine mesh of her panties. Her ass crack was lusciously visible through the sheer fabric, like the cleave of a peach. As much as I wanted to take a bite out of her, I tore her panties down instead.

'Oh!' Davina squealed, despite the mouthful of pearls.

The moment her ass was bare I smacked it good, watching her lovely cheeks ripple in response. I hadn't realised how pink her skin had gotten while her panties were on, but my goal now was to turn them red.

'Do you know how hot you look?'

She moaned "Mmmm" around the pearls, wiggling her ass in my lap.

'Do you deserve another spanking?'

Her bum bucked up in the air as she cried, 'Mmm-hmm! Mmm-hmm!'

I couldn't bear to tease her any longer. Letting my hand fall against her exposed ass, I slapped her so hard she started inching forward, out of my lap.

'Not so fast, little lady.' I kept one leg under her tight belly and wrapped my other one around both of hers, locking her in place. 'You think you can get away that easy?'

'Mmm!' she hollered, so urgently I knew the pain was real.

'Three more,' I said. 'I'll do the countdown, since your mouth is busy.'

I got a throaty chuckle out of her for that one.

And then I surprised her with a quick smack. 'Three.'

'Mmm!' The sting of it was audible in the strain of her voice.

I traced my palm around her sizzling ass. Which was hotter – my hand or her flesh? We seemed to get each other's temperatures rising, and although I loved spanking my girl I was almost glad I only had two to go. My palm couldn't take much more.

With Davina locked in place, I smacked her ass. The sting ran up my arm like a bolt of lightning. She cried out around the pearls and I could feel her pain in my body. It was getting to be too much for both of us.

One more. Just one more.

'Gimme,' I said, tugging the pearls from my girl's mouth. They came out slippery and wet. Perfect.

'They're going in my ass?' she asked, sounding partly terrified and partly exhilarated. 'God, Greer ...'

'Hold your cheeks open, babe.' They were rosy red, and she hissed when she touched them. 'Wow, Davina, you've got the prettiest little asshole.'

She chuckled as she arched off the ground. Her breath came harder, faster, as I ran the pearls down her crack. I can't overemphasise how alluring she looked with her garters undone at the back, her panties pulled down to her thighs, and a string of pearls cascading between her rosy cheeks.

'Keep spreading them,' I told her. Her arms were shaking, but I wouldn't keep her in that position too long. She moaned when I poked the pearls into her ass, more and more, filling her with gleaming spheres until there were only a few poking out. 'That's a good girl. You can let go now.'

Davina's hands fell in front of her, and she sighed in moderated relief.

'Ready for *one*?' I asked as a courtesy.

'Yes,' she cried. 'Please yes!'

I took a breath and lifted my palm from her ass, but I didn't spank her. She might have been ready, but I wasn't. This had to be memorable. It had to be perfect. I took another breath and held it.

'Please?' she asked in a whimper.

I released my breath and took another. Third time's a charm. I brought my palm down on Davina's ass and the shock was like fireworks. She screamed, arching so high off the floor she reminded me of one of those carved mermaids on the front of old ships. She slumped back down, whimpering, and her pure emotion gave me needs I couldn't set aside any longer.

'Stand up,' I said, releasing her legs. 'Stand. I want your pussy. Now.'

Davina scrambled to her feet, panting, almost gulping air into her lungs. Her ankles gave out in those high-heeled shoes, but I caught her before she could fall. Diving between her thighs, I snuffled her pubic hair like a wild hog. I felt crazy with lust, like I couldn't control myself. The musky-sweet scent of her pussy was my love drug, and I parted her lips with my thumbs, thrusting my face into her wetness.

She held my head as I pressed one cheek flush to her clit and then turned, teasing her with my lips, circling the other cheek against her clit. I could feel her all over my skin, but that wasn't enough. I had to taste her too.

Parting my lips, I lapped at her pussy. She pushed down on my head like I was a crutch, like her legs wouldn't support her otherwise. I tried to go slow, lick her at a reasonable pace, but I was beyond restraint. My tongue had a mind of its own, and it felt no pain. Davina squealed as she fisted and twisted my hair.

Still, no pain. Everything was for Davina, all for my girl. I wanted to make her come so hard her legs would be out of commission for a week.

Then I remembered the pearls in her ass, and I knew I'd better work them before she came all down my chin. Releasing her pussy lips, I wrapped one arm around her thighs and sought the string of pearls with my other hand.

'Oh Greer!'

Whenever she said my name, everything inside me rattled. I pulled on the pearls, but they resisted, so I refocused my energies on her clit. Splaying my tongue against it, I shook my head side to side, making her hiss and whine. She was getting close to the brink. I knew the signs. So I gave the pearls another tug and felt her resistance weaken.

'Baby, you get me so hot!' Davina cried, and I looked up at her, past her dusty rose mesh bra and crimson lips, into her huge hazel eyes. 'I'm gonna come, sweetie. Suck my clit. I'm gonna come!'

It was obvious who had the control. I couldn't resist her. She asked, and I obeyed, sucking her clit between my lips and teasing, taunting, building suction. Her ass eased up, letting me pull a few pearls through its tight ring, and then a few more. I sucked her clit like a nipple, then I sucked it like a cock. That really got her going. She bucked against my face, giving her all, tightening her ass and then releasing more pearls.

I kept at the string, and I kept at her pussy. Her moaning and shaking made me wild, and I bobbed between her thighs like I was giving her clit a blowjob. I licked and sucked and smashed my lips and cheeks and chin against her pussy. She gave me pearls when I pulled, a few at a time, stringing me along.

'I'm gonna come!' she cried. That became her mantra. She chanted it again and again as my jaw ached and fingers tugged. The pearls worked their way out of her ass a little more with every pull, and I knew just what would put her over the edge.

I thrust three fingers up her snatch and she howled, arching onto her toes. She was so wet they slid in without a hitch, but I spread them a bit as I fucked her. Every time my hand came up, it smacked me in the chin, but I just kept at her, beckoning her orgasm with my mouth.

Screeching desperately, Davina plunged her pussy down on my face, stroking against it in sweeping circles. She pulled my hair unapologetically, and I ate her harder, licking and sucking in alternation. With her lips spread across my face like a mask, I could hardly breathe, but I didn't care. The only thing in the world that mattered to me was Davina's pleasure. She was everything to me, and I had to make her come.

Backing off for a moment, I looked up at her and read the pleasure painted across her face. Her eyes were closed and she was panting, muttering nonsense. And then she must have realised I wasn't licking her and my fingers had stilled inside her pussy. She looked down and, when she met my gaze, her whole expression changed.

She smiled and said, 'I love you so much. You know that, right?'

I could have said, 'I know you do, babe,' or, 'You mean the world to me.' I could have said a lot of sappy things, but in that moment I wanted to take charge. That's why I challenged my girl by saying, 'Prove it. Come on my face.'

Shoving my face between her thighs, I went at her clit so furiously she screamed. The harder I went at her, the more feverishly she praised my efforts. Her fingers were back in my hair, tugging hard, and that's when I yanked the string of the pearls from her ass. The pearls put her over the top. She hollered my name, stroking off on my tongue, flooding my mouth with pussy juice.

'Oh yes, Greer! Yes!' Davina squealed and yelped until her affirmations transformed into, 'No, Greer. No more.'

My jaw was killing me as I backed away from her brilliant red pussy. I'd worked her so hard she fell onto the couch and then bounced back up, hollering, 'Ouch!'

I laughed. 'Let's see that ass.'

She turned and gave me a good look. Her cheeks were still pink, and the garter straps hung limp down that rounded flesh. Dropping the pearls on the carpet, I swatted Davina's ass. She shrieked, tumbling to her knees, bum in the air, face on the couch cushion.

'Had enough for now?' I teased.

She turned to face me, and her smile was deliciously coy. 'For now.'

I sat beside her on the floor and we breathed together, sharing a conspiratorial grin. 'So, how'd you enjoy your first foray into vacuuming?'

She laughed, turning her face into the cushion. 'You're silly, Greer.'

'That's not much of an answer,' I teased, nudging her with my elbow. 'Get used to playing domestic diva. After dinner, you're washing the dishes.'

'Before dinner, you're washing my necklace.' Davina leant over, laughing again, and kissed my cheek, then bit my earlobe. 'If I'm forced to do chores, I'm doing them in pearls.'

The Wedding Singer
by Anna Sansom

'Thank you, ladies and gentlemen. We're going to take a short break now while you enjoy the buffet. Join us for more dancing soon.' I turned off the microphone and stepped down from the stage. Buffet time! The guys were right behind me as we wove a path through the wedding guests and toward the table bearing a range of sweet and savoury delights.

I filled my plate and headed back toward the small table that had been set aside for the band. That's a nice touch, I thought. Often we end up hanging out beside the stage or going outside for a cigarette just to fill the time between sets. I don't smoke but the guys do, and I'd usually rather join them than be left on my own in a room full of strangers.

I'd just sat down and was trying out a savoury pastry when she came over to the table. She touched me gently on the shoulder and I looked up with crumbs on my lips and the half-eaten pastry in my fingers.

'I'm really enjoying your music,' she told me. 'I hope you're having a good time too.'

I hurriedly swallowed the dry pastry and answered, 'Oh yes, it's a lovely party. I'm glad you're happy with what we're playing.'

'You will play my special request too, won't you? It is such an important day for me and to hear that song would be the cherry on the cake. The cherry on the *wedding* cake!' She laughed and I joined in.

'Don't worry; we've got it on the list. There's no way I would disappoint you on this big day.'

'Thank you. I'd best get back to our guests.' The satin of her dress rustled as she stepped away, and I watched the curve of her buttocks move against the tight fabric.

'She's hot!' Danny had joined me at the table and was watching appreciatively.

'Danny!'

'Hey, I'm a hot-blooded man, what do you expect? You think I'm going to ignore a beautiful woman at a wedding?'

'I think you should try and ignore *that* woman.'

'So what's in this?' Danny held up one of the pastries, examining it.

'Dunno. I think mine was crab. But it could have been chicken.'

'When do we get to the cake?'

'Danny! We're the hired help, remember? We're here to entertain, not to act like badly behaved guests.'

Danny looked down at my heavily laden plate and plucked off one of my sandwiches. 'So I see,' he said. 'Guess you won't be wanting this then?'

I grabbed the sandwich back from his plate and stuffed half of it in my mouth.

'God, watching you two is like watching a chimps' tea party!' John sat down in the empty chair between Danny and me. 'Will you guys show some respect?'

'Great spread,' Mike added as he joined us at the table, and the four of us quickly ate our food.

Danny finished eating first and pulled out his packet of cigarettes. 'I'm going out for a smoke,' he said. 'Anyone coming?'

'Yep.' Mike picked up his last sandwich and put it in his pocket. John stood up and reached for his jacket.

'You guys go ahead,' I told them, 'I'm still eating.'

Tonight I preferred my own company to hanging out with the guys. We'd been playing a lot of gigs lately and I was getting bored of the wedding circuit. They were all the same: a bunch of straight people trying to be nice to the family and exes they didn't get on with; a few suits and fancy dresses; love songs from ten to midnight; then home alone to my small apartment and being reminded, yet again, that I hadn't found *my* "special someone".

I picked over the remaining food on my plate and finished my drink. I checked my watch: another ten minutes and we'd be back on. Best get some more water from the bar while it was quiet.

The party guests were seated around tables, eating and chatting. I walked over to the empty bar and held out my glass. 'Could you fill this with water for me, please?' I asked the man behind the bar.

'I don't suppose I could tempt you to something stronger?' Her voice was a soft whisper against my ear and I turned to face her. She was smiling.

'Uh ... Thanks, but not while I'm playing.'

'Maybe later?' She raised one eyebrow and leant in close. 'Or maybe I can get you something else instead?'

'Oh, I've had plenty from the buffet, thanks.'

'Yes, I saw. But that's not what I had in mind. I've got something to give you.' She placed her hand lightly on my elbow and guided me toward her. 'Come with me. We'll go somewhere private.'

Was she about to hand over the cash? I wondered. I hated that part of the job. It usually happened right at the end. We'd have all our gear packed up and the bride and groom would thank us, then there would be that awkward silence. Maybe they sometimes genuinely forgot, but I was usually the one forced to say, 'Uh ... Em ... There's just the small matter of – uh – sorry – payment.' And, as if that wasn't bad enough, the guys always insisted I count the money there and then – just in case someone had made a mistake. The possibility of someone offering the money up front was something I couldn't refuse.

I left my glass on the bar and followed her out of the main hall. She stopped beside the elevator and pressed the button.

'We'll go upstairs,' she told me. 'I am reading you right, aren't I? We share a common interest, a common habit you might say.' And she laughed again.

A common habit? Her pupils were dilated and she gazed at me without blinking. I knew where this was going. 'I don't take drugs,' I blurted out. 'If you've got something upstairs I don't want to know about it. I don't even smoke. Or drink – much. We should really go back. I need to be ready for the second set.'

'Silly, I'm not offering you drugs. Why would I spoil such a wonderful day with drugs? I want to remember this day for the rest of my life. But I do have something special for you upstairs. Think of it as a wedding favour.' She laughed, and stepped into the waiting elevator. 'Are you coming?' She stroked her fingers down her throat and allowed them to dip into the line of her cleavage.

Oh. Now I got it. I watched her fingers brush along the top of her dress as the doors closed behind us.

Her suite was on the 12th floor, and I looked around me guiltily as I followed her inside. She kicked off her shoes, walked over to the drinks tray, and poured herself a measure of brandy. With her glass in hand, she turned to face me.

'Now, if I can't offer you a drink, what can I offer you instead? How about this?' She reached across and slipped one strap of her dress down off her shoulder.

'What about your husband?'

'Don't worry about him; he's completely preoccupied with the guests. He won't even notice I'm gone.' She stepped toward me. 'But we don't have much time,' she whispered urgently before pressing her lips against mine.

Her ferocity caught me off guard. She pulled me into the bedroom, set her glass down beside the bed, and tugged at my clothes. 'I want you,' she told me. 'I've been watching you all night. It was as though you were singing just for me. Don't make me wait any longer. Make love to me.' She threw herself onto the bed and held her arms outstretched.

It was true: I had been singing every song for her. She was truly beautiful and, from my raised platform and central position, I had been able to follow her every move all evening. Now here I was alone with her, and she wanted me.

I took a large sip from her brandy glass. The guys would be wondering where I was.

I looked at the woman on the bed. Her dress was hitched up around her thighs and I could make out the lacy tops of her stockings. Her breasts were held high, constrained by her bodice, and I longed to release them so I could take her nipples between my lips. She spread her legs some more and I could see the thin band of her underwear lying snug against her crotch. She half closed her eyes and looked at me from beneath long lashes. She licked her lips slowly. This was the most obvious come-on I'd ever experienced.

Her blatant hunger and lust awakened my own. The air was scented with desire and I was made heady by it. She may as well have drugged me: she was having such an effect on me that I felt euphoric. The unexpectedness of this encounter, and the consequences of being caught, excited and aroused me. My juices were flowing and my clit was hardening in anticipation.

'You'll crease your dress,' I told her. 'Come here.'

She stood up and turned with her back to me. I found the zip in among the satin folds and eased it open. The dress slid down her body and she stepped out of it. I picked it up and laid it over the back of a chair. Then I turned to face her. She was pulling at the fastenings of her basque. 'We don't have time, lie down,' I instructed.

I lay down on top of her and kissed her while my hands roamed freely over her body. She gasped and wriggled underneath me. My fingers found the edge of her knickers and I pulled them to one side. I worked my fingers between her lips and dragged them slowly through her slickness.

'Ah.' Her breath caught in her throat as I made contact with her clit.

'I want these off,' I said as I tugged at the flimsy fabric of her underwear.

She lifted her hips off the bed and I pulled her knickers straight down and over her feet. I tossed the damp fabric over in the direction of her dress.

I stroked up her thighs, feeling the contrast from the lace of her stockings to the smoothness of her flesh. Her inner thighs were silky, like the satin of her dress, and I trailed my fingertips across them, stroking upward, nearer and nearer to the heat emanating from her cunt.

She held her breath as I got closer, finally releasing it in a long groan as my fingers reconnected with her lips and her clit.

She arched her back and pushed her torso up against mine. My fingers slid inside. 'Yes,' she hissed, as my fingers beckoned to her.

I didn't want to hurry the experience. I knew the others would be waiting but I also knew how much I wanted to savour this woman. I wanted to feel her get wetter and wetter, and tighter and tighter around my fingers. I wanted to see the flush of excitement pink her chest and throat. I wanted to strip her of all her clothes until she was fully exposed to me – until I could drink in every inch of her and cover her entire body with kisses and caresses.

Her breasts were unavailable to me and I had to make do with feeling their form through the constricting fabric. Her neck and throat teased me: naked flesh that was too delicate to take between my lips. I must not leave any evidence of this encounter.

Instead, I moved my face toward her cunt.

She opened her legs wide and directed my mouth to her clit. I stilled my fingers inside and licked lightly over and around her. She pressed my face harder against her and I sucked on her clit. Now she tried to draw away from me, but I licked again and picked up the rhythm with my fingers.

'Too – good,' she gasped. My smile was hidden in her folds but I heard her giggle.

I teased her clit some more: sucking, licking, blowing warm air over her. Then I began to hum. The vibrations from my lips made her hips dance.

'Too much!' She laughed, and her thighs trembled around my shoulders.

I brought myself up to look at her. 'Maybe I'll just fuck you then?'

She nodded and I pushed my fingers deeper inside her. There was room for more so I slipped in a fourth finger.

Her throat and face were flushed, and she bucked beneath me. I was mesmerised. Her full breasts strained against the tight-fitting basque, and her hands clawed at my back. 'Do it,' she urged. 'Do it to me.'

I fucked her slowly and forcefully; my eyes locked on hers, my breaths quick and shallow.

'This is so good,' she panted. 'Keep going, please keep going.'

I quickened my pace a little. God, I wanted to see her come. She bit at her lip, watching my arm move between her thighs.

A knock at the door made us both freeze.

'Room service,' a woman called out.

Another knock, and then the sound of a key scraping inside the lock.

'No!' I shouted. 'No room service!' Remembering my manners, I added, 'Come back later, please.'

'OK. Sorry to disturb, ma'am.' To my relief, the key was withdrawn.

'That was a close call,' I said.

'Adds to the excitement,' she replied. 'Are you going to finish what you started?'

I moved my hand again, my fingers motioning inside her this time while I worked my thumb onto her clit. She was so wet and I could feel my own cunt throbbing and a pool of moisture hot between my legs. I still had all my clothes on – even my shoes – and I loved the contrast of seeing her in only her underwear. I felt powerful and desired: it was an irresistible combination.

I picked up the pace again and she bucked beneath me. We were both breathing heavily, panting in time with each other. Her breath came out high, and was punctuated with the word "yes" over and over. The effort of my fucking came out in the grunts that accompanied my breaths. I never wanted to stop.

'You're going to make me come!' she shrieked.

I kept going, keeping time with the beat of the pulse roaring in my ears.

She closed her eyes; I watched the story of her orgasm play out across her face. My fingers were held tight and I squeezed my own muscles as though she were inside me.

I collapsed on top of her and sought out her mouth with my own. She sucked my tongue into her mouth the same way she'd sucked my fingers into her cunt. I let her kiss me. She toyed with my tongue, tasting herself on me.

Her kissing gradually became less insistent and I could feel her body relaxing underneath me. I began to move my hand out.

'Not yet. Please.'

'We have to go back downstairs,' I reminded her.

'Just a moment longer. Please.'

She closed her eyes and placed her hand on top of mine, pushing me gently back inside her.

'You feel so good inside me. I don't want it to be over.'

I could see the time on the clock radio beside the bed.

'I don't want anyone to come looking for you.'

She sighed. 'OK.' Her hand wrapped around mine and she slowly pulled me out.

I gave her a deep kiss, and then rolled to the other side of the bed. I watched as she stood up and retrieved her clothes.

'Wet on wet.' She laughed as she pulled on her damp knickers. Then she stepped back into her dress. 'Can you zip me up?'

I helped her with the zip, waiting while she reapplied her lipstick. Once fully reformed, she stood in front of me and took hold of my hands. 'Can I see you again? I want to touch *you*.'

I hesitated.

'Please?'

I let go of her and reached into my pocket. I handed over one of the band's business cards. 'That's me,' I said, showing her the phone number. 'You can call me any time.'

She took the card from me, raised the hem of her dress, and slipped the card into the top of her stocking. Then she handed me the glass of brandy. I took a sip and handed it back. She took a larger mouthful. 'Back to the party then.' She sighed.

'I love women,' she declared as we rode back down in the elevator. 'I don't know why I ever got married. Still, everyone loves a wedding, don't they?'

I smoothed my clothes down one more time just as the elevator doors slid open. Danny, John, and Mike were loitering in the foyer. Danny saw me first and strode over. 'Where have you been? We need to get back on,' he growled.

'It's OK,' she told him, 'it's my fault.' Then, turning to face me, 'You will play my song, won't you?'

'We'll make it the first on the list,' I replied. 'Come on, guys, we've got people to entertain.' I waited until the rest of the band had walked ahead of us, then let my hand brush casually down her back and cup her backside. She gave me another ravishing smile and headed back to the party guests.

I took the stage and I flipped the microphone to "on". 'Ladies and gentlemen, welcome back to the show. Hope you enjoyed the buffet and are in the mood for love! This first song is a special request from a very special lady.' She moved to the front of the crowd and stood smiling up at me. 'There she is: *the mother of the bride*!'

Danny counted us in and Mike played out the opening line of Ella Fitzgerald's *You Do Something to Me*. She danced in front of me, just for me, and I sang her song, just for her.

I love weddings.

The Senator's Daughter
by Valerie Alexander

The senator's daughters were always embarrassing him. I suppose all political offspring have a high public profile, but four beautiful girls who like to get into trouble were a special kind of media magnet. So when the senator – or, rather, his wife – hired me to paint his library, I knew I was walking into an interesting household. Not that I would have shared stories; I was a decorative painter, hired by wealthy clients to adorn their homes with special effects like marbling or Venetian plaster, and my success depended on my discretion as much as my talent.

Everyone knew the senator, of course. He had been considered presidential material at one time, the handsome ex-football hero who married a model and now supported all the right causes, until he was caught nailing a call girl and three other mistresses tumbled into the media spotlight like toys falling out of an overstuffed closet. He'd kept his job but lost his halo, and now he was mainly famous for his spoiled and beautiful daughters, who seemed intent on keeping up the family tradition of scandal.

The biggest scandal yet broke three days before I was to start working in their house: the oldest daughter, Molly, had just announced her pregnancy by an NBA basketball player. So I was relieved when the senator's wife called me and told me, somewhat tensely, that the family would be gone while I worked. Their assistant would let me in.

I was relieved not to have to deal with their family tension – but I was kind of disappointed too. I'd wanted to see the famous bad girls for myself. Of course, I reminded myself, the oldest daughters, Molly and Michaela, were in their 20s and probably didn't live at home. Megan, the one in college, might have her own apartment as well, so probably only the youngest, Madison, still lived at home. Certainly none of them had been around on my initial visit, when the senator's wife showed me the library and how she wanted it painted.

I knocked on the carved oak door. An assistant answered. 'Hi, I'm Summer,' I said. 'I was hired to paint the library.'

She looked over my blonde ponytail and coveralls. Like a lot of people, she seemed momentarily flummoxed at having a girl contractor. 'Oh right,' she said after a moment. 'I was told to expect you. Come in. But no one's here but me and Mica.'

'I know. It's OK, we already went over everything.' This was really how I preferred to work. Having a client looking over my shoulder before I was finished was never fun.

'Great.' The assistant seemed relieved. 'If you need anything, I'm usually in the office down the hall.'

The house was massive. Solemn black-and-white family portraits lined the walls; four brunette daughters surrounding their tanned parents, the senator flashing his famous killer smile. The girls were all gorgeous but I didn't pay much attention. As a bi girl, I liked dating femmes enough, but rich girls had always gotten on my nerves. They tended to use people, in my experience.

'Who are you?'

One of those rich girls curled around the hallway corner now, seductively rolling her back against the wall like a cat. I vaguely recognised her. The oldest and most famous daughter, 24-year-old Molly, was dark-eyed and willowy like her model mother; but this one had her father's green bedroom eyes and his dazzling smile. Her petite but voluptuous body strained at her skimpy nylon camisole and matching boy shorts. It had to be Michaela, the 21-year-old.

'I'm Summer,' I said. 'Your parents hired me to paint the library. I do special effects.'

'Oh God. Please tell me my mom didn't hire you to do some crazy Egyptian shit.'

I tried not to smile. From the cool marble-floored rooms around me, it was obvious the senator's wife had a serious Ancient Egypt fixation. The house was filled with Pharoanic art, from framed papyrus scrolls to statues of Anubis guarding the dining room archway.

'No. More of a green marbled look.'

She leant her head against the wall and studied me dreamily. I knew her gaze, her head tilt, were probably practiced. The senator's oldest daughters seemed to be professional seductresses, from what the media reported.

'We've never had a girl contractor before,' she said. 'How long have you been doing this?'

'Since I dropped out of art school a few years ago.' I was trying really hard not to look at her tits. The last thing I needed was one of the daughters complaining to her parents about the pervy bisexual painter they'd hired. 'Look, I'd better get started.'

She was still lingering in the shadowy hall when I brought in my equipment. 'I'm Michaela, by the way,' she said, sauntering ahead of me in a way that showed off her sumptuous ass. 'But everyone calls me Mica.'

'I'm Summer. Hi.'

'I'm the only one here this week,' she said. 'Madison's at equestrian camp and Megan's in Prague. My parents are gone too. So it'll just be us,' she said, giving me that deep green stare. 'If you get bored, let me know.'

I forced a polite smile. Was she really hitting on me? Girls hardly ever came on to me; everyone assumed I was straight because of my shoulder-length blonde hair and make-up. It was a stupid assumption, but unfortunately a lot of people still thought in stereotypes. Probably Mica just flirted with everyone. God knows the media would have blasted it everywhere if the senator had a bisexual daughter.

'Thanks, but I'm on the clock.'

She disappeared into the vast, shadowy house. I got started priming the library walls, telling myself I hadn't really been attracted to her. Some rich political princess was the last kind of fling I needed; she'd probably just lie there and make me do all the work. Still, her green eyes and pillowy hourglass of a body kept returning to my mind. She looked so soft and pampered, but was so obviously predatory. It turned me on more than I wanted to admit. It could be just a mindless fuck, I told myself. One hour buried in her soft skin and silky-wet pussy, and then it would be like it never happened.

As I worked, the daughters' reputations came back to me. Molly had supposedly slept with her father's security staff, and had been packed off to Europe after her second DWI. Mica was known as the frosty, stuck-up one who spent her time shopping and at salons. Where Molly tended to be photographed falling out of a taxi, or slurry-eyed in a club booth, Mica's photos were of her posing with scads of shopping bags outside high-end stores in her trademark heavy mascara and pink lip gloss. Not that she was scandal-free; she'd been in the gossip columns last year after her sociology professor left his wife for her, only to find himself dumped a month later.

Megan, the 19-year-old, was catching up on her sisters fast – she'd made a name in high school by renting out a hotel suite for an after-prom party that was raided by the cops, and then was expelled from her first college. It was a wonder 15-year-old Madison hadn't been locked in a convent, just to be on the safe side.

A sudden sharp buzz startled me. 'It's me,' said a disembodied voice. 'Mica. Can you come upstairs? I have a professional question for you.'

It was the house intercom. Unsure of how to work it, I just cleaned off my hands and headed up the big, winding staircase. Mica was leaning over the banister, her boobs bulging out of her skimpy top. 'Thanks,' she said and led me down the hall.

Her indigo bedroom was the size of my apartment, her bed an elevated platform of pillows. She led me into a bathroom that was all gleaming marble tile with a spa-sized shower and a working fireplace.

She leant against my back. 'I just want your suggestions on how you'd redecorate this, if I asked you to,' she said in my ear.

I stepped away from her. 'It looks good the way it is.'

'What about the bedroom?' She led me back to that

sprawling bed. Her boy shorts rode up her crack, showing off her smooth, tanned ass. 'Different colour scheme?'

'Why don't you tell me what you want?' I countered.

'What I really want,' she said, 'is to see you out of those coveralls.' She cornered me against the wall, unzipping them. 'You look like you have an awesome body. Why cover it up?'

'Cleaning paint off my skin is a bitch.' But I let her pull them off me like I was hypnotized.

'Nice,' she murmured. She slid up my tank top and bra like a greedy child unwrapping a present. I didn't move. I felt lightheaded with disbelief. Girls never threw themselves at me and I never slept with clients, but somehow both were happening.

Mica cupped my small breasts. 'Yours are the perfect size,' she decided. She lightly pinched my nipples. 'I would love not to be saddled with these monsters.' She pulled off her camisole and pressed her soft tits against mine. They were definitely natural, full and round and dropping just a bit.

I found my voice. 'Uh, Mica, I'm sure you do this all the time …'

'You're thinking of Molly,' she said in a voice laced with irritation. 'She's the slutty one, I'm the studious one.'

Right. She looked studious, rubbing her nipples over mine. 'Look, you know you're hot, but your parents are paying me …'

'Fuck my parents,' she said and kissed me. 'This is just a little break.' Her tongue flicked my earlobe before returning to my mouth. 'No one has to find out.'

As she undressed me, I groaned and gave in, scooping up her luscious tits. Maybe this was fast and crazy but she was right – no one had to know. I'd fuck a beautiful girl with no drama and no repercussions, then go back to work.

Mica pulled me toward her bed until I fell naked on top of her. All I could think was that she was the softest girl I'd ever lain on. She squirmed underneath me with an impatient grunt. 'Here, lie like this,' she directed. She propped me against a pile of pillows, then opened my legs. It wasn't like me to be so passive but she seemed to have the entire script written out in her head, and so I let her lead. Somehow this entire seduction felt planned, not spontaneous at all, as if I was simply a prop in her stage production. But hey, if she wanted to use me for sex, I wasn't going to argue.

And then I quit thinking, because she was sliding down between my legs, her voluptuous breasts brushing over my thighs. I sucked in my breath, my clit suddenly stiff with excitement. A moment later, her hot tongue washed over my pussy. I groaned. This clearly wasn't her first time with another girl. She teased my clit until it was almost painfully swollen, then sucked and nibbled my pussy lips until I was twisting on the sheets, begging her to make me come.

Mica laughed. She drew my clit between her lips again and sucked it, her deft fingers teasing my pussy. My hips were bucking, shamelessly begging for more of her. It had been a long time since someone mastered my cunt so effortlessly, but Mica knew exactly what to do. Just how many girls had she slept with? Her mouth and fingers worked me over until my pussy seemed to melt into throbbing, molten honey. Groaning, I got up on my elbows and revelled in the sight of that famous, exquisite face eating my cunt.

She caught my eye. That killer smile flashed up at me, smeared and sticky with my wetness. A thunderbolt rolled through my body, and then an intense orgasm was searing me, blissful and squeezing her fingers in rhythmic waves as I groaned.

I collapsed back on the pillows, winded. My entire body was trembling.

Mica climbed up me, sliding her wet cunt along my stomach. 'You better not be *too* tired,' she said and kissed me. I could taste myself on her full lips.

I shook my head, and then she was straddling my face. Her cunt was soft and small, resting on my mouth, and very wet. Her tiny lips were already open and swollen. I let my tongue unfurl between them as the taste of her, sweet and briny, filled my mouth.

Mica moved back and forth on my mouth, holding onto the massive oak bedframe and tossing her long, dark hair around. It was quite a show. Her tits dangled over me, her thighs spread wide as she humped me with abandon. I filled my hands with her ripe ass and moved her closer, tilting her forward so I could work my fingers into her quivering slit.

A guttural moan shook from her throat. 'Deeper,' she begged. 'Yeah, just like that.'

Her cunt closed around my hand, hot and trembling. My tongue circled her clit as my fingers moved inside her, trying to stroke her velvety walls in tandem with my tongue. She shuddered, a small, wet gush erupting onto my lips.

'Faster,' she muttered, sliding closer to my nose. She was riding my face like a hobby horse now, humping me so hard that my tongue and fingers were tossed around in her moving, thrusting chaos. She was gasping and clenching my head between her thighs, and I could feel her pussy swelling around my fingers – and then she was coming, whimpering and smearing her pussy all over my face in a rhythmic, shameless demand.

Mica slid off me and fell on the bed. Heaving a long sigh, she threw her legs open and grinned. 'God, that was good,' she said in satisfaction.

I wondered if I should go. This whole episode had been so crazy, like a fantastic but slightly dangerous dream. But, to my surprise, Mica rolled over and kissed me. I pulled her against me, revelling in her softness as her tongue delicately traced my lips.

'I love the way my pussy tastes on your mouth,' she murmured. 'I wish I could have sex with myself. Do you think that's narcissistic?'

It was pretty much exactly what I expected from a girl as rich and gorgeous as Mica, but I shook my head. 'No, it's natural.'

'I love fingering myself in the mirror. I taped it one time, but then I deleted it. I'm so afraid of my computer being hacked.' She looked at me calculatingly. 'Are you going to tell anyone about this?'

'What? No. I know how the media follows your family. That's the last thing I would do.'

Her green eyes studied mine. 'I actually believe you.' She

sounded surprised and a little disappointed.

'Not that it isn't worth bragging about,' I assured her. 'You're so ...'

'Horny?' She kissed me again and worked her fingers into my pussy.

I closed my eyes and luxuriated in the skill of her small fingers. Girls were always so much more talented with their hands than boys. Mica buried her face in my tits, sucking on my nipples with a tenderness and skill that made me throb. I didn't think she could make me come a second time, not so quickly, but her nimble fingers coaxed my cunt into a creamy, pulsing warmth. I rolled onto my stomach and spread my legs, letting her finger me from behind. I stroked my nipples, a sensual euphoria filling my blood. This was my favourite position for coming and, as she used both hands on me, tweaking my clit and moving her fingers deep in my pussy, my second orgasm broke through me, a hot stream of ejaculate washing out of me without warning.

'You squirted,' Mica giggled. 'Look, you soaked the sheets.'

Suddenly I was self-conscious with embarrassment. 'I have to get to work,' I muttered, and pulled myself out of bed. I felt so dazed and saturated with sex that I could barely think.

Mica followed me. 'Look, my parents are going to be gone all week. They won't know if you started today or tomorrow.'

Good point. I nodded, and she pulled me toward that fabulous shower. 'Come on. Get cleaned up and you can start over tomorrow.'

As she soaped me up, I couldn't help feeling like her pawn. She had set her sights on me and gone in for the kill as efficiently as a panther. The whole thing felt suspiciously easy, like she was in complete control and I was just her toy. But I forgot all that as she leant naked against the tiles, her long, dark hair plastered to her nipples. God, she looked hot wet.

She reached into her collection of bath gel and conditioner bottles, pulling out a blue waterproof vibrator. 'I'm not done yet,' she explained with a languourous smile. She lifted one manicured foot onto the shower ledge and played with herself, opening her lips and showing me the brighter pink of her cunt.

'Please, Summer?'

I twisted the vibrator dial and pressed it against her clit. She sighed happily, arching her back against the tiles. 'Do you like fucking me?' she asked, fixing me with her eyes.

'Of course.' I sensed that wasn't the lavish compliment she was looking for. 'You're the sexiest girl I've ever been with.'

She smirked and pushed her shampoo bottles aside, seating herself on the shower bench. Leaning back, she spread her knees wide. 'Get on your knees,' she purred.

From her smug face, I suspected this was what she'd wanted all along – me, the hired hand, kneeling naked between her legs and licking her clit while I drove the thick blue vibrator in and out of her cunt. She arched her back and moaned, playing with her nipples. She looked every bit the princess being serviced, and again that feeling of being used passed over me. I knew I was probably just a toy to her, as much as the vibrator disappearing into her pussy.

But the truth was that I liked it. It turned me on to be selected, undressed, and taken sexually like this. I sucked her clit, circling it with my tongue as I pressed the vibrator in her wet and steaming puss, and it was with real pride that I felt her come, squealing and writhing against the shower wall.

I sat back on my heels, grinning. Mica looked disoriented and dazed. Good. Finally she wasn't quite so in control. I rinsed off, and turned off the shower, wrapping up in one of her thick purple towels. But by the time she climbed out of the stall, she had recovered her confidence.

'Not bad,' she smiled. 'I've never had that vibrator used on me quite like that before.' I groped for my clothes and she snatched away my bra. 'No – I want this as a souvenir.'

'Fine.' My wet hair dripped over my tank top, my nipples visible through the wet cotton, but I wasn't going to argue. No one was around to see.

Mica glanced out the windows as if checking for her parents, then slipped into a green transparent bra and panties. 'Why don't you go home for the day?' she suggested. 'You can just start fresh tomorrow.'

Good God, she was controlling. What a pain in the ass she

would be to date. But working really was the last thing I felt like doing so I shrugged. 'OK,' I said. 'I guess I'll see you tomorrow.'

The smile she flashed me was polite but detached. Yep, she was done with me. She'd had her fun and now she was ready to dispense with me, no romantic goodbyes necessary. Downstairs, I checked on my gear in the library, sealing up the primer, then headed out the front door.

'Summer, wait.' Mica ran into the yard in just her bra and panties, her tits bouncing. She kissed me hard and deep, pushing up my tank top and liberating my tits, kneading them hungrily. It was all very exuberant and completely unsensual but I kissed her back, flattered by this sudden erotic ferocity. Maybe she really was more attracted to me than I knew.

Then something flashed, followed quickly by another flash, and I saw someone move in the hedgerow. A photographer. Oh fucking fuck. I quickly pulled down my top as Mica settled back on her feet with a satisfied look.

'Perfect,' she said. 'Molly might be pregnant but being the bisexual sister will get way more coverage.'

Her father's killer smile flashed over her face and she flounced back in the house. The photographers were still snapping pictures of me as I covered my face and made my way to my car. I had most definitely been used, and not just for sex. I'd been her hapless pawn in a much more devious game. But my entire body was still tingling and I found that, despite everything, I was smiling.

Sealed
by Elise Hepner

'Why did I find this in my box, Marta?'

With a delicious thud, I jumped up, sitting on the long, plastic folding table, and dragged my eyes away from my boss's steady glare. A lick of pleasure twisted in the pit of my stomach. She held a plain white envelope in my face. Another day – another campus mailroom pay cheque I worked too hard to earn. Emily continued speaking, but I hadn't heard a word. More of my focus strayed to the slick constriction created by my latex lingerie, pressed up against my pussy. A delicious sense of security bit into my damp flesh. Underneath my skipping pulse, I knew with my secret armour in place the bitch couldn't touch me.

Not unless I wanted her to, anyway.

Beneath the tight, collared shirt I'd picked out that morning, my nipples peaked, shooting an erotic spark down my spine. My point of focus shifted to a file cabinet behind her head. Maybe I could pretend that every breath into my lungs didn't sting from her scent of gardenias and peppermint while she shuffled in her platform heels like a tottering penguin. But calling her names wasn't going to change anything. Even if it was only in my head.

I supposed I should answer for myself. If only to stop the tirade that had only wound me up further until I seriously might pop off the table and run for cover. Anything to make this stop. To make Emily less aware of my growing arousal while she raged until her face turned grape juice box purple.

'Haven't been in the mailroom until five minutes ago, and

that was to inventory packages, Emily.'

A quick flit of my gaze back to her face revealed tightly pursed, vamp red lips. With a faked casual ease, I leant back on my hands until my sensitive, pebbled nipples brushed against my cotton shirt. Each measured breath was a chore. Her black brows knitted together and I cocked my head to the side with a clueless shrug. No movement I made – no matter how subtle – could distract me from the wicked clench of my thighs. Or the thrum of my blood past the cinched vinyl moulded tight along my hips.

Did she think I was lying? Part of me enjoyed the idea of toying with her temper. How far could I push before she snapped entirely and gave me the tongue-lashing of a lifetime? That last thought might have gone too far. A mental image of my boss between my legs licking for all she was worth slammed my eyes shut as I bit back a low moan. God, was I pathetic or what?

'You're not giving me a damn thing to work with here, Marta.'

'I don't know anything about this,' I reiterated in well-pronounced words so she'd better understand me.

Maybe that should have stopped the argument. But it wouldn't – not unless I had pertinent information on the sleazy, sexually explicit letters boss lady had been getting from a secret admirer every week during her shifts. Even if I did know something – nothing would pass my lips. Emily worked into a frenzy was a small pleasure amidst the dullness of my regular job.

Plus, with her arms crossed along her polka-dot day dress, supporting her ample cleavage, I had a good enough view down the front of her dress to see a hint of her old-fashioned nude bra. Subtly sexy. And I liked this game way more than I should have.

Her light green eyes narrowed, the little gold flecks around her iris shining against the onslaught of the yellow overhead lights. While she measured me with her gaze I tried not to wilt. Mentally, I dragged myself kicking and screaming away from the idea of this woman and I locked in some kind of forbidden lust fest. Things like that didn't happen – regardless of my kinky downtime.

Unleashed, repressed sexual energy turned Emily into a pitbull on steroids at work. It had even started to show in her meticulous, vintage wardrobe, with small creases in her dress's full skirt. Next would be her perfect, thick black curls – all tangled and flying away from her skull like she'd been given the ride of a lifetime.

And wouldn't I like to be the one offering that ride?

My tongue traced the line of my lower lip and the small touch was so silky-smooth that every muscle in my body tensed. This had to stop. How in the world had I thought that wearing my special secret to work would distract me from the irate sex kitten only a few feet from my swinging feet? Somehow it hadn't crossed my mind that latex lingerie would only make this more tempting.

What a dumbass. Each tap of her heel on the vinyl floor reminded me of the error of my ways.

Emily was more tightly laced than Scarlett O'Hara's corset.

Was she still speaking? From the set of her mouth it'd looked like she'd settled down enough to think clearly again. But there was darkness in her eyes I couldn't read. What in the bloody hell did this dame want from me? I shifted back on the table, white-knuckled grip on the rim. I'd probably have a textured mark all along my palms when this was over – something to remember her by, I supposed, considering I'd probably be fired in the next few seconds.

Not many people got away with talking to my boss like she's a dumb three-year-old.

For some inane reason, Emily drew closer to me. Large spots of pinkish colour washed across her dimpled cheeks and I blinked back the sexual imagery crowding my over-caffeinated mind. Her hands dropped to her sides, crinkling the layer of crinoline beneath her dress. I released my grip on the table with a tight inhale. But I kept my hands moving at all times. If my fingers were occupied with flitting little patterns and strokes across my slacks then Emily's blunt rage couldn't reach past my tightly wound arousal.

Then maybe I wouldn't be tempted to do anything stupid – like fuck my boss.

'I did it.'

Emily was startlingly close now. I watched the soft rise and fall of her pale, perfectly shaped breasts and tried not to be obvious. Someone had to take the blame for this insanity, and I was in the mood for a little trouble. Why not? It's not like I'd just talked to her in the most respectful manner ever. The more I thought about it, the better my emanate unemployment sounded.

Not exactly whip smart, am I?

Besides, getting fired would give me more time to stroke myself alone in my dorm room, and I didn't really need the job anyway. It was only an excuse, a cover, a ruse, whatever. This dumb pay cheque was a way to parade around my secret latex fetish in public without getting caught. I tempted fate with every slick, rubber step. And with my boss advancing on me with a dangerous glint in her eyes I had a feeling my last day was about to give me the fantasy of the century as she geared up to give me an epic tongue-lashing.

It's not just Emily that turns me on.

Personal space got dicey as the irate Glamazon stood between my outstretched legs. A tease of her sensual body heat through my slacks jerked me into sitting up like puppet strings were attached to my back. It was enough to make me instantly wet. Our eyes locked, but she hadn't moved an inch.

Could she tell? I couldn't help thinking I was holding a lit firework between my legs.

She took small, choppy breaths as her nostrils flared out. Kinda cute. Her fists rested just below my knees and I wondered if she'd hit me. At least it'd give me a chance to pop her one in return for the hell she'd put me through at this job. My nerves were shot, trying to explore what she was going to do to me now I'd lied and she thought it was the truth.

Emily just stood there in my personal space while I tried to keep my hands busy. A solid effort to get my mind off rough, sexy fantasies where she'd dominate me and make me come until I was hoarse and grovelling for more. But I'm not an idiot.

I patiently waited for my firing. Ironic, that the woman who wouldn't ever shut up was eerily silent.

'What are you going to do about it?' I goaded her on, unable to help myself, sick of limbo.

'What – what am I –?' she sputtered out.

What did I expect? Not Emily's unreachable anger that quickly shifted to wide, drowning Bambi eyes. Boss's puckered, cherry red lips in an "o" of shock that morphed into a coy, unreadable smile. Her sweet breath played across my cheeks. That was the only thing that registered as I became aware of every inch of my flesh.

What could she do to me here – doors locked, after hours, and the next shift not due for two hours? Her perfectly manicured hand landed like a ten-pound weight on my thigh. In an instant my throat was tight. Did she – had she felt –? A quick shiver and I glanced away.

'You?' Her nails gripped my flesh until her flowery perfume became enticing and my whole world flip-flopped. 'How did you find the time to write such infuriating, enticing prose? I know your schedule like the back of my hand – there isn't room to breathe, let alone compose filth in different handwriting so you wouldn't get caught.'

Without a doubt, she knew I was lying.

It was easy to see her doubt in the half-lidded glance she'd pinned me with until – honest to God – a blush heated my cheeks. But there was also something else in her stare I could appreciate. Curiosity. It kept her hand on me while I came to terms with the loud racket my heart made in the centre of my chest. Neither of us looked away. Was she trying to figure out how much she could get away with? I wouldn't tell her she could do just about anything and I'd fold beneath her with a damn sigh.

When she slid her palm up toward my thigh, I knew she liked whatever idea she'd concocted because her impish grin said it all. But I hadn't come to terms with the fantasy of my exposed secret.

'Wait, I – I –'

'Shhh.'

One hand cradled my cheek like she'd comfort a startled animal. Her other hand moved up my simple slacks until she sensed the thick, latex barrier between us. A spark of friction drew my lower lip between my teeth. My rubber protection held all my heat. It took every bit of my willpower not to squirm.

As her palm rested on my secret, exposing me as surely as any X-ray machine, her laughter made me flinch. Emily's fingers tightened against my skull until I couldn't look away from her erotic gaze. Her single-minded intensity was a sensual gift without any ribbons or bows. Swift fear spiked across my tender flesh, leaving adrenaline heavy in its wake.

One finger slid underneath my protection until I drew a tight gasp into my lungs. An inescapable shudder as I wrapped my legs closer around her body. I measured her wicked grin. Would she have the balls? If I could have picked anyone to explore this shit with, I would have chosen Emily. Her fingers left a permanent, invisible brand of heat that made every part of me alert to her every movement.

A smooth wiggle of her finger – and her touch was gone.

Latex fell back against my skin, a stinging, satisfying punishment and the constrictive *slap* made my ears ring. It was as if every part of me sensed the sharp echo of pain. A lusty burn vibrated through my cells. I nuzzled my cheek into her soft, slick palm and a moan slipped out of my mouth.

Perhaps I hadn't always been willing to carry this secret. Certainly my less than covert longing for this woman showed what lengths I'd go to part with it. Emily leant in against my chest and smoothed her silky thumb across my heated cheek.

'I know. I know what you want,' she purred against the sensitive lip of my ear.

Those simple words arched me like a bowstring to her subtle commands.

Another snap left me seeing stars. But it was her heavy breathing that pushed me further down into myself. Forced me to acknowledge what I'd challenged for so long. This was never meant to be a secret. Lingerie was meant to be used – to be played and toyed with until two people couldn't take it any more.

I didn't need to see my boss's sparkling eyes to know her pleasure. Emily's fingers trembled against my cheek.

I didn't say thank you.

Instead, I croaked out, 'Yes.'

'Get. Down.'

Her luscious purr trembled down into my toes and it wasn't even the fact she signed my pay cheques that sent me sliding down from my perch. A skin to skin slow lower to the ground until my feet touched the floor. Against my breasts her nipples were hard as her weight shifted to push me back into the table. Whatever was coming – I wanted it. Not a doubt in my mind. But I never expected for it to come to this, with my hormones at a boiling point and one of her hands always lingering on my flushed flesh.

'Turn.'

Did I stall? I must have taken too long with my blink because her hand along my cheek pushed my whole head sideways. All my body could do was follow. Until I clasped my fingers around the pebbled, cheap plastic and waited for another delicious sting. That – reveal – was a stripping of sorts that had nothing to do with actual nudity, but I was exposed and vulnerable. When my gaze trained on a cliché motivational poster in front of me there was no other excuse I needed to tell myself so I'd obey her every wish.

Her slow, hot, breaths trickled down the nape of my neck as her hands slid around my waist from behind. Before I could catch my breath the snap and zipper of my slacks were undone as she dropped them to my knees. The sensation of the soft fabric's steady friction made me moan. But nothing prepared me for the pleasure of her bare fingers along my waist, lightly playing along the line of latex until she reached my lower back. It was a blessing that I was standing still because my whole world tilted on its axis.

So soft. What a contrast to her rolling, wicked laughter against the shell of my ear. I fastened my gaze on a dull patch of the white table as I licked my lips. It was her move now. Pressed flush against me, her small mouth secured over my earlobe with the harsh pressure of teeth. And when her finger penetrated the barrier between where the latex and my skin met, my inner walls clenched tight until I slightly hunched against the table.

Any more and there would be nothing left of me.

'One more, what do you say?'

Without looking behind me I could almost picture her eyebrow raised in an anxious question. A face she used often when she knew employees wouldn't like what she was going to tell them but they'd have to do it anyway. My pussy contracted in time to my runaway pulse. I waited. On the ledge of impatience, one foot in the air. One more drop of her finger and she wouldn't need to touch me again.

'Are you ready?' she coaxed while her skirts tickled the backs of my thighs.

'Please,' I rasped.

'Mmmm.'

Her finger shifted back and forth – left to right – teasing the powerful blow I yearned for until I was about to scream, no matter if people heard me. The slow drag across my flesh was torture. Who knew a small touch could be filled with so much promise? Her lips dragged up the taut line of my neck and I imagined a red brand from her lipstick – marked for the world to see below my short, boyish haircut. My stomach flopped and her tongue lashed out.

That small, basic graze raised goosebumps as a whimper trickled through my lips. Never in my wildest dreams – well, maybe some of them. But there was reality to think of! And this certainly couldn't be it. Not as her hand shifted and cupped my tiny breast, playing with my über-sensitive nipple until I kicked out with a mini-temper tantrum. Her hands clasped everywhere. Against my back her heartbeat pounded while she made a yummy, satisfied noise on the spot between my neck and my collarbone.

'You better come for me. You at least owe me that much, you little brat.'

Emily's finger scooted out from underneath my underwear, and a resounding snap of needling tension shifted until my knees went weak. The whole room fell away. My ears rang with the perfect slap. As her nails bruised my breasts and she curved her front to my back, an orgasm tumbled through my body as my pussy clenched with the aftershocks of my pleasure. The back of my thigh stung like a bitch.

But there was no denying my simpering smile.

'There better be more notes where that came from, because I like where this is going. And after today I fully expect you'll want to keep your job, won't you?'

Can I get a resounding yes to that?

Without a doubt this damn job was the best thing to ever happen to me.

Well, except for the invention of latex – but was all in how you used it.

Rehearsing with Katarina
by Elizabeth Coldwell

Katarina regards herself in the mirror that runs the length of the small rehearsal room, checking her poise is precise. With a glance to her left, she indicates to me that I should mimic her exactly, rising up on my toes and raising my arms to the same angle. We've been rehearsing this same routine for close to two hours now, staying behind after all the other dancers left for the afternoon, and I've had enough. But Katarina demands perfection, and that means I have to stay here until she's finally convinced I've got everything right.

Landing the role of her understudy in the revue was a definite step up for me, both in terms of prestige and financial recompense. I've been one of the chorus dancers at Le Salon d'Or for just over a year now, delighting a regular mixture of seasoned punters and curious tourists with our exotic routines. I'll be honest, it wasn't what I planned when I set out on my career. I always saw myself in the corps de ballet of some well-respected dance troupe, dreamt of maybe even working my way up to the level of prima ballerina, but it became obvious fairly early on that I was never going to make the grade. It doesn't help that my body blossomed in all the wrong ways, leaving me too top-heavy to conform to a ballerina's elegant silhouette. So, instead, I found myself taking a job in one of Paris's most famous exotic revues, wearing very little more than a plumed headdress and a crystal-encrusted G-string, performing for an audience who are allowed to look but not touch. It may not be high art, but nothing else comes close to the feeling of pure power that comes from holding a group of salivating men spellbound with your moves and your looks.

When Katarina's previous understudy, Mireille, left to go and join a show in one of the big resort hotels in Las Vegas, competition to take over her role was intense. I didn't think I'd get it, but as Katarina herself pointed out, we're exactly the same height and we do bear a certain facial similarity, though my tits are fuller than hers and her legs are a little longer. And once we have our heavy stage make-up and wigs on, you will barely be able tell us apart. She clearly likes the idea of having a twin, an obedient shadow. That's why I'm here now, following the same moves over and over, imprinting every step, every hand gesture into my muscle memory. My limbs ache, and my throat is dry, but there's no stopping till she is satisfied.

At a command from Katarina, the jangling piano introduction strikes up again. 'Two, three, four,' she barks, giving me my cue, and we begin the routine again, stepping out with sinuous, precisely timed movements. I count through the steps in my head, concentrating on moving with the same almost predatory grace as Katarina displays. Even in her baggy, sweat-soaked grey T-shirt and black leggings, she looks fierce, sensuous, sexy. When she performs this particular dance on stage, in only a pearl-backed thong and a bra made from strings of pearls that contrive to leave her nipples and almost all of her breasts bare, every man in the room wants her. Hell, I want her – and I've never even been with a girl.

I watch her in the mirror as she moves, hoping that somehow a fraction of her self-assurance will transfer itself to me. She grasps the back of a white-painted wooden chair before pirouetting and kicking her leg high in the air. We've been working on this move all afternoon, and I still can't quite get the timing right. Katarina comes to a stop as the chair I've been holding onto skitters across the floor, clapping her hands and bringing the music to an abrupt halt.

'How many times, Jodie? How many times?' She's trying to be patient, but the exasperation is evident in her clipped Russian tones. Like me, she didn't make it as a ballerina, but studying at the Bolshoi gave her an impeccable technique she'll never lose. I hope she appreciates quite how hard I'm trying to match it.

'I'm sorry, Katarina.'

'It's simple. Watch me again. Simply turn, and so –' Her leg comes up in a straight, perfect line. Watching her stretch and extend her body, I can't help but notice how the crotch of her leggings is moulded to the lips of her pussy. She must shave herself pretty much clean – we all do, so not a wisp of hair can emerge from our skimpy costumes – but the thought has never intrigued me the way it does now. I'm just tired, I tell myself; my mind is wandering. Nothing more.

'OK, yes, I've got it,' I tell her. This time I will get it right.

Katarina calls for the music once again, but our accompanist, Madame Myskow, has risen from her piano stool. Her wizened old face wrinkles further as she purses her lips. With a shake of her head she says firmly, 'I'm sorry, *chérie*, but it is past six o'clock.' The woman has been at Le Salon d'Or longer than any of us has been alive, accompanying generation after generation of dancers in the rehearsal room, and she knows the terms of her contract of employment inside out. As soon as six rolls round, she's gone.

We watch her shuffle out of the room, a tiny figure huddled in the black astrakhan coat that will protect her from the January chill. If I leave now, I'll have time for a soak in the tub and a light supper at the bistro across from my apartment before I have to be back here for the nine o'clock show. Loosening the tension in my neck with a couple of slow rolls of my head, I say, 'Well, looks like that's it for the day. Same time tomorrow?'

'Oh no, Jodie. We have not finished yet.'

'But we've got no music ...'

Katarina looks at me like I'm a slow-witted child. 'We don't need it. You have never danced without music before, moved purely to a beat?'

With that, she sets the metronome that stands on top of the piano ticking back and forth, before dragging my chair back to its correct place and coming to stand in her starting position once more. Suppressing a sigh, and any thoughts of supper and a bath, I go to join her.

'Two, three, four ...' Katarina launches into the routine yet again, and I follow. Despite my objections, the lack of music doesn't seem to make a difference – the damn tune is burned into my brain by now, anyway. What has changed, I realise as I glance in the mirror, is that now Katarina watches me, lips compressed, expression neutral.

'OK, OK, stop!' she orders, in the moment before I go to grasp the chair back. 'Jodie, you need to relax. You have the technique – I knew that when I recommended you for my understudy – but you think about everything too hard. You have to be freer in your movements, and what's most important, you need to own your body, not let it own you. Look …'

As she speaks, she reaches for the hem of my T-shirt, and pulls it over my head. Too startled to stop her, I watch her reflection in the mirror as she cups my breasts, clad in the sturdy bra I always wear to offer me support when I'm practising.

'Look at how you truss yourself up,' she comments. 'You don't do this when you are on stage, do you?'

'No, but –'

'So don't do it now.' She unclips the bra, pulls the straps down off my shoulders and tosses the garment to the side of the rehearsal room with a grimace of disdain. 'See how much better that feels, how natural it looks.'

Her words direct me to look in the mirror. I'm so used to going topless on stage, but now the sight of my bare breasts, nipples tightly peaked, causes a blush to rise to my cheeks.

'Don't be ashamed, honey.' Katarina's voice is soft in my ear, something like genuine affection in her tone. 'You have beautiful tits, so round, so full …' Her hand brushes the undercurve of my breast, just for a moment. Is she coming on to me, or does she really just want to help me improve my performance?

Before I can decide, or even begin to consider how I might feel if it's the former, Katarina has removed her own T-shirt and bra and is standing beside me, bare from the waist up. Her nipples, I can't help but notice, are just as hard as my own. I could put it down to the simple friction caused as our bodies move and stretch in the routine, but it's more than that. There's a tension in the room I can't ignore; when our eyes meet in the mirror, I fight the urge to turn my head and look away. She hasn't turned off the metronome, and still it continues to tick, as though counting down the moments till something of great significance occurs.

'OK, honey.' Katarina smiles at me. 'Now we are equal.' She cups my breasts, feeling the weight of them in her hands, then does the same to her own, clearly coming up short in comparison. 'Or maybe not.' She chuckles. 'Now, let us try again.'

She counts us into the routine, and this time I let my inhibitions go and simply move with the beat. As we move, I catch glimpses of us in the mirror, only in my mind the glass has been replaced by an audience, watching and savouring the sight of our bodies in motion. I can't help wishing Katarina had gone further, and stripped us down to nothing, not even the skimpiest pair of panties to hide our modesty. The thought of treating a crowd of voyeurs to a flash of my bare, smooth pussy turns me on like I can't believe – it's further than we'd ever go on stage, but if I was in some seedy strip club in Pigalle, I'd be showing everything off twice a night at least.

More than that, I want Katarina to see it. I've no idea why, but something about being here when everyone else has gone, dancing half-naked with this imperious Russian beauty, has roused my blood and set a beat pulsing between my legs, faster and more insistent than that of the steadily ticking metronome. Driven on by fantasies of exposing myself entirely to her, I spin and swoop, not even thinking about what my next move should be. I kick my leg up in perfect time with Katarina, high and proud; the chair stays steady, and I relax my grip on its back as I dance around it. Katarina lets out a delighted whoop.

'That's it, Jodie, you did it! See, what did I tell you? You just needed to be free.'

Almost before I know it, she's caught me in an embrace. Our bare breasts rub together, sending the most delicious flashes of sensation down to my crotch. My pussy lips feel swollen, sticky, and I don't need to look at my reflection to know there's a damp spot in my leggings.

When neither of us makes to pull away once that initial moment of congratulation passes, I'm pretty sure this is heading somewhere. It's an open secret that Katarina's into girls, but I've never seen her come on to anyone in the dance troupe before, especially not someone who's as straight as I am. Or thought I was, because there's no denying that being so close to her excites me. Breathing in the mixture of fresh scent and lily of the valley that exudes from her skin, feeling the softness of her breasts against mine, lingering in her embrace, I know I want her. But what if I'm reading too much into the situation, and now I've nailed the routine she's just going to call it a day and head home to get ready for tonight's show?

Her next action stills all my questions. Brushing a strand of hair away from my face where it's come loose from my ponytail, she plants a kiss on my lips, so light I almost don't feel it.

'Jodie, I knew you were the right one …'

I think she means the dancing, my appointment as her understudy, but I can't be certain. Her mouth is on mine again, stopping any reply, but I've had more than enough time to back out if this situation was making me at all uncomfortable. Any doubts are melting away under her touch.

Her hand moves to caress my breast. I catch my breath as she kneads the tender flesh in small circles with her palm. Our lips meet once more, Katarina's guiding, mine following. She uses her tongue to prise apart my lips and our kisses grow wetter, more passionate. The metronome ticks faintly in the background, but I'm moving to a different rhythm now. I'm hypnotized by the feel of that searching mouth on my own and the hand that teases and pinches my nipple relentlessly.

Katarina's mouth snakes a wet trail down my neck, making my moan in response. Closing my eyes, I throw back my head; a submissive gesture that bares my throat to her.

She moves lower, till her soft mouth suckles on my nipples, stiffening the already hard peaks even further. My groans of pleasure fill the rehearsal room, my breathing suddenly ragged as Katarina's roving hand snakes up my thigh. Her fingers trace small, spidery circles, their motion unerringly upward. When she strokes over the rapidly dampening crotch of my leggings, I know there's no going back. The sheltered part of my brain, the part that's never thought seriously about the pleasures of girl fun, is vaguely suggesting I should push Katarina's hand away and call time on her antics – the clock is ticking ever closer to tonight's show time, after all. But the wanton side of me, the side that revels in dancing in only a G-string for a greedy, expectant audience, is silently urging that hand to slip into my leggings and touch my liquid pussy.

Silence won't get the trick done, though. I need to voice my urges. In a small, breathy voice that doesn't sound like mine, I beg, 'Touch me, Katarina. I want your fingers in my pussy.'

Her mouth releases its sucking grip on my nipple. 'Are you sure, honey?'

'I've never been more sure of anything,' I assure her.

Katarina smiles and, crouching down, eases my leggings and underwear over my arse and thighs. When everything is around my ankles, I kick them off, the garments tangling together in a ball that lies forgotten as Katarina surveys her handiwork. I sprawl back on bare floorboards that have been scuffed by the feet of a thousand dancers. My nipples glisten with saliva and my cunt is open and saturated. Her expression tells me how much she loves seeing me in this abandoned state.

She stands, hands on hips, letting me in turn admire her, bare-breasted and magnificent. Then she quickly strips out of the rest of her clothes, before coming to join me on the floor.

Her hand cups my pussy, giving it a loving squeeze. One finger pushes up into my hole, another rests on my clit, letting me get used to the sensation before she begins to play with me in earnest. She takes hold of my head and guides it to her breast, inviting me to suck at her big nipple, the colour of damask roses. I take the hard bud in my mouth and lick it, as Katarina's fingers dabble in the pooling juices that coat my puffy, swollen lips.

My thighs loll open as I lie back, encouraging her to straddle me. Katarina's finger rolls over my clit; the powerful shock of the sensations she's creating low in my belly cause me to close my teeth hard on her nipple. She doesn't wince or complain;

she's made of tougher stuff than that. This is the woman who's danced *en pointe* till her toes bled, who's kept me here for hours after the end of our usual rehearsal to drum her show-stopping routine into me. If anything, pain only stirs her on to do better, try harder. She merely smirks and encourages me to carry on with my oral ministrations.

A wave of tension begins to build in my belly, under the relentless force of those clever, circling fingers. My head swims, and I'm begging Katarina not to stop, my voice muffled against the soft flesh of her breasts. When her only response is to withdraw her hand and pull away, I whimper in frustration, then sigh, as the fingers are replaced with a hot, urgent mouth. For the first time in my life, my cunt is being licked by a skilful female lover. I've been eaten out on so many occasions before, but nothing has ever felt quite like Katarina's sighing breath at the mouth of my channel, or the unique pressure of her muscular tongue against my clit. Maybe it's true that the only person who really knows what turns a woman on is another woman. Whatever, this is bliss, this is ecstasy, I never want it to stop ...

My world turns upside-down as Katarina propels me into a breathless orgasm. I grind hard against her nose and mouth as I come, surrendering to pleasure like I've never known.

When she rises up in a crouch, reaching for her leggings to start dressing, I'm oddly disappointed. She's given me everything and had nothing in return.

'What about you?' I ask. 'Don't you want to come?'

She grins, my juices still wet on her lips. 'Honey, I dance better when I'm unsatisfied. But tomorrow, come back for another rehearsal, and we'll see.'

With that, she shrugs on her T-shirt, efficient and professional once more. But tonight I'll watch her dance, spotlighted on the stage, and learn more of her tricks to keep an audience spellbound. And tomorrow Katarina and I will rehearse again in private. What she'll teach me then, only she knows, but I've already shown her what a keen and willing pupil I can be. I'll do whatever it takes to please her - and no woman can ask for more than that.

Also from Xcite Books

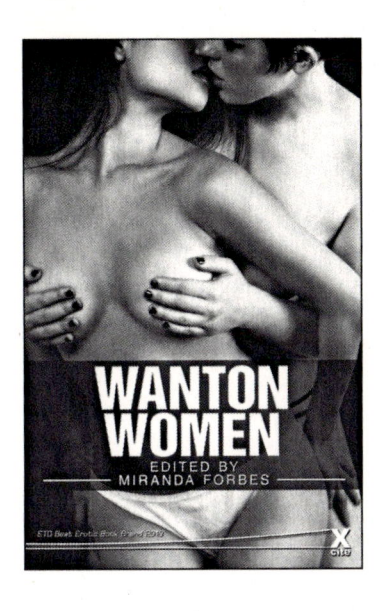

Wanton Women

Twenty hot tales about ladies who lust... after each other. From vulnerable virgins to femme fatales to misbehaving minxes, these wanton women all have one thing in common. They don't need a man to satisfy them in bed – or anywhere else for that matter! Wild women or just girls getting it on, these stories are guaranteed to tease.

ISBN 9781907761683   Price £7.99

Best of Both

Why limit yourself to one gender when you can have two? A collection of 20 stories celebrating the bonuses of bisexuality. From one-on-one loving to foursomes and moresomes, this anthology ticks all of the boxes, in every possible gender combination you could imagine! These bi-curious and bi-veterans know exactly what they want. They want the best of both worlds ...

ISBN 9781907761669   Price £7.99

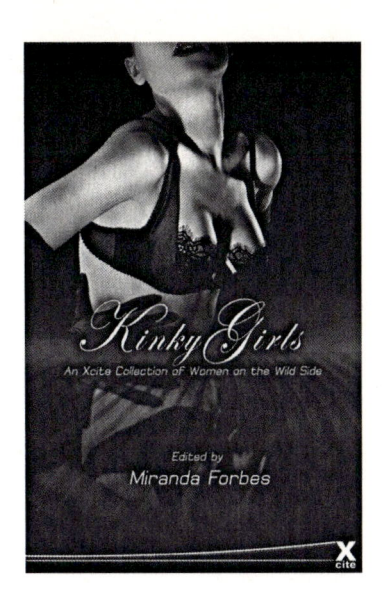

Kinky Girls

Women who act on their most shameful fantasies and embark upon the most daring misbehaviour, is still the most enduring and timeless theme in erotic fantasy, and loved by male and female readers alike. And this collection takes the idea of a kinky adventurous woman to the max. A collection of 20 original, varied, outrageous, eye-watering and utterly sensuous stories from the best new voices and established authors around today.

ISBN 9781907016561   Price £7.99

Xcite

Xcite Books help make loving better with a wide range of erotic books, eBooks and dating sites.

www.xcitebooks.com
www.xcitebooks.co.uk

facebook

Sign-up to our Facebook page
for special offers and free gifts!